HERMIT

A Novel

Praise for HERMIT

O. Gene Bicknell's *HERMIT* fuses suspense and intrigue into a gripping, poignant thriller that deftly handles the "effect of isolation on the human mind". *HERMIT*'s Sergeant Jackson Eagle has the skills of Lee Child's Jack Reacher and the intelligence of Tom Clancy's Jack Ryan. But it's Sergeant Jackson's heart that carries the story.

—**Ann Carpenter,** Screenwriter

Hermit is so much more than an adventure story and a story of survival. It reveals the inner conflict of Special Forces veteran, Jackson Eagle, as he struggles to aid survivors of a plane crash deep in a remote mountain area. His experience as a POW and an unfortunate run-in with law enforcement, force him into the mountains, but feelings of compassion for a mother and her injured child bring him intense human contact as a helper, teacher, guide, and rescuer. It's a story that will pull you to the very last page as you witness extraordinary journeys of all three main characters and ultimately understand the power and the draw of being a hermit.

—**Steven A. Scott,** Ed.D.
President, Pittsburg State University

Praise for HERMIT

Gene Bicknell's novel *Hermit* started out with a POW being rescued — and drew me right in to the story. The details, the words used to describe Jackson's feelings, just made me love his character — his horrible injuries made me hurt for him. But the story is not just about a rescued POW. It's about a brother taking care of his sister. It's about a man's heart healing. And it's about a man helping a young boy heal — and grow — and become a man on his own. Every line of this story kept me enthralled. I could not put it down, and I could not stop reading it. I highly recommend *Hermit* to all readers.

—Rebecca Allison

When I picked up *Hermit* — I could hardly put it down! The characters are so real — you can feel, smell, taste, and sense their vulnerabilities, fears, joy. From the very first page, this book grabs you. You want to know more about Jackson; his life, his solitude, his suffering and how he has come to terms with the torment and loneliness his life has become. As Jack's life becomes more than that — as the book progresses — I found myself wanting to cheer him on toward a better, more normal life — whatever normal may mean for him. I hope there is a sequel, as I feel there must be more to his story!!

—Julie Hejtmanek

Praise for HERMIT

In his new book, Gene Bicknell brings out the relational truth that we thrive in community with others rather than self-isolation. His characters compel us to consider our relationships and affirm that we are our best selves when helping others. The pages turn fast as action and interaction blend masterfully on this journey of redemption. One must imagine the author's intimate knowledge of perils from being alone too long and how compassion for others lifts us out of troubling circumstances.

—**Rev. Marshall Nord,** Chief Communications Officer
PathLight International

Requests for permission should be addressed to: Ascend Books, LLC, Attn: Rights and Permissions Department, 7221 West 79th Street, Suite 206, Overland Park, KS 66204

First Edition
10 9 8 7 6 5 4 3 2 1

ISBN: print book 978-1-7369431-6-8
Ebook ISBN: 978-1-7369431-7-5

Library of Congress Control Number:2021939115

Publisher: Bob Snodgrass
Editor: Camile Cline
Associate Editor: Jennifer McDaniel
Publication Coordinator: Molly Gore
Sales and Marketing: Lenny Cohen
Dust Jacket and Book Design: Rob Peters

Publisher's Note: The goal of Ascend Books is to publish quality works. With that goal in mind, we are proud to offer this book to our readers. This book is a work of fiction. References to real people, events, establishments, organizations, and locales are intended to solely enhance the fictional story, provide a historical perspective, and give the book a sense of reality and authenticity. All main characters, events, dialogue, and incidents in the novel are the creation of the author's imagination.

Printed in Canada

www.ascendbooks.com

HERMIT

A Novel

O. Gene Bicknell

For Rita

Preface

As human beings, we were created for community (Genesis 2:18). And in Ecclesiastes 4:10, Solomon describes how vulnerable we are when we're alone, "Pity anyone who falls and has no one to help them up." There's strength in numbers, he added, for "…one may be overpowered, two can defend themselves. A cord of three strands is not quickly broken." (v. 12)

This is just as true for us spiritually as it is physically. God never intended for us to fly alone, vulnerably isolated. We need relationships with each other for encouragement, refreshment, and growth. (Corinthians 12:21)

Prologue

In the perfect darkness, Jackson concentrated on slowing his breathing. The indescribable pain penetrating every inch of his body, the sounds of gunfire, the shouting in Arabic. He blocked out each distraction until it only took up a small part of his consciousness. As his panting calmed, slowing to deep breaths, the Ranger focused solely on what he knew. The sounds of chaos were getting closer.

"Process what you hear, son," Jackson could hear his father say. A U.S. Special Forces soldier like him, his father served his country well as a Ranger trained in survival. Between the Army's training and his father's, there was little Jackson couldn't endure. Explosions rocked the little cell deep in the bunker of what he surmised was an abandoned tenement. Dust and rocks fell onto Jackson's head and shoulders. He sat up despite the broken wrists, shoulder blade, collar bone, ribs, and right femur. What wasn't broken screamed in pain as if it was about to snap. He had to be in a good position to discern what was happening, so he sat quietly gritting his teeth.

Three explosions in rapid succession opened a large crack above his head, peppering him with small pieces of rubble and choking dust. A single shaft of light shot down. Jackson barely registered the final two blasts which caused a single, high-pitched ringing in his ears. He shook his head to clear the sound and shake off the rubble, and then looked up as he recognized a few errant gunshots. As footsteps approached outside his cell door, Jackson curled into a ball, untouched by the stream of light.

"Clear!"

English.

Jackson closed his eyes and remained still. His breathing was barely audible. The ringing in his ears was still so sharp and painful, he was sure the whole world could hear it.

He heard a loud grunt and the sound of a large piece of furniture scraping across the floor. A moment later, the door opened filled with a light so blinding that it penetrated Jackson's eyelids, erasing the darkness. He dared not breathe or open his eyes.

"Damn."

Jackson's eyes flew open. Before him, four Rangers were standing there, staring at him as they looked over the cell. After taking a moment to focus, he recognized the heavy armor, desert fatigues, and insignia like he had been swaddled in them. Given his father's training, he practically was.

"Sgt. Jackson Eagle?"

"Yeah," Jackson croaked. He could taste the dust and ozone on his overgrown beard. He could tell from the soldiers' eyes he looked as bad as he felt. Emaciated and filthy, his eyes were deep-set from weeks of alternating neglect and beatings,

Jackson tried to shift in order to stand. Three of the Rangers knelt to keep him steady and support him in place.

"Don't worry, Sarge. The medics are on their way with a stretcher. Hold here for a bit and we'll get you out." For the first time in weeks, Jackson allowed himself a deep breath. He felt the tension in his shoulders relax, and he leaned back against the walls that held him captive. He closed his eyes and pictured the green of home.

Chapter 1

"D~ear~ J —"

Every one of her letters started that way. They always had.

But what came next caught him off-guard like a punch to the gut. Nothing could prepare him as he read what would be her final letter — a letter that abruptly ended with a casual "See you around."

Now, heading back home after all those years in the service, he pictured her handwriting on the plain, white paper as he looked down at the snow-tipped mountains.

At least she was brief. Hadn't drawn it out like a long knife between the ribs despite feeling wounded.

He touched his shirt, feeling for the ring suspended from a chain he wore around his neck. He wasn't quite ready to get rid of it just yet.

Her letter arrived just weeks before he was captured. Once the Taliban's bounty reached a high enough figure to interest the stealthiest in its militia, it was only a matter of time before they finally got him.

As the plane edged past the Snowy Range, Jackson closed his eyes, trying hard not to remember, but unable to forget.

The memories during the day and the nightmares after dark were worst at Landstuhl, east of Stuttgart. As his bones set and the sedative-induced fog wore off while recuperating in the U.S. Army clinic, his mind found all of the misery he'd packed away during his ordeal. He volunteered for any advanced training he could — Airborne School to become a HALO paratrooper, Commando training for elite Special Forces units — it was a natural progression that led him to a specialized skill set. One of the Rangers' most-lethal snipers, he'd been marked for termination by the enemy for more than a year. Yet, he always evaded capture. Until that night when the sneak attack went south, and his team was pinned down. He stayed on the roof, covering them long after he should've bugged out.

The ring lay heavy on his neck. "I'm dreaming."

He could feel himself slipping further into the nightmare even as he struggled to reach the surface.

"Take cover!"

"Shoot!"

"Target one o'clock."

"Kill shot!"

He could hear the shouting in his ears, but he wasn't sure who was yelling.

"Is it me?"

He kept firing at his target even as he felt their hands on his belt and shoulders. Jackson knew they wouldn't kill him right there, so he ignored all of their commands to put down his weapon. A few of his guys fired up at them. He could hear the popping sounds as the bullets flew over his head. One of his captors caught one in the back and began roaring in pain. The next second, he felt him grip his shoulder and belt. With the help of three others, the man rolled Jackson over the edge of the four-story building. A first-floor wooden awning and his right femur broke the first part of the fall. Both wrists snapped as his six-foot-three, 220-pound frame crashed head-first through an empty barrel and into a storage cellar.

Suddenly, he jolted awake and looked around. The flight attendant was two rows ahead of him, stretching toward him and shaking his shoulder.

"Sir, please, you're scaring the other passengers," she said. Jackson blinked and looked around. The elderly couple beside him had shrunk as far against the window as they could get. Several passengers had left their seats and were bunched up in the aisle near the lavatory. Others were peering around the flight attendant. The row across the aisle from him was empty.

A woman and teenaged girl sitting diagonally across the aisle looked startled. They both looked at him for a while before apparently deciding he was okay. The woman gave him a final sideways glance before returning to her book. Jackson thought he detected a hint of pity but couldn't be sure.

The remaining passengers slowly returned to their seats after being reassured by the flight attendant that they would be okay. Jackson mumbled an apology and closed his eyes.

After a few minutes, the whispering died down.

A moment later, he felt a gentle tap on his shoulder. He accepted a bottle of water from another flight attendant who had come from the front of the plane.

As he reclined in his seat, Jackson felt the sun's heat penetrating his face and seep into his sinuses. The yellow-gray bruise around his left collarbone was almost gone, but he knew it would be tender for months. A reminder of the special torture inflicted on him within days of his capture.

He closed his eyes. His mind was drifting again.

He began dreaming of Diane was pushing him on the swing. He could feel himself going higher and higher, his tan little feet stretching toward a bright blue sky. She was laughing and not paying attention to how high she was pushing him. Jackson shifted a little to look down at her. The top of her head and her two, long black braids were all he could see. He noticed her head was down, and she was pushing with all her might.

Just as he started to get scared, she suddenly pushed him too hard , sending him kind of sideways through the air. For a moment, Jackson couldn't tell if he was falling off the roof or the swing. But when he landed, he jerked, sitting straight up in his seat. He looked around, but no one noticed this time. He massaged his collarbone. It had fractured at the exact same spot when he hit the ground. Diane.

Diane had cried as their mother drove them to the hospital. He just looked out the window of their old station wagon, gripping his arm and never making a sound. She hated it whenever he got hurt and was so upset that she was the reason this time.

"I'm so sorry," she sobbed. "I thought you were having fun. I didn't mean to."

A passenger on the flight swooshed by. The sudden rush of air roused Jackson again. He took the magazine from the back of the seat in front of him and flipped through it. Images of snow-covered peaks, sandy beaches, and skylines of ancient cities. One reminded him of his time in Germany — after the rescue.

When he first arrived in Landstuhl — broken mentally and physically — the doctors there sedated him to keep him immobile. Diane tried many times to contact him, and eventually they spoke once by phone. But with broken wrists and a busted collarbone, he had to listen to her by speaker phone.

Jackson closed his eyes again and let himself relax. "You're safe," he told himself. "The pilot is in control. You don't have to be in charge right now."

Her face swirled just above the surface. The pain dissolved.

"I'm coming to Landstuhl," she said.

"No, stay home and wait," he told her. "I'm okay."

The memory made him smile. Jackson was roused a little as he felt the plane bank, but kept his eyes closed. If she saw him, he worried she would never let him out of her sight again. He remembered that look when they first buried their dad, then their mom, just a year apart. He had flown back both times — first from Afghanistan and then Iraq — before his final mission took him back to Afghanistan. His dad died of an infection near his heart. Undetected for months, it was too late by the time the doctors determined why his body was failing. His mom and sister had cared for him at home. His mom almost never left their tidy home, partially tucked away in the great woods where he'd also spent his childhood learning to play and hunt.

Diane honestly thought he would stay and help her with their mom, but he was clear from the beginning. He felt her pain as they said goodbye after the funeral.

He kissed his mother's cheek for the last time then. She'd been diagnosed with a brain tumor just before their father passed. Though he couldn't quite believe it, he could see in her eyes that she was already resigned to it. Diane and Jackson debated with her. It was operable, but she just couldn't go on without their dad. His illness had taken all the fight out of her. She was ready to join him.

It was hard for Diane to let go. She loved all of them fiercely — had cared for their parents with the patience of Job.

It had been hard enough convincing her he had to go back after their mother's funeral — and he was in perfect health then. The government flew her in for two days each time he was moved to a different hospital, first into Ramstein and then into Reagan. She was covered head-to-toe in hospital garb at Landstuhl. He couldn't see her face, but he recognized the sound of her voice. It reminded him of their mother's voice. He couldn't recall saying two words the entire time she visited him at the German hospital. He maybe said four at Walter Reed.

By then, he was out of a few casts, less restricted and able to amble around a bit. He was sitting in a rolling chair. *I'm dreaming again*, he thought. She wheeled him out by the fitness center and past the ball field on one of those hot Maryland dog days. The heat. He blinked his eyes and reached up to turn the dial on the air above his seat. The coolness cleared his head and sharpened his memory of that time.

"You're not working with your counselor," she said as she pushed him along the wide sidewalk past the buildings. He didn't respond.

"Jack, Dr. Jefferson needs you to focus on your mental recovery, not just your physical."

Jackson thought she sounded like the therapists who tried getting him to open up. "You need to address your nightmares."

"I'm okay," he said, hoping she would change the subject, but realizing she hadn't flown 2,000 miles just to drop it. She stopped by a bench, pressed the brake by the chair's wheel, and sat down in front of him.

"You're not, little brother. Don't you want to come home?"

The look on her face and the pleading in her voice broke through. Jackson remembered hanging his head.

"I don't know... yes, I do," he finally said.

"Okay, then," Diane said. " Let's focus on the positive. Your PT says you're making really good progress. Can you channel some of that effort into your conversations with the shrink?"

He nodded, sighing deeply. "I'll try.

After that, he threw himself into recuperating and then strength training. Just like he did during his military training, he challenged himself with each new hurdle. Once his physical therapist cleared him to move on, he set new goals, whether it was more reps or heavier weights, more laps or longer runs.

He tried to do the same thing with Dr. Jeff. The good doctor knew all of a soldier's tricks, though, and at time tried some unorthodox methods to get Jackson to open up. He found it was much more difficult setting goals when his own mind was the obstacle. Jackson shared as much as he could bear, trying to unpack an overwhelming sense of isolation that crept into his every thought following his imprisonment. Eventually, the doctor cleared him to go home.

He remembered how Diane couldn't get off work when he was released from Walter Reed and mustered out of military service at Fort Meade. The ceremony was brief, but those who attended the ritual could not help but be impressed. Decorated with high honors and in peak physical condition after his ordeal, Jackson masked his mental state well. He accepted the decorations, ribbons, and medals with grace and few words. He looked the very picture of a modern American warrior before quickly changing into his fatigues for the trip home.

"You don't want to go grab a drink and celebrate a little?" Myers, a member of his Iraqi team , asked. Several guys from his old unit had shown up to congratulate him and marvel at the fact that he was still alive. Jackson watched them as they waited by their cars in the parking lot. He knew they wanted the full story, but he had worked too hard for too long to bury it deep in the recesses of his mind.

"I'm not much for celebrating, Paul," Jackson said. "Thanks, though. Hey, take it easy. And thanks for coming." After giving him a slap on the back, he stepped into the military vehicle designated to take him to the airport. As Jackson strode toward his gate at BWI, he could hear some of the new hardware clanging around in his duffel bag.

The plane began shuddering and the "Fasten Seatbelts" sign pinged on. He looked around, noting how accustomed everyone was to flying. Most of the passengers were dead asleep, even the children. He thought back to Diane, who he would see in just a few hours.

He knew he caused his older sister worlds of grief anticipating his return this final time. He was a different man than he was when he enlisted. With Valerie probably married now, what would he do?

Jackson started contemplating his options at Walter Reed more than two months ago. He was all patched up, but he'd had weeks of PT and boredom to give his mind free range. Whatever he did, it wouldn't involve walls or a ceiling, he knew that for sure. Indoor plumbing was for Fobbits too. He had been roughing it with his pop and Crow granddad since he was old enough to ride a pony. Trapping, fishing, hunting, camping, cooking wild game. Surviving. The retired sergeant major taught his son well. Maybe he could head up to Alaska after the meet-and-greet back home in Idaho and become a fishing guide. He needed a new life, away from all the old reminders.

After a layover, he stuck his right foot out into the aisle of the smaller aircraft. The nerves around the healing bone shot darts through his quad muscles and he massaged his leg, hopeful it would soothe it. The long flight hadn't helped.

"You get injured?" an older gentleman across the aisle said, gesturing at Jackson's leg. Jackson noticed him studying his fatigues and the bright Ranger insignia on his sleeve as they had made their way onto the plane.

"Huh? Oh, yeah," Jackson responded, starting to pull it back.

"No, no. It's not bothering me," he said, pausing. "Thank you for what you're doing for our country."

Over the years, Jackson had gotten used to this response from civilians.

"You're welcome," he said, smiling and nodding. Then he settled back as the flight attendant started his spiel.

As he closed his eyes, he told himself again that he would stay just long enough for Diane to get bored of him. They would fall into a routine, and then he would spring the news on her about leaving. He just needed to devise a plan.

Chapter 2

Jackson looked for his sister after grabbing his oversized duffel in baggage claim. "By the info kiosk," her text read when he'd finally flipped open his cell. Diane rushed him as he turned the corner, and he wrapped one arm around her in an awkward response. He hadn't been hugged in years. Despite doctor's orders upon his medical discharge, Jackson gave in to the embrace, squeezing her tight and lifting her a foot off the ground. She laughed, kissed him on his clean-shaven cheek, and hugged him back.

"Hey, hey! Welcome home, little brother," Diane's dark eyes sparkled and the little creases around them deepened as she looked up at him.

"Wow, you look better than I thought you would," she added and smiled, tenderly taking his arm and steering him toward the sliding doors.

"Gee, thanks," he said.

Diane filled him in on the new Arapaho Glades Mall as they passed by and all the scuttlebutt about her high-school classmates, guys and girls he'd looked up to when he was an ungainly preteen. He noticed she carefully avoided talking about any of the classes between theirs and especially his own. No need to open still-fresh wounds.

"And there's our new office," she pointed to a sturdy building that looked like it belonged in Colonial Williamsburg rather than rural Idaho.

"How is the old codger at Burke, Stewart these days?"

"Still driving me insane. Don't get me wrong. It's easier than when I started with him, but he still can't follow the deadlines that I clearly mark in his calendar." Jackson looked at his pretty sister, who any man would be thrilled to have as a wife. But he knew she was married to her job. Her work-husband, Reg Stewart, rarely gave her enough latitude for a life outside the firm.

Jackson knew that caring for their parents had taken all her extra energy. She briefly dated a few boys in high school and one in college, but none of them held her interest. When Jackson would press, she admitted to regularly getting asked out on dates, but she was just hoping to find someone intelligent enough to keep her attention. Diane felt like she had time. Jackson told her there was a whole big world out there, much of which he'd already seen, because they both knew Arapaho Glades offered limited possibilities.

She caught him smiling at her and gave him a nudge. "Stop. You asked," she smiled at him again. "I'm glad you're home, bro. You need a break and I need someone to talk to besides the dog."

"Lady's doing okay then, huh?" Jackson asked.

He looked out the window as they made their last turn toward home, up the gravel road that wound through the

massive Western white pines, larches, firs, and spruce trees
dusted with snow. As if on cue, the basset hound bounded off
the front porch of the modest, two-story home toward the Jeep.
Lady's energy belied her age, Jackson thought, watching her
circle the Jeep, barking and jumping in excitement.

"There she is," Jackson said as he rubbed the dog's head and
scruffed her neck. As he stood up, he could see the faded paint
on the yellow house and the dense woods that seemed to be
swallowing it whole from all sides.

A large homemade banner bearing the words "WELCOME
HOME JACKSON" hung across the length of the porch.

"Thanks, sis," he said, pulling his bag from the back seat.

"You know, it's not every day my hero brother comes home
for good." She turned and gave him a smile as they walked up
the steps. The door, as it always had been, no matter the time
of day or night or season, was unlocked.

"Hope you're okay in your old room. Sheets are clean, and I
dusted a bit. Even polished your medals and old trophies."

Jackson set his duffel bag inside the front door, taking in
the familiar old photos of their grandparents, parents, and the
two of them when they were younger.

"Place hasn't changed much," Diane said. Jackson took a
deep breath and let the moment fill him up.

"It's home."

Standing close to the big picture window that beheld his
favorite view in all the world, Jackson gripped his favorite
mug and took a sip of coffee. The house was quiet. Even Lady
barely acknowledged his rising. He'd already been around a
couple of days so the thrill had worn off, he figured. Through
the frosted pane, he looked beyond the edge of their yard

and deep into the forest. Something was drawing him away, pulling at his soul like a magnet.

A few hours later when Diane finally came downstairs, Jackson had the whole kitchen fully deployed. Every coil on the stove was heating up all the necessary ingredients for huevos rancheros and waffles with winter berries. Their grandmother's nesting bowls were freshly washed and resting in the drying rack. Diane couldn't find even a grain of flour remaining on the cutting board their father made from the felled bigtooth maple by the driveway. Jackson saw her inspecting her kitchen and grinned.

"Clean as you go, that's what the Army taught me," he said.

"Glad I went shopping," Diane told him. " When did you learn to cook?"

"Experimentation…and Mom's cookbooks," Jackson gestured to the neat row of stained spines resting on a shelf near the window.

After Diane tasted a little of everything on her plate, Jackson decided it was time to broach the subject of leaving.

"So, I'm thinking of heading out to do a little bow hunting. Maybe some fishing, too."

Diane blinked, then said, "Not today?"

When Jackson didn't answer immediately, she added, "Remember? I told you. It's Saturday." Jackson tilted his head slightly, furrowing his brows.

"Arapaho Glades is a little town," she explained. " Everyone wants to see you. We're heading over to the Tavern around seven." The pleading in his sister's eyes wore down Jackson's resolve.

"Okay, tomorrow then. But I really don't want to go tonight. I have an idea: Why don't you go and tell everyone how great I look and how good I feel? You've always been a better talker anyway."

The eye roll from his older sister told him everything. He figured he'd pack for his hunting and fishing expedition, head over to the Tavern to grip a few palms, then hit the rack early so he could get going before sunup. He couldn't wait to get out for a few days.

As the last rays of the day crept through his window, Jackson's childhood room filled with light. He knelt by the chest in the corner and carefully inspected the worn bow and quiver of arrows, an old hatchet, various knives, and all types of survival gear.

"I'm out of the shower! You should start getting ready!" Diane called.

Jackson frowned and continued digging in the box, pulling out items and stuffing them into his hunting pack next to the new aluminum arrows he'd purchased earlier that day at REI. He had already packed the new cooking gear, jerky, cans of beans, canteen, a few Crow waterskins, and new subzero cold-weather gear in a hiking frame by the front door.

"I think I'm just gonna stay here...tonight," Jackson turned to see his sister, wrapped in a towel with another around her hair atop her head, appear in the doorway.

"Jack, people want to see you," Diane said. The whole town missed you. Everyone thought the worst. Especially me!"

He just looked up at Diane.

"C'mon," she said. "Just come, have a beer, say hi, then you can go home."

"But, sis, you know me. I told you I didn't want a welcome-home party. The sign out front was enough for me."

Jackson looked down at his chest.

"Besides, is *she* going to be there?"

"Maybe… I don't know. I didn't invite her, but it's like, the only place in town to get a drink and dance a bit. Besides Jack, after how she broke your heart, I won't even speak to her when we're both in line at the store."

"Well, I appreciate that," he said.

"So, how about this: Since I won't take no for an answer, *if* she shows up, I'll kick her butt." Diane flashed a sassy smile.

"All right, one drink. You can go on ahead in the car. I'll walk over in a bit."

Diane nodded, satisfied with her small victory, and scampered down the hall. Jackson grinned and shook his head. But soon his gaze fell upon the Purple Heart and Bronze Star on a shelf with his other medals. He turned them over, and slipped them into his breast pocket. Then he swiftly bent down and picked up the pack, heading for the door.

"You drive a hard bargain," he yelled into the hallway.

Chapter 3

As Jackson zipped up his new jacket and stepped out into the darkness, he reveled in the bite in the air. Just a few hours in the cozy home was a few too long. He strolled past the forest that nearly surrounded the driveway, past Miss Rita's house on the left and, further on, the Carmichaels' A-frame on the right. The lights of the little town were bright against the dark, enveloping sky.

It didn't take ten full minutes for the red Tavern sign to come into view. In that time, the ring and chain around his neck started feeling heavy and cold. Jackson walked along Main Street — its shops closed and mostly dark — but he could see the Quilting Basket's window display illuminated after hours, as well as Grant's Shoes. There was a street light on every corner, and so Jackson carefully avoided the glow around each circle of light as he strolled slowly, taking in the sights.

He saw Herb's Burgers, the restaurant he took Valerie to. It was their place and kicked off nearly every date. A few people sat in the booths. Folks he didn't recognize. "Everyone I know must be at the Tavern," Jackson thought.

Even her. Man, he had thought she was the one. But the things he'd seen overseas changed him. He knew now why it wouldn't have worked. He loved her — more than anyone — but he could never let anyone get close to him. Not again, anyway.

The bad thoughts started creeping in. He'd kept them at bay most of the day, excited about the hunting trip. Now, his mind went from one dark place to another as he stuck to the shadows, his memory swirling through each trauma as if it were the first time.

The sound from the Tavern was loud, and Jackson stopped and blinked a few times to focus. He could see some of its patrons out in the street, smoking and laughing. He figured he had a good minute before they noticed him coming down the dark sidewalk.

As he stepped around another pool of light near the Tavern's parking lot, the sound of a man and woman arguing reached his ears. His sister's yell didn't register as her voice for a moment.

"Stop that! Somebody, help me!"

As he approached the parking lot, he heard her shouting again, and she was in distress. He peered through the crowd of cars and could see Diane struggling inside the Jeep. Jackson approached quickly and saw that Deputy Tom Denny, a guy on his high-school football team, had her pinned and was yanking at her jeans. She was being assaulted.

In a rage, Jackson's combat training, exacerbated by the stress of his imprisonment, took over. He grabbed the deputy's head and shoulder and pulled him off Diane. Pressing him against the door, Jackson hit him again and again. Denny fell and tried to crawl under the car to get away. Diane stood back and watched as her brother transformed into someone she almost didn't recognize. He pulled the deputy from under the car, but, as he did, Denny drew his pistol. Jackson was leveling to hit him again when Denny brought up the gun.

In an instant, Jackson grabbed the deputy's arm and the gun. The pair spun around twice as they wrestled to gain control. Falling together toward the pavement, the gun discharged. The muffled sound didn't register with the crowd of laughing party-goers near the door of the bar.

When Jackson jumped up, ready to go at it, Diane's attacker didn't move. A pool of blood spread across the deputy's shirt. Dumbstruck, Jackson stood motionless. He was shocked back to the reality of the moment and couldn't comprehend what he had just done.

"Get up," he yelled. "Get up!" When the deputy didn't respond, Diane came to Jackson's side.

"I think he's dead," she said. The image of a tiny, dark cell flashed in Jackson's mind.

"I've got to get out of here," he responded.

Without looking back, Jackson and Diane climbed into the Jeep. They didn't speak as they got in. She moved through the gears, quickly gaining speed through the town's streets. Jackson looked at the blood on his hands, then forced himself to look at his sister's face as tears streamed down her cheeks and chin.

"Kay needed a scarf for a ski trip and I had the perfect one in the Jeep," Diane was sobbing, talking as much to herself as to Jackson. "Tom is bouncing tonight. He followed me out. Last week, he tried to kiss me when I left. I slapped him."

"It wasn't your fault, Diane. It'll be okay." Jackson looked out the window, trying to believe his words. It took fewer than three minutes to arrive home.

Side-stepping Lady as she entered the house, Diane quickly and silently gathered a few things for Jackson's packs. She didn't need to be told what he planned to do. His plans hadn't changed. He was going camping.

Jackson went to the back of the house and strode through the yard toward the little stream bordering Miss Rita's property and theirs. He washed his hands in the freezing water and did his best to clean the blood off his jacket. Then he shook and came inside, grabbed the packs by the door, and waited in the Jeep while his sister locked the door. He closed his eyes and Diane was silent for a long time as she drove.

He needed to plan and stress never helped him think. He rested his head back and tried to relax, visualizing everything he would need to do. He saw an aerial map in his head and sorted through the sections with the densest forests, that weren't along any flight paths, had few roads, but lots of game. Places his granddad had said to avoid because a body could get lost in such a confusing maze where everything looked the same. Jackson figured the dense forests could save him, if he was smart and moved quickly.

He pictured trees so close together that their canopy was endless green. Among their trunks, he saw caves of all sizes, burrowed into by animals for their homes, but large enough for his necessities and him. The cave he chose would need to look like it was in-use or used recently by a wild animal. It would need to be secluded and well-hidden. Not far from a water source, and nowhere near paths made by elk and moose. And he'd need to stay there for a very long time. He would need to live like a wild animal. A dark thought took hold.

"Where will you go?" Diane asked as she rounded the last foothill and headed toward the mountain pass. Jackson was still working it out, so he said nothing.

"What should I do?" she tried a different tack to pull her brother out of his reverie.

"Just tell them the truth."

"I'm coming with you," she said.

"No, you're not."

"Jack, I can't lose you. Please."

"I know how to survive out here. You don't. I'm comfortable in the forest and I'll be fine. Go to work like normal. Act normal. Wait to see what happens."

"How will I get in touch with you?" Diane started to cry again.

Jackson remembered the little cell phone in his back pocket. He pulled it out and threw it into a streambed as they sped over a wooden bridge.

"You won't."

"Jackson, I just got you back." His sister was sobbing now. And slowing down.

"Pull over. It's okay. It'll be okay," he reached out and hugged her after she stopped the car. When she settled down a bit and wiped her eyes, Diane looked up at him with the look he was dreading, a look of hopelessness . He hugged her again, longer, but then held her away so he could look into her eyes. "Diane, I'll miss you, too. You're all I've got left. I have no choice, though. I've killed an officer of the law. They'll send me to prison. I know what it's like. I won't be confined. I just can't let that happen. "

"You're the last of my family, and you'll always be in my heart. I love you dearly, but I'd be no good to you locked up," he told her. Jackson waited until his sister had pulled herself together and had given him a small nod.

"Let me drive, okay? I know where I want to go in," he said.

The drive felt like the start of a mission more than a retreat. Silent beside him, Diane watched the trees' shadows pass. He could tell she was numb. This night would take days, if not weeks, to recover from. It took all his attention to recognize the landmarks leading him to a small cut-in by the road. He had been there only once with his granddad, but the path into the woods led to a beautiful little rivulet — a crick his granddad called it — surrounded by some of the tallest pines he'd ever seen.

"Wait here."

He left the Jeep running and walked through the overgrowth, picking his way through the rocks and deadfall until he needed his flashlight. Another twenty yards in, his light bounced off the little waterfalls, and Jackson knew he'd guessed right.

"This is it, sis," he said when he'd returned to the Jeep. He started unloading his hiking frame and pack from the back. Diane got out and gave him a hug.

"But how will I contact you?" she asked more insistently, hoping for a different response.

"Forget about me, sis. Let's just remember the fun we've had. You're the best sister a guy could have, and you'll always be my hero."

Diane nodded, wiped a tear from her cheek, climbed into the driver's side, and drove away. Jackson watched the red taillights fade in the distance until he could no longer see them. Then he turned into the perfect darkness of his new home.

Chapter 4

"Get a move on, son."

He recognized that gruff voice. It was his father's. He'd heard it so many times.

"But where am I supposed to get moving to?" Jackson thought.

Far away, he could hear the rat-a-tat-tat of the steady fire he'd endured on so many missions.

"I don't want to get moving. I need to stay right where I am. "

"Home. Am I home?" Suddenly he was covered in a cold sweat.

"Dinner!" "Mom? What was she doing in the middle of a fire fight?"

He felt different. He was playing outside with Diane. He was on the swing out back, and she was pushing him.

"Mom?"

He began wandering around, calling for her. No response. He called again.

Awareness of something else started to creep in.

"Am I dreaming? But where am I? Where am I supposed to go?"

He tried to remember the last thing he did when he was awake.

"Crawl into the corner of the cell? Rest back against the headrest? Scoot down under the blanket in his room at the house? Bed down on a floor of pine needles?"

"Get yourself together," he muttered, then grew quiet. He listened. No sound. Had his mother gone? And where was Diane? Where was his father?

"Hey! I'm here!" he yelled. "I'm not going to disappear," he ordered himself. "Get your ass up! "

"Here! I'm here!" He kept calling until he was nearly hoarse. The sound of his own human voice did little to comfort him in the vast darkness and silence.

No one answered. Had he lost his mind? He wished he would.

He was sinking, pulled down into a black abyss. Disoriented. The despair was crushing.

The moon slipped behind a bank of clouds.

"Okay, now my eyes have to be open."

Sparks from the fire popped, floating up into nothingness. He was in his sleeping bag on top of a bed of the softest pine needles.

"No, this ain't right," he thought to himself. Spectral scenes began playing out before him. "Not right at all." He started shaking himself awake, but couldn't be sure if he was dreaming it or actually doing it. "There's a word for this. But not English. Apsáaloke?"

"Déjà vu," he thought. "Is this the same dream in the same night? Or a different night? Or am I awake and only thinking about the repeating nightmares?"

As his mind tried to unwind the knot, he sensed movement. He stilled his mind in its dream state and slowed his breathing. He needed all his faculties alert, even if he was asleep.

He was in the hole. Not the same one they rescued him from. He could feel smooth concrete beneath him as he lay there. Not a dirt floor, like his final resting place in Afghanistan. This one had light. Easier access. To electricity. Water. Pain.

He knew they were watching him through a small, barred window in the heavy door. Then, as now. He could feel it, sense it. His eyes didn't need to be open to know.

But something even more sinister had taken root in his psyche. He recognized this even as he slept. It wasn't his captors, not mortal flesh.

He tried to stop it. Shake himself out of it. He slipped farther down the hole.

There was no way to tell how many miles he hiked in nearly a week. He had backtracked and switched back and climbed. He'd made sure not to leave any straight lines and as few footprints as possible. Not a twig was broken or fallen leaf torn after he passed by. He often waded through creeks for miles when he did need to walk in the same direction for some distance.

On the first full day on the trail, he'd encountered an abandoned campsite. "Young hunters," he had thought to himself. Beer cans, spent ammo, a soggy loaf of bread, and a mangled tent pole had been left behind. The trunks of a few trees nearby had been shot to shit. "Maybe not even hunters. Kids out messing around." Jackson traced their movements around the campsite until he was confident they hadn't gone in the direction he was heading. The forest grew darker and more ominous as he left the area. A person must intend to get lost in order to penetrate the forest where Jackson was going. He took comfort in that fact.

The darkness of the forest contributed to dark thoughts as he walked. He replayed the fight with Tom Denny, the gun, the feeling of impact between them. He hadn't been sure at first whether he'd been shot. He had been shot before, in combat, and had kept fighting then. He would've kept fighting this time too. Until he knew Diane was safe and Denny had gotten the message. But he hadn't meant to hurt him permanently. Finally.

The waking nightmares followed Jackson as he crept farther and farther into the wilderness. Every time he covered his tracks, he felt like it was one more minute lost to the future he had imagined. "I'm finally out. I could do anything I wanted. I wanted to be off the grid, sure. But never this off the grid."

He recalled the few days with Diane and his plans to spend more time with his only living relative. He imagined moving out, but maybe not too far away. He could be a wilderness guide out of Arapaho Glades as well as anywhere. "I'd stay close. Go over for dinner once in a while. Hang out on holidays. Barbecues with friends." The idea of missing it all depressed him even more than the memories of his torture and imprisonment at the hands of his enemies.

The guys in his unit had been his family after leaving home. He remembered one barbecue in particular, on a beach. Pretty girls in bikinis. He was still in love with Valerie then, so he had kept his head down and helped with the grilling. His buddies were in top comedic form. He remembered thinking at the time that it was a great day. Maybe his best day. It had bothered him at the time that his best day didn't include Val. He'd thought about that when he'd read her letter.

Jackson never minded being alone, but he did miss his brothers. They had been a tight unit. A few had given their lives for the others. His thoughts grew dark again and he let the horror wash over him just as he fell into a restless sleep.

His sleeping nightmares became most intense after days spent thinking about what he had endured, done, and might have been. One morning within the first few days, he awoke with the sensation that he'd faced down a full-grown bear as he rested against a tree during the night. He shook himself to rid the ridiculous notion from his brain.

"I need to make a pact with myself," Jackson thought as the sun rose on the fifth day. "The minute I start thinking about something bad, I need to stop, take a deep breath, and look around at this incredible place. I'm missing it. I've been given a gift."

Throughout the rest of the day, Jackson struggled with keeping his promise. But by the time he pitched the tent and got comfortable, his mind was sending out fingers of hope for the beauty of the next day. His nightmares were less intense that night and he woke feeling more optimistic, yet knowing it would be a long row to hoe. Maybe years.

It was just as he had pictured it. He would've missed it if he hadn't tried to follow the woodpecker, its red head and striped body flitting among the low branches. "Is this the same one?" he wondered. A woodpecker woke him nearly every morning on his trek into oblivion. First gunfire, then his father's voice. Sometimes it was the other way around. Last night had been the worst, so he was glad to awaken and hear the birds calling and hunting for food. Bed of pine needles. "That's much better," he thought to himself.

After he disappeared his campsite, packed up his gear, and strapped it on his broad back and shoulders, he looked around to decide on the best route. "I'll follow the woodpecker," he thought, and, for most of the day, he did. A few times he lost the woodpecker and followed his own feet and instinct.

He let his mind wander again, even though he remembered his therapist's warning. Back into the same patterns. He replayed and replayed his misery, like a hellish earworm he couldn't shake out of his skull. But the sameness of his surroundings left little to the imagination, so he walked and thought.

"What a year. Valerie had all but said yes, all I had to do was ask. Then we'd move in, make plans, get married." Jackson was as sure-footed as any full-blooded Crow warrior. His footfalls made no sound. He didn't look at the ground as his eyes swept the area for a glimpse of the little red head.

"Find a job. Get a house." He considered the change that Val's letter had brought. "Hang out with Diane until I was sure of my next step, that would've been nice. But in just a few days, my whole world has fallen apart. Everything is against me. An off-duty deputy. Unbelievable."

Jackson ducked as he travelled through a tunnel of leaves and branches. It was the only way through; boulders and trees blocked any other path. He imagined poor Tom Denny lying on a shiny table. He remembered Tom's mother. Her voice carried at games. She was always shouting something incomprehensible to poor Tom. Jackson could hear what her crying would sound like, sobbing poor Tom's name.

Tom who tried to rape Diane.

Jackson paused and shook his head, and then continued crouching through the verdant tunnel.

He imagined his arrest, Diane's denial that he had been involved, the proof by the prosecutors. Judgment...sentencing. He needed to stop and straighten up. His breathing had become rapid. "The doctor warned me about this."

He didn't linger on the transfer to the prison or what his cell would look like. His mind went almost straight to the torture. Never mind that he would be in an American prison for the involuntary slaughter of Tom Denny. If he was in a cell, there would be torture.

He recalled the beatings most vividly. The doctors had given him a dozen redirection techniques whenever his mind wandered to that dark place. None of them really helped. He promised himself he would keep trying and, for a moment, he quashed the painful thoughts.

"But I'll never have a normal life with a family of my own." He had come out the other end of the winding, leafy tunnel and straightened up. A streak of red caught his eye and he followed it until he found a small stream. He shed the packs, crouched, and dipped his cupped hands into the icy water. He splashed it onto his face and felt the week's growth of beard. "Never have a wife. No kids."

He rocked back and slumped onto the dead leaves. "Vulnerable. At the mercy of nature." He didn't have to wonder what a lack of interaction would do to him. He'd experienced it for months first-hand.

He heard a sound behind him and turned to see Dr. Jeff, wearing his purple V-neck sweater vest, leaning against a tree.

"Everyone is trying to survive, Jack," he said. Jackson held his breath. He thought he was awake. "But to survive, you need nourishment. You need to interact with other

people. You need to connect. You can't stay in this hole."
Jackson blinked.

The trees stood solemnly around him, not being anything
but trees growing out of the ground. "I won't ever know what
it's like to have someone. Even the trees have one another.

"Maybe I shouldn'tna never left. Val asked me not to go.
She was the only one. Everyone else patted me on the back
and told me to go kick some ass. Now everyone was going to
welcome me back. But her. When I went away, I married the
military. That's the whole story."

He opened his pack and took out some jerky. Dinnertime. He
could almost hear his mother's voice. After he finished eating,
he laid back and gazed up at the gray sky. The only sound was
water rushing over the stones in the streambed. He closed his
eyes, willing himself to stay awake. "I need to find my home."

Jackson stood up, brushed himself off, and looked around.
The stream was deep and almost too wide to leap across. He
decided to follow it through the trees and see if it would be
his water source.

Branches seemed woven together over his head, perfect for
full coverage. He began searching in earnest for his new home.
He checked out every nook, no matter how small its opening,
to see if its interior space would be large enough. He'd almost
given up when he spied a door-sized opening farther along, on
the edge of a little glade, halfway up a rocky bluff, bordered
on either side by two enormous oak trees. The trees grew at
the base of the rock wall and their branches grew across the
opening, nearly obscuring it from view.

Setting his pack by a large elm, Jackson clambered up to
a slab of rock, fairly flat, but hidden by the angle below, that

jutted out from the opening. It sloped away from the opening very slightly and he knew the cave would never flood. He spent the better part of an hour clearing the rock, leaves, and branches that had fallen along the entryway.

"Granddad would approve," he said as he poked his head between two large branches and into the large cave. It was a palace, so deep that he couldn't see the back of the cave, with a ceiling high enough that he could stand upright. He whistled and heard the echo bounce through smaller chambers at the back of the cave.

"I'll trim some branches tomorrow," he thought. "Tonight, maybe the nightmares will take a night off." It was past nightfall when Jackson pitched his tent in the little glade and bedded down inside.

Rising the early the next morning, Jackson felt better rested and attributed it to some small modicum of hope he'd developed just as he was drifting off. What was I thinking about? He tried to remember his last thought before sleep overtook him. "Oh, right. Maybe I'll discover a village of wood nymphs tomorrow." The idea made him grin. "A whole neighborhood of wood nymphs. Wouldn't that be crazy."

For the first several hours of the morning, Jackson scouted the area around the glade to ensure that it was as secure as he hoped. It was. During his reconnaissance, he discovered many species of birds, fish, and wild game traversed the air, stream, and land. He would never want for food or water.

But he thought he might have some competition. He had heard wolves howling through the night. He hadn't heard them any of the other nights, although he was pretty sure they were near. He'd seen tracks of deer and elk, with the broad paw prints of Timberwolves interspersed with them. "I'll get that cave cleared out today."

Walking to the streambed, he stripped down and took a bath in the freezing water. Refreshed, he grabbed some clean pants and shirt from his pack, dressed with blazing speed, and settled against the elm with some beef jerky for breakfast. He regarded the bluff, the jagged rocks, and the cave opening while he chewed. He began to draft a blueprint in his mind of best locations, inside and out, for all he would need to survive and maybe even thrive in his new quarters.

"Water to cave, outhouse, fire pit inside...or outside...for cooking. Maybe two firepits?" He needed to keep the animals at bay. And he didn't want to draw them in by the smell of cooking rabbit or fish, or venison. Once he had cleared out the inside of the cave, he would examine it for openings for smoke holes.

Jackson noticed a flat, grassy area near the side of the bluff. He got up and examined it. Several very large trees with great canopies grew in the area, but not as closely. He needed a fixed table for skinning his catches and preparing and preserving meats, herbs, and anything else he could forage. A natural wall along the outside of the cave was well hidden nearby and could serve as a storage site. He would build a small roof and shelves and hooks for his equipment, all easily obscured by branches and dirt. The cut oak branches would do nicely for the table, storehouse. And maybe, one day, a smokehouse.

"And outhouse. Digging a latrine is typically first duty. So to speak." Jackson grinned at his little joke. He began marking off the size with his steps to get an idea of distances from the entrance to the cave, the stream, the best location for the latrine. He figured he could build something secure, but moveable, so that he could pick up the small building and transfer it to another site if he needed to. He thought pine wood might suit better for its lightness. It may not withstand many winters and not block the cold as well as solid oak would, but it would do the job well enough. And, as he turned around and looked up into the trees, he wagered there were certainly enough pines in this forest to build a hundred outhouses.

The morning slogged by. Jackson cleared off the ledge and began stacking rocks there as he removed them from the cave. It was slow and back-breaking work. But Jackson was used to this kind of labor. He had built walls and forts at the far edge of their backyard as a boy.

After a few hours, he straightened up and surveyed the inside of the cave. He'd made good progress and was only a few feet from the back wall. He pictured a large bed there. He'd have to get busy tracking bear for their skins. Would make for good bedding in winter. He'd need a large one to cover the opening too. It would protect against dangerous creatures when he was off hunting or sleeping. And the pelt would be thick enough to block out the cold and snow in the winter and rain during the spring and summer.

After a quick lunch and a little rest, Jackson resumed clearing out the main part of the cave. He had spied through the dimness at least one more chamber off to the side. He had cut some branches off the oaks and could now move easily in and out of the cave. He used one of the thinner branches to poke along the cave's ceiling, to check for a possible smoke hole near the entrance—he found a good one—and make sure it was sturdy with no risk of collapsing.

As he reached the smaller chamber, he noticed moisture along the cave walls and even a little rivulet seemingly coming through the rocks. He pushed his staff against soft moss and dirt along the ceiling. As he pressed, some rocks and dirt tumbled down. Jackson jumped away in time and then peered up through to see a small shaft of light.

Immediately, he left the cave, clambered up the side of the bluff, and reached the top easily. He found a spring and paced the distance to where he thought the hole would be in the small chamber. There was a mossy patch not far from the spring. He poked down until he could see the inside of the cave chamber. "Rain will get in here," he thought. "The spring could even overflow."

Jackson spent the rest of the day and evening thinking about the problem of the hole in his smaller chamber. He still hadn't worked out a solution as he strung his tent across the main opening and rolled out his bag. He fell asleep quickly, but woke often through the night to listen to animals scratching or rustling by. When the howling started, the scratching stopped. For a while. Wolves are the apex predator here, he considered. Except for me. After falling deeply to sleep, the best sleep he'd had in ages, Jackson awoke when the sun was already well up, its rays sending a soft orange glow through the tent fabric.

He looked around the large space and felt satisfied. Quickly dressing, he walked to the stream to get a drink and relieve himself. "I've made the right decision to make this place a home," he thought as he surveyed the area again. "There are a lot of possibilities for making this into a pleasant place. And I'm far enough away and deep enough in that I can't be spotted from land or air. Better get back to my shack. Jack's shack." Jackson smiled at the name for his hermitage.

"An aqueduct to impress the Romans," Jackson said aloud as water from the spring began flowing into a small reservoir he'd crafted in the closet-like room of his cave. He'd found another, smaller chamber a few days after moving in, but determined it made a better pantry.

It had taken several weeks for Jackson to try dozens of solutions for getting water into the cave. Each one failed. For a while, he gave up on the natural hole in the ceiling of the small chamber and looked for other ways to bring water in. When those didn't pan out either, he turned his attention to finishing the latrine, building traps, furniture, and tools, and storing items he needed to keep safe and dry for long-term use. "My whole life," Jackson thought. "This hunting knife has to last at least 50 years. Unless I die sooner".

Somehow, that thought comforted him. Maybe he would be spared this life of isolation and loneliness by a quick death. A bear mauling or fall off a steep cliff. "Simple exposure would do the trick." He wiped sweat away with the back of his wrist as he tied elk sinew he'd cured in the sun around sticks to make a rabbit snare. "I need to wipe these thoughts away too," he thought.

The water from the spring could be turned on or off inside his cave. And the tent had come in handy for collecting rainwater and providing a shower, of sorts. The whole mechanism would take some tinkering. "I've got the time to get this water source, filtration system, and drainage working perfectly," Jackson figured. He applied the same diligence and creativity to each task, realizing that no interruption except his own basic needs

would interfere with turning this rough cave into a palace. Or
at least a very comfortable living space.

Chapter 5

The pack had thrived for generations by staying far from any scents or sounds that were unfamiliar. The big alpha that had established the pack's territory looked as wise as he was. White fur sprouted from his long ears and gave his muzzle the look of an ancient shaman. The other wolves had nothing to compare their leader to, however. They had never seen a human in all their years roaming the mesa, the canyons, the deep forests, and the streams that bordered their territory.

As each generation matured, wolves wandered away or into the pack to mate. More and more wolves were born and more packs established. The wilderness teemed with the wizened old wolf's offspring. And many packs roamed the mountains, valleys, and glades that the first wolf had discovered.

So, when a young wolf happened upon the scent of something strange, she followed her nose without thought of danger. She knew how to steer clear of mama bears and stayed off the trails and out of the rotted logs where the rattlers sunned...and waited. She was the descendant of the great alpha who had claimed the land. When she stood atop the bluff, all she surveyed was hers.

When she hunted, her brother, a deep gray wolf, usually ran ahead, and she, a lighter gray and tan, followed more cautiously behind. But she left the pack and boldly followed the scent that day. It didn't take long to find the source. And the noise. And the delicious taste that filled her mouth as it lumbered through their claim.

The creature looked huge. Not as big as a bison, but nearly as tall as a bear on its hind legs, reaching up to scratch high along a tree trunk. Its body had shiny things all over that glinted in the sunlight. It was easy to spot, even from across the valley. Though it tried to be stealthy, it clanged and shuffled, scraped and even moaned, occasionally, as it made its way.

After observing the creature for several hours, the light gray and tan wolf grew bored and jogged to the stream for a drink. Another scent caught her attention as she lifted her head and she was off, regaining her pack, readying for another hunt.

A few days later, the creature crossed her trail again. This time, it was bedded down for the night and a small fire smoldered in front of it. The wolf quickly backed away and rejoined the pack, losing interest once again. This went on for several years. The young one strayed to investigate the scent that was becoming more and more familiar. The creature had claimed a territory near a glade full of berries and it was always easy to find there or out on the trail, hunting.

In time, her light gray mate began following her when she would stop and sit at the edge of the glade. The pair was between litters and she was curious to see what the creature was about. The creature fascinated her and, though she felt cautious, she knew no fear.

Late in the fall, the wolf and her mate discovered the creature sitting in front of a blazing fire, which was very unusual for it. It typically built small fires with only a few twigs, but on this bitter night, out on the trail, the creature had constructed a fire in a meadow. As usual, the scent from the campsite was divine. The cooked meat drew many predators to the meadow. All but the wolf pair slunk away. The fire and the strangeness of the scene were enough warning for the others.

The two wolves had often observed that the creature mumbled to himself. The wolves had even heard it howling, whether awake or asleep. Occasionally, it jumped from behind trees and leaped onto rocks, barking orders. But that night, they witnessed a creature that was deep in a stupor.

As they approached, the creature didn't move a muscle. Its face was covered with dark brown fur. But its eyes glinted red in the bright firelight. The pair came closer, assuming the creature was dead. Its eyes never blinked. Just stared straight ahead into the flames.

They crept to the side opposite it and regarded it through the flames. Ready to bolt, they lowered their heads and tried to penetrate the flames to see whether the creature was as easy a target as they had first assumed. The mate let out a low growl, but she turned her head to quiet him. She didn't want the creature to be alerted. The game lay beside it. They would have to get closer.

After some time, the creature lifted its eyes. A moment of shock crossed its face. But then it didn't seem the least concerned to see the deadly visages of the wolves baring their teeth and staring back at it through the flames. In fact, it seemed to brighten, as if greeting old friends for a spot of tea.

The odd response provoked deep, guttural growls from both wolves. But instead of retreating, or lunging, they widened their stances, raised their hackles, dipped their heads lower, and waited. The creature watched them carefully. After what seemed like half the night, it reached out slowly and tore chunks of rabbit meat from the spit laying beside it. The wolves watched every move.

"Want some?" the creature offered the chunks. A deep warning rumble emanated from the chests of both the wolves. The creature kept its arm still and continued to hold out the meat. When the wolves didn't move, it added, "Go get it." And it tossed two pieces of meat far enough away that the wolves had to trot back to the edge of the meadow to gobble them up.

The meat was as delicious as it smelled. The wolves were drawn to the creature, but they needed to get back. This was odd behavior, even for them. They stood far back and off to one side of the firepit so as not to obscure their view of the meat. And the odd wolf.

For that is what he was, she realized as she stood by the safety of the trees and her mate. He was a wolf that ate rabbit, like them. A wolf that howled, like them. A wolf that hunted, like them. A wolf that slept among all the living creatures, like them.

She glanced at her mate and he led the way back to their young ones. She sensed that he understood this about the odd wolf too. Lone wolves don't survive on their own for long. This one could hunt and even gave food. Yet this one needed protection too. It would be a long night considering the odd wolf they had just encountered. One thing she felt for sure. He was no threat.

The memory of the cooked rabbit stayed with the pair all the next day. She watched as her two-year old pups bedded down in the shallow cave not far from a stream. She knew they were ready to leave the pack and find mates of their own. They could fend for themselves quite well, but the gray and tan wolf would miss them.

The pair was comfortable wandering off. They didn't want the other wolves to follow. It was likely they wouldn't come to the same conclusion that she had after years of studying the creature. So, when it was quiet, the two gray wolves departed to catch the scent of the odd one.

It didn't take long once they tracked back to the meadow and followed the odd wolf's hunting route. He could hunt, but he didn't hunt like they did. He could bring down large prey alone. They needed the entire pack to take down the elk and deer that roamed the forests.

He had cleared off a wide space under a large pine and was cooking another rabbit. They growled a warning as they approached, but the odd wolf barely seemed to mind. He continued to sit quite still under the tree and only turned his head enough to watch them cross his field of vision. Her mate left her side and prowled around the back of the tree against which the odd wolf sat. When he emerged through brush on the other side, he was close to the odd wolf and sniffed at him. Then he growled.

She trotted closer to the two and sat down. She waited. The light gray wolf walked to her side and spread his paws out, keeping his head down and baring his teeth. The odd wolf continued cooking the rabbit. She licked her jowls and he noticed. He seemed to bare his teeth too, but not in a threatening way.

After a while, the odd wolf used something shiny against the meat, then tossed the pieces in opposite directions. She lunged to the piece closest to her and her mate sprinted across the tree roots to grab the chunk nearest him. They ate eagerly, then ran into the woods, stopping and turning around only when they were sure they couldn't be spotted.

The routine continued for many months. When one of the wolves would pick up the scent of the odd one, they would head off in his direction. Eventually, their pups were grown and gone in search of their own mates and the pair found a den close to the glade. They began walking with the odd one in the woods. Noises he made became familiar to them and they responded to his calls and whistles. They helped him to hunt. They played with him. They brought him their kills to cook and share. Without full realization of what was happening, the three had become a pack of their own.

She went into heat again sometime after they had begun sleeping by the odd wolf's bear-skin bed. The den was almost too big for the three of them. She knew it would be just the right size for the growing pack. So, when it was time, she wandered off with her mate in tow. Some nights, they would hear their pack-mate calling and whistling for them. A few times, he got very close, but they kept their distance until the new pups were ready to travel. Then they trotted into the glade and scrambled up the bluff. After they'd sniffed around the entrance to the cave, they crept up to him as he slept under his bear skin and nuzzled him until he'd awakened. His delight cheered the wolves. They played all day until the pups were exhausted. The routine continued with the new wolves learning the calls and whistles of the original pack. When the matriarch finally passed many years later, she was satisfied that her progeny was in good hands and well cared for.

The odd wolf adopted the stealthy ways of the wolves. Sometimes he ate, slept, and hunted at times the wolves never would have, but the wolves and their leader adapted to each other. And though they couldn't converse, they could communicate. As successive generations grew up with the alpha, they seemed to have learned how to read each other's thoughts.

Chapter 6

As Catherine Esquivel picked up the empty duffel bag, it felt like it weighed a ton. Not because it was made of sturdy fabric, with many pockets and indestructible zippers, which it was, but because her boy would be off on his spring break trip with his dad soon...and she would miss him.

She opened the door to her son's room in their condo near downtown Denver. The stench nearly pushed her back into the hallway.

"Oh, gross," Catherine muttered as she scanned the room, pressing the back of her hand against her nose and trying to determine which clothes were clean or clean enough to go into the duffel. Travis Scott, Post Malone, MGK, and Juice WRLD posters filled the walls.

She fought the urge to neaten as she rummaged through more piles of clothes, papers, binders, and random gadgets Tucker strewn around the room. Catherine folded all she could fit into the duffel. Just as she decided against looking for underwear to pack, her iPhone rang, and she pulled it from her back pocket. Her heart sank as she recognized the name appearing on the screen.

"Hi, Richard," Catherine tried to sound bright and carefree.

"Hey, Cat." Pause. Catherine waited. "So, I just got a call, and the company is sending me to Bangkok on Monday. Bad timing, huh?"

Without missing a beat, Catherine said, smiling, "Not really. Tucker loves Thai food." She set the duffel bag down and began pacing through the open spots on the floor.

"Cat don't be ridiculous," he said. "You know I can't take him."

Typical.

"You are unbelievable! One week a year, Richard. That is the only obligation you have to your only son. One week!"

Catherine sucked in her lower lip, trying to regain control. Just the sound of her ex-husband's voice was enough to trigger an outburst.

"You tell him,"she said when he didn't respond.

"I sent him a text. Maybe I can free up some time this summer. It'll work itself out…"

"You're an ass, Richard," she said. Catherine hung up. She waited for the familiar shift of the ground under her feet whenever her hopes for Tucker and dreams for herself were smashed by her ex. Catherine learned to control the feeling a bit ever since Tucker was small, but she still felt the seismic ripple. She stamped one foot, picked up the duffel, and grabbed Tucker's hiking boots from the closet.

"Pivot, Catherine," she told herself. "Don't let Tucker wallow. Don't you wallow. We'll make my on-site to Idaho an adventure."

After booking the RV and clearing the plan with Lewis Franklin, her supervisor in the Roseburg Forestry Engineering department, Catherine finished packing the last of their perishables in several small coolers, along with paper plates, cloth napkins, paper towels, toilet paper, and reusable forks, knives, spoons, cups, and containers. Then she returned to Tucker's room and found a drawer of clean underwear and socks. She added his bag to her pile by the front door.

Tucker was lanky. He didn't exactly know what that meant, but Lewis, his mom's boss, had started using the term every time he saw him. And always with its companion: tall. He stretched out his long legs as he sat on the bench near the parent pick-up loop and watched the guys—sophomores, most likely—spin and kick the soccer ball near him on the pitch. It was a perfect spring day in Colorado and everyone was excited to be out for break. Tucker didn't care much. Just exchanging one miserable existence for another, he figured.

His earbuds in his ears were turned down low, hidden beneath his black hoodie. He wanted to look uninterested, but still able to hear the players. He wished he could play.

A guy in green rammed the ball with his head and it took a bad spin, bouncing across the pitch and rolling under Tucker's bench. He looked under the bench and then up at the expectant faces of the four guys coming across the grass to retrieve it. He half-hoped they would ask him if he wanted to join in.

"Hey, can you toss that back?"

Reluctantly, Tucker picked up the ball, stood, and rolled it back underhanded. It stopped short.

"Don't exert yourself, Esquivel," called the boy in green with a Fly Emirates logo on his chest. Another boy started coughing and choking, mimicking an asthma attack. As he gasped, the other boys laughed.

Tucker sat back down and pulled the hoodie around his face, looking down and ignoring them. Or at least trying to. Tucker was used to being alone, but, once in a while, he felt that tug. He was sick of being lonely. He wanted to be part of a team…or something. He wasn't quite sure. But being alone sucked. A little brother or sister was out of the question since his parents divorced when he was still pretty young. Mom ruined it. He was certain of that. His dad wasn't around much anymore, but he remembered how much fun he would have on visits.

Tucker frowned. The last few vacations were duds, though. Either they were cut short because of some other commitment his dad forgot about, or his parents argued about some insignificant detail, canceling the trip. It was always his mom's fault. So, Tucker tried not to get his hopes up too high. He learned not to expect much so he wouldn't get hurt.

Out of the corner of his eye, Tucker saw his mother's silver pickup truck roll toward him.

"Hey, T, how was school?" Catherine asked as he stuffed his backpack in the rear of the cab. He shrugged, noticing the duffel bag on the floor. He unzipped it and started sifting carelessly through its neatly packed contents.

"Did you remember my PS?" Catherine didn't respond, acting as if all of her attention was on the left turn out of the loop.

"You packed my hiking boots," he said. "Dad and I never go hiking." Tucker looked at his mom for the first time since he got into the truck. This wasn't going to be good.

"Your father had to go on an unexpected trip, sweetie," Catherine said, realizing he never received his father's text message. Or one was ever sent.

"But don't worry, I have a great trip planned."

"Life sucks," Tucker said just under his breath so his mom couldn't hear. But she did.

"I know exactly how you feel," she thought to herself.

"I thought you said we were going to Idaho," he mumbled as they drove up to the RV rental center.

"Yes, that's where Roseburg is sending me...I mean us," she recovered quickly. "Lewis agreed to cover the cost of the RV for the week rather than put us up in a motel while I survey the land.

We'll rough it. It'll be fun!"

Tucker opened his mouth, closed it, shook his head, and scanned the lot to see which camper would be his new home for a week.

Touting all the amenities, the fifth wheel camper the rental agent offered them had opposite effects on mother and son. Tucker grinned as his mother pulled out of the rental lot, towing the RV behind her truck. At 13, he hadn't completely crossed over to surly teenager, so Catherine was glad that he was happy. She could've done without all the bells and whistles, but she knew she'd appreciate the 55-inch TV toward the end of the week, after they'd played every card game they could think of.

"It's a long drive, nearly due west and then north into the range," she said, gesturing at the GPS on her dash. "We should get there on Sunday. I want to take in the scenery."

Tucker shrugged. His hoodie pulled up; Catherine couldn't

tell if he could hear her through the music.

"Maybe I'll take you up in the plane to look over the harvest area," she raised her voice, hoping to be heard. Tucker's grunt assured her he had.

Free from distractions, Catherine made better time than she anticipated. Riverview RV Park popped up on the GPS to arrive late Saturday afternoon. Just a few more hours now. Her cellphone rang.

"Hey, Lewis."

"Hey, Catherine! How's the trip going so far?" Lewis sounded out of breath.

"We're close. We'll get there around dinnertime," Catherine answered. "You at the gym?"

"Treadmill at home," he said. Catherine heard her boss huff a few more times before he gasped. "Hey, have you crossed into the Pacific Time Zone yet?"

"Yep. I'm excited," she said. A whole week away from home, roughing it. Surveying unspoiled forests. A change of scenery."

"You need it, but more than that, you deserve it" Lewis said."

"Thank you for letting me bring Tucker."

Catherine looked over at her son, who was in the same position he'd been in most of the trip — asleep with his hooded head pressed hard against the window.

"Well, Richard didn't give you much of a choice when he canceled…" Lewis said.

"Yeah, yet again. Anyway, thanks," she said. Catherine was grateful to have a boss like Lewis at Roseburg. He was always a little distracted, but he was a big teddy bear who gave her a lot of latitude. He sounded winded now.

"And remember to keep your mouth closed while you're on the flat and even on the increase," he said. Breathing through your nose will help expand your lung capacity."

Deep breaths from the other end and Catherine grew concerned. Finally, Lewis gasped, "Phew, got it. Listen, I gotta go. But please call me when you're all settled."

Catherine smiled as she pressed the phone icon on her steering wheel and thought of Lewis, overweight and trying to get back into fighting shape, as he called it. She coached him when she could, offering encouragement at work and texting him health and fitness tips whenever he needed a boost. She ran hurdles and the 440, plus relays, in college. She was glad she still ran three to four times a week since her work took her all over the country. She was often sprinting through airports and taking miles-long walks through potential harvest sites at high altitudes.

When they were in college, Richard ran with her. Or — to be more accurate — a little ahead of her. "You sprint 90 feet, maybe once or twice a game," she would tease him, pointing out that he really had nothing to prove as a baseball player. After college, they thought their physical compatibility and dedication to fitness made them a great match, so they got married. It seemed like the thing to do. All of her friends were getting engaged, and she'd dates Richard at least as long as they dated their boyfriends. But Richard had the ego to match his handsome face. He wanted to stay on that Big Man On Campus pedestal he'd ascended to in college and have women fall at his feet. Catherine and he rarely touched and said I love you even less. She was ambitious and had big plans. He took a sales job and traveled for long stretches. When Catherine answered a call from a woman she didn't know, he didn't deny knowing who she was. Tucker was five years old. Catherine told him she was done and moved with the boy to Denver.

She shook herself from her reverie as she pulled the truck and RV up to an old trailer on cinder blocks.

"Whoa, five-star accommodations," Catherine said. "Roseburg really spared no expense on this trip, huh?" Tucker shifted in his seat to get a better view out the dusty window.

"Tucker..." Catherine warned, as she opened the door and started to climb out.

"Woo-hoo. Spring break," he said unexcitedly.

"Help you folks?" said a man as they pushed open the screen door and walked into the RV Park office. Tucker's eyes widened to take in all of Edwin — or so said the name stitched on his shirt — while his mom approached the counter.

"Oh! You must be Mrs. Esquivel!" he said, setting down a large beef sandwich onto a deli wrapper, before she could respond.

"Mizz."

"Edwin. Howdy." He licked the mayo off his fingers and offered Catherine his hand. She reluctantly took ahold and and shook it.

"What brings y'all to Riverview? Lemme guess. Fishin'?"

"I'm a forestry engineer," Catherine said, wiping her hand on her jeans. "I do surveying."

Edwin sifted through the papers on his desk and located her rental form, reading it carefully.

"For Roseburg Forestry? That's right." He slid the form across the counter.

"Looks like you're all paid up. So just sign here, Mizz Esquivel. You'll be in Site 11."

After signing and returning the paper to him, Catherine waited.

"Don't I get a receipt or something?" she said.

"Oh, we do all that electronically," Edwin said, looking away. "Through the e-mail."

"I'd like one for my records, if you don't mind," she insisted.

"All right. I'll just print one out for ya. Just figured I'd save a tree, is all," Edwin said, chuckling.

As he shuffled into another room toward a printer covered in black smudges. Catherine shook her head, then said, "It really doesn't save..."

She noticed Tucker looking at a rack of pamphlets and bumper stickers. He held up a "God did not create the stump" bumper sticker to her and smiled.

"You know what?" she called. "I don't need one."

"It's already printin'," Edwin shrugged, pulled the paper from the printer, and handed it to her. "You all need anything, just knock, holler, or kick my tires."

Tucker nodded and put the bumper sticker back in its place. Catherine murmured a thanks and headed out to find Site 11.

Chapter 7

The sumptuous dinner of mac and cheese, hot dogs, and peas stood on the fold-out table before them. Catherine could tell Tucker was getting frustrated.

"Put the phone down," she told him.

"Reception is terrible here," Tucker said, slapping the phone against his palm.

"It's time for dinner," Catherine said. "Please put the phone down." She was getting frustrated, too.

"C'mon, Mom. It's almost working," Tucker said with a mild whine in his voice he hadn't used in a couple of months.

"Nope. I want to eat and get a good night's sleep so we can head out early and fly around a little bit."

Tucker set aside his phone and dug in. He was ravenous.

"You're going to love it," she added, trying to lighten the mood.

"Mom, it's called spring break. Not spring job. Can't I just stay in the camper?"

"No. This is a vacation. I know it's not your ideal one, but it's the best I can do under the circumstances until I get some actual time off."

"Yeah, like that'll ever happen." He looked at his mom after a moment.

"What if I said chopping down trees is against my beliefs, and I refuse to go on principle?" Tucker said, raising his eyebrows, testing.

"Okay, Mr. Tree Hugger. Then you can do the dishes, so we don't have to use paper plates tomorrow."

After dinner, Catherine retreated to the back of the RV to review the land she would begin surveying in the morning. She received an e-mail message from Rufus in her office on Friday evening the Piper Arrow 200 at the small regional airport was fueled up and ready so she could head out first thing on Monday. She decided it would be fun to take Tucker up a day early.

Peeking in at Tucker in the back of the RV and seeing he was sound asleep, Catherine pulled on her jacket and went outside. She wandered around the campground for a while, noting the many vacant sites, and just a few long-term campers. Weeds grew around the flat tires on the RVs. But lights shining out from the few extended-stay campers confirmed they were. The grounds were relatively clean, still, Catherine got the feeling that it wasn't a popular vacation spot.

Feeling a little spooked, she started to turn back. She scanned the far trees and couldn't shake the feeling she was being watched. Just then, she saw a man heading her way.

"Hey," he said.

"Who's there?" she responded.

"Oh, it's just me, Edwin," Catherine could see that it was the campground manager.

"Taking a walk, are you?" he said when she didn't respond.

"Yes, I'm stretching my legs after the long drive," she said starting to walk past him.

"Well, you're a mighty pretty lady, and I thought you might want to have a drink with me." Edwin took a step closer, keeping her from passing. Catherine could smell his strong cologne.

"Just got myself cleaned up, and hoped you'd be lonely," he said. Catherine's eyebrows shot up as she took a step back.

"Didn't see a wedding ring and, well, you see, I get mighty lonely out here myself."

Catherine smiled politely and began walking back to the RV.

"That's a very generous offer, but I'm afraid I've got to get back to my son and get some rest. Thanks for offering, though!"

She was now ten paces beyond their meeting point.

"Hope I didn't offend you," Edwin said, "But I guess it doesn't hurt to ask."

"You're a nice man, Edwin, but I'm not interested. I'm here to work. Have a good night," Catherine said, trying to appear casual as she walked back to the RV.

"Goodnight, Mizz!" Edwin called.

"Pack a snack and some water, just in case," she called to Tucker as she unhitched the camper from the pick-up truck the next morning. "And a blanket. I don't know how great the plane's heater will be."

As they drove away, she looked back at the RV and smiled. Despite the little run-in with Edwin, this was going to be a great week. Catherine hadn't felt certain about a lot of things lately, but she felt good about this.

Within half an hour, they pulled through the open gate near the hangar where the Piper Arrow 200 sat. Once she parked, her phone sprang to life and three texts from Lewis came through in rapid succession.

"Did you find the RV park okay?" which was followed by "All set for tomorrow?" and finally, "Helloooo?" Catherine laughed and texted a message: "All set. Be back in touch Monday evening or early Tuesday."

She enjoyed working with Lewis, despite all of his foibles. He was easygoing and actually more of a peer than a supervisor.

Tucker had already gotten everything out of the cab and was walking around the small aircraft.

"We're going up in this thing, huh?"

"Don't be a hater. It's cute," Catherine told him.

"Hope its cuteness helps us stay airborne," Tucker said, loading the water bottles and snacks into the cargo space between his feet.

Catherine checked the gauges, asking Tucker to remove the wheel blocks. Once he was back and strapped in, she turned the key and the propeller spun to life. She smiled broadly and turned to Tucker, who glanced around anxiously.

"You're not nervous about flying with me, are you?" she said playfully. "Putting your life in my hands?"

"By now, Mom, you've pretty much proven that you can do anything," Tucker told her.

The small prop plane taxied down the runway and executed a picture-perfect take-off into the glorious blue sky. It was ideal for flying, and Catherine was thrilled to be off-road for a change.

It took nearly an hour to locate the mountain range where Catherine would begin her work the next morning. Tucker wore the plane's headphones and kept his hoodie down. Catherine peeked over frequently, happy to see that he was drinking in the view. He pointed out landmarks and pretty vistas to her throughout their journey.

"Are we flying over the one you're going to cut down?" he asked her.

"Harvest," she corrected. "It's just east of here. But look, see that whole span…"

Catherine gestured to a big rock plateau and, beyond it, lush green forest.

"One of the last old growth stands in this part of the country."

She banked the plane to the west. Ahead, the snow-capped peaks of the range were visible. She flew straight toward them. The closer they got, the more spectacular the view, with giant slopes of pure, white snow.

"Feel free to drop me off right there for some snowboarding," Tucker joked.

She grinned at her son and then checked out the mountain as she began flying parallel to the peak.

"You really think you could drop out of a helicopter onto a 10,000-foot mountain and snowboard down?"

Tucker seriously considered the question, then he gave the most brilliant smile.

"I could so do that."

"I would so never let you. Not with those lungs of yours," Catherine said, smiling. But immediately saw that Tucker wasn't amused. He turned away and pulled the trail mix from the bag by his feet. Conversation over, she surmised.

The plane shuddered suddenly. Catherine looked back to the west and was surprised at the sight of spiral clouds forming.

"Looks like we got some weather after all," she said. Lenticular clouds."

Tucker looked through the windshield, eyes wide. The plane felt like it hit a speed bump — up then down — and Catherine was glad they were both strapped in.

"What do they mean?" Tucker asked, trying not to let worry creep into his voice.

"Squalls maybe." Catherine tried to turn away and flew just below the mountaintops. Suddenly, the engine sputtered.

"What does that mean?" Tucker asked in the same tone, his voice rising a bit.

Checking the gauges, she saw the fuel tanks and engine temp were normal.

"I'm switching fuel tanks to see if this one is getting water." A moment later, Catherine shook her head.

"What?" Tucker asked, truly alarmed.

"No, the other tank doesn't help, and we'll need it to get back."

At 6,000 feet, the plane was dipping and diving, with Catherine struggling to keep it level. As best as she could, she made a beeline for the airport.

"Still not running smoothly," she said, switching on the radio. She reached the dispatcher, giving the plane's call letters and approximate location, although she felt like they were blown way off course." At least I asked flight safety to keep us on radar before we took off," she thought.

"We're having a bit of engine trouble here," she said into the handset. "I'm flying visual flight rules. We should be seen on the controller's screen."

Catherine gave her location again, but the static became more persistent as the mountains obstructed the radio waves.

"Mom, is something wrong?" Tucker looked straight at her in order to get a sense of the danger they were in.

"We're losing altitude. Between the down drafts off the mountain and the engine stalling out, we may need to land somewhere else."

She tried signaling several more times, but the dispatcher's voice was crackly and kept cutting out.

"What's your location?" the dispatcher's voice finally came through loud and clear. The engine died, and soon the plane began sinking through the clouds.

"May Day," Catherine said, keeping the panic out of her voice. "My location is south southwest of …." The dispatcher's voice crackled, and the radio went silent. "May Day, May Day, May Day," she repeated, trying everything to restart the engine and gain altitude.

"We're too low. The mountains are in the way," she said calmly.

"Mom," Tucker said and gripped his armrests tightly, watching the tops of the trees reach up toward the little plane.

"Tucker, we might have to make an emergency landing, honey."

"A what?"

The ground was coming up fast. Catherine looked for an open space and spotted a narrow creek bed. She tried steering toward it.

On rare occasions from his vantage point on the ground, Jackson could see airplanes high in the sky as they passed. On the very rarest, he could just make out the sound of their engines if they flew low enough. With so many high peaks and deep valleys, most airplanes stayed high and away from danger.

Through the years, his awareness of a world beyond his hunting and fishing grounds had dimmed. His memories faded, and he'd become completely absorbed into the life he'd chosen. Into the nature around him.

On this day, he heard the plane before he saw it. He never heard anything mechanical or man-made here in the forest, so hearing it so close to his home set off alarms in his head.

"Are they looking for me?" he wondered.

The plane's engine was in trouble. The sound gave him pause as he walked through the dense woods. He closed his eyes and could hear the helicopter as it lifted off into Afghani air space, carrying his broken body away from his place of torment. He opened his eyes when the engine suddenly died.

"Don't worry, baby. Everything's going to be fine," Catherine said, attempting a smile as she calculated the glide ratio. It could get them to the creek, strewn with small rocks and relatively straight for the landing she needed. They were heading into the wind now, which was good. She adjusted the flaps to slow their approach and gently raised the plane's nose.

"The tail will hit first," she said to herself, pinning the automatic landing gear retraction system. Wheels down would cause the plane to flip, and she didn't want that. Tucker put his head down over his knees like he'd seen in the movies. He put his arms over his head, trying not to pay attention to the sound of the plane crashing through the treetops. He tried not feeling the plane shudder as it dropped suddenly.

Without a moment's hesitation, Jackson ran with the two wolves at his heels as he watched the treetops sway in the distance. He heard the cracking of timber as the plane's wings and fuselage smashed through the trees, and he gauged the distance to the last place he saw the plane as it was going down. The wolves overtook him, knowing instinctually that he was running toward danger, and so they ran ahead to cover more ground. He knew he had to help. He didn't want anyone to be as broken as he'd been many years before. Jackson knew the sound of the crash would be absorbed by the density of the trees. There was no one in these woods anyway, and he was hopeful the groundcover was wet enough to keep a fire from sparking.

The tree limbs nearly sheared both wings off of the Piper and the ground came up so quickly that the impact knocked Catherine and Tucker unconscious in their seats. The plane slid along the rocky creek bed, and, at its bend, into the trees. The trunks of the concentrated old giants completely removed both wings as the Piper bounced from side to side, finally coming to rest beneath a tight canopy.

The compression popped open the windshield and the passenger door to the cockpit. The plane's nose tilted up off the ground, and Tucker hung partially out of the plane. Both he and his mom were still secured by their seatbelts.

Chapter 8

The day started like any other for the past fifteen years. He'd awoken to the sound of the woodpecker. He used to wake up in a cold sweat, imagining that the rat-a-tat-tat of the bird searching for food was instead the final bursts of ammo from an automatic pointed directly at him, time after time, before he did his job and collected that pay. On other mornings, he thought he heard his father's voice, echoing through the cave, "Get a move on, son." That's how he'd woken him up every morning back home. "Get a move on, son!" called up through the staircase, followed by "Time's a wastin'." His dad was more reliable than an alarm clock.

Distant voices and images plagued him for the first four years of his self-imposed exile. His parents, his sister, his grandfather. And then sometimes it was his brothers in arms — some still alive, others long dead — who visited him, waking and sleeping. He never minded being alone, but he did miss the men with whom he served. Their voices played in his head, and he heard them in the rustling of a squirrel or in the whisper of the wind.

But on this day, so many years later, he stretched, testing the air outside his blanket of bear hides, and reached for the doe-skin shirt and long pants he wore when the weather was only moderately cold, before rising with the sun.

Carved by water and deposits over the millennia, the massive cave had three rooms and was ideal for every season. He cleared out rocks and moss with his own hands and swept the dirt floor with brooms of pine and spruce. The coolest section of the cave, set back from the living space, served as the small pantry, holding the jerky, roots, dried herbs and berries, and other plants he liked to keep convenient during the coldest months. A nearby spring ran into a trench he lined with small rocks to funnel water into a little wooden trough in the other space, which had a floor drain. He called that his W.C., (water closet).

The cave entrance was extended by limbs from high in two giant trees. He shored up the logs with rocks and smaller branches and he'd leveled and packed the earth within and just beyond the space. It was well-camouflaged by nature. The trees and rocks around his home made it blend into the landscape on the edge of a glade, unseen even by someone standing in the dead center of the partially covered meadow.

An eight-foot bear hide served as the door. In his fourth year, he'd been out hunting, crouching against a tree, stock still. He hadn't been quite human, but he wasn't the full animal he eventually would become. A bear meandered up, sniffed at him, but he remained still, lost in a trance that had become his own private prison, revealing the depth of his insanity. The bear raised up and stood over him, testing this creature who smelled like the forest, but was unlike anything it had ever seen. He simply mumbled to himself, unaware of any danger, while the bear nudged him. Then he smiled, his eyes unfocused, as the bear moved on. He could never be sure if the bear covering his door was the same one.

Just inside the entrance was one of two of his firepits, this one for cooking. The other, was located outside several paces beyond it outside, was a sentinel fire for keeping warm. It had a clear sightline of the entire area. He kept his occasional fires small, just enough to provide some light, heat, and protection from curious creatures.

Jackson tied back his long hair. Both wolves — large for their species — looked back at him as they loped along the little path beyond the cave. It led to a stream, which was the reason he'd chosen this place for his home.

He looked around and remembered the first time he had found it. It took seven days to reach. A hard march with little rest. Jackson covered his tracks, changing directions often. And like always, he chose the more challenging route whenever he came upon a fork in his path. He didn't wish to be followed. This part of the woods was teeming with life, so he made his movements like those of a bear or buck. He assumed they would use infrared if anyone was tracking him.

In late afternoon on that last day of his retreat, he discovered the stream leading to a meadow. It wasn't until after dinner that he'd spotted the mouth of the cave cut halfway up into the rock bluff. He pitched a tent in the little glade and fallen asleep to the sounds of the woodland animals on that first night.

Now, the wolves knew the man's routine well. He gathered the icy spring water in an old waterskin while they drank from the stream, and they would be off on a new adventure.

"I think we'll go hunting today," he said to them. "What do you think?"

Neither wolf looked back this time, but simply stood, waiting for him to gather his bow and quiver. "Maybe rabbit. I better take some snares," he said, filling a pouch with the necessities from an old rucksack. He grabbed another small pouch and pulled a few berries from it and popped them into his mouth. He attached both pouches to either side of his belt, covered the entrance of his dwelling, and walked back into the sunlight. The cave entrance disappeared from view.

"I hope it's deer today and I bet you do too," he said to the wolves which always stayed within earshot when they went hunting or hiking. Jackson, lean and agile even as he was about to enter his 40s, began climbing over a rocky outcrop on the other side of the glade. The dew on the ferns would be dry by the time they reached the closest hunting ground for the kind of game he wanted.

A fire erupted in the instrument panel. One moment, the dust settled, the birds resumed their chirping, and the creek babbled just beyond the crash site. Nature had reset back to normal. The next, a poof and small, growing flames began shooting into the cockpit. First, it took out the radio, then it started tearing through the rest of the gauges.

Skidding to a stop before the wreckage, Jackson stood for a moment as the two wolves backed up a few paces. They sensed danger and so did he. "Enemies. Not my kind of creatures," he thought to himself. "What were they doing here? Did they come to ruin everything I've built? Take away my mountain? My family?"

The man backed away slowly until he saw the glow of the fire inside the cockpit reflecting off the face of a man. Not a man. A boy. He realized that the woman beside him bled from cuts to her face and arm. Confused and afraid, the man went through every scenario in his mind. Every instinct shouted at him to help. In less than ten seconds, he knew what he had to do.

Jackson unlocked the seatbelt and gently lifted the boy from his seat. Fearing further injury, he carried him gingerly through the forest and laid him at the base of an enormous spruce. He ran quickly to rescue the woman. The fire seemed to have eaten through the panel and was fizzling out, but the man knew it could be damaging the interior of the plane. Jackson was cautious as he approached, allowing his training to take over. Calmly, he released her from her seat and lifted the woman, who must have been about his age judging by the features not obscured by her wounds and raced to the base of the spruce. He laid her down gently, saw that both were breathing, and doused the last bit of fire with water from his waterskin. Once his job was done, he retreated into the woods.

Tucker floated. It wasn't what he expected, but he was relieved. It was the opposite of the slam he'd felt when their plane smashed into the ground and bumped over the rocky creek, too shallow to absorb much of the impact. He knew his mom did her best to slow them down and head toward a clearing in the forest. But his back, neck, and shoulders were in agony even as he floated.

Then he was resting on the soft pine needles and the scent was wonderful after the acrid smell of the burning cockpit.

"Mom!"

Tucker struggled to open his eyes. Peering through the slits of his eyelids, he saw the back of a man rushing away from him. With long hair and covered in buckskin, the man looked strong, even from the half-second Tucker concentrated on waking up and seeing him.

"But where was Mom?"

The fog in his brain overtook him again, and he let his eyes close.

" I'll sleep and figure it out soon, Tucker thought before losing consciousness again.

The man stood behind an old western white pine. The wolves laid panting behind him, unconcerned by the humans not far away.

"They look okay, right, guys?" he said, turning to look at the wolves. Then he turned back. They weren't moving, and he knew this was a bad sign.

"Shouldn't they be waking up?"

Jackson wondered again what they wanted here. He wanted them to leave, but he worried about them too. He couldn't understand why he cared. The only creatures he cared about were his family—the wolves. He remembered the day those first wolves returned. He had been frantic, wondering why they left and worrying about them like a concerned father. The three were inseparable before then. But they returned, proudly strutting up to his bed, pups in tow. He recalled picking up one of the wee pups and stroking its soft fur. Nothing would destroy his family. No one else mattered. Yet, the woman and the boy were so small and defenseless. They had no weapons, no water.

The man untied the pouch containing his day's worth of provisions from his belt. He couldn't afford to leave the waterskin, but the creek was nearby if they needed it. If they could get to it. He approached them slowly, crouching low and staying downwind, always in the shadows of the massive trees.

He placed the berries and jerky by the woman and began backing up. Just as he returned to the white pine, the woman opened her eyes.

"Hey, can you help us? My son..." he heard her call. But he closed his eyes tight, turned around, and ran with his wolves back toward home.

Chapter 9

"Mom. Mom?" Tucker's voice strained as he tried to rouse his mother, but she was unconscious. He thought he'd heard her call out, but, by the time he'd forced his eyes to open again, she was out cold.

He looked himself over, touched his face and head, felt his ankles and elbows. He noticed the bone above his left eye felt tender and his back was still killing him. "I'm okay though," he said aloud, mostly to reassure himself, then turned to his mother. Half her face was covered in blood, but wherever it came from must not have been deep. He looked her over. He couldn't tell how badly injured she was. He put two fingers along her neck to check for a pulse. He wasn't sure. Then he put his ear against her chest. He thought he heard a heartbeat...

Shifting his weight so he could sit up and take a look around, Tucker noticed a haze coming through the trees. Was it smoke?

The notion sent Tucker into an unbidden flashback. The May Day, the tree tops, the cracking and breaking, the crash. He took a moment to remember the details. They came at him rapidly, the scenes changing so fast he could barely process them. "If we're in the middle of nowhere, I've got to call for help." Tucker reached inside the pocket of his hoodie and retrieved his phone. No bars, no service. He tried calling his dad anyway. Nothing.

Then he remembered the radio in the cockpit. He'd watched his mom work it. He was sure he could figure it out. Checking his mom again before rising slowly, Tucker took a few tentative steps. His left foot hurt a little. He took a few more steps until he felt strong enough to walk normally through the dense forest. The smoke was thick, but he could make out the gleam of the white plane in the clearing.

Black smoke billowed out of the plane. Tucker hesitated, unsure of the danger. He had to get to that radio, though. He went around the back of the plane and saw that the entire tail was missing.

The cockpit was visible from the other side of the Piper. Tucker acted fast while the breeze blew the smoke away from him. He looked in through the door and saw that the radio was completely charred. Then he grabbed the pack and blanket, along with a water bottle. They weren't too hot to the touch and he carried them quickly back to his mom.

Tears welling in his eyes, Tucker grabbed her by both shoulders.

"Mom! Mom! Are you okay? Talk to me!! Say something, Mom," Tucker's voice rose an octave as he tried to wake her up. He suddenly wished he hadn't been such a brat. "Mom! Wake up! We gotta get out of here!" He felt the panic rising as he realized he may never leave this place. He felt for a pulse and put his ear to her chest again. She was breathing. "Thank goodness," he said to himself.

A branch cracked in the distance and he had the worst feeling that he wasn't alone. Was something or someone watching him? He thought back to the plane. How had he gotten out of the seat? He sensed a presence lifting him out and carrying him here. Was that presence still out there? Catherine stirred beside him.

"Mom?"

"We're going down, sweetheart. Don't worry about me," she said before passing out again. Tucker looked around again for help. But there was none.

He rose again and noticed his arm and wrists ached too. As he circled the tree, he spotted a small hill two dozen paces away. He thought he saw a partially covered hole about four or five feet up a small incline and beyond a ledge, but couldn't be sure without taking a closer look. He looked back at his mom before he went to investigate. "I'll be right back," he thought to himself.

Tucker staggered toward the small cave, still unsteady from the crash. He took two large strides up a small slope to reach it. The opening was no more than three feet wide and more like a letter box than a doorway. He checked inside. It was deep enough to fit them both pretty comfortably. "Better than being out in the open," he thought. He hurried back to his mom, trying to catch his breath. He'd noticed just before the crash that it was coming too rapidly. He'd tried to ignore it, but now he couldn't. An attack was imminent, he knew.

He reached for his inhaler beside his phone. Two quick puffs. Nothing. He examined the inhaler and noticed a puncture in the bottom. "Great. Can't worry about it now." Carefully, he checked his mother's head again. He worried about moving her, but he thought it would be dangerous out in the open. Setting aside the bags from the cockpit, Tucker slid his arms gently under his mom's arms and tried to drag her toward the cave. No give. Not even a little. He released her arms and slumped beside her. He tried to calm his breathing.

"I'd trade 'tall and lanky' for 'big and brawny' any day," Tucker gasped aloud, feeling defeated. Catherine was slender, but also slightly taller than the average American woman. Tucker realized it would take a miracle to lug her unconscious form to the cave, up the incline, and push her in through the narrow opening. Especially if he didn't want to add to her injuries. He didn't even really know what all her injuries were.

"Oh, God. Please help me. I gotta get Mom safe."

Tucker reached under Catherine's armpits again and made sure he had a good hold. Then slowly and very carefully, he pulled with all his might until she was in the right position to drag her backwards toward the cave.

After five small steps back, Tucker let go and put his hands on his knees. The pain was excruciating. Tears welled up in his eyes.

"Just give me enough strength, Lord, to make it 15 more feet. Okay, 20," he amended after looking over his shoulder. Tucker lifted his mother up as before.

He staggered a moment, then got his footing and began to walk backward toward the rocky hill. After four more steps, he dropped his mother's arms suddenly and fell backward. His breathing was becoming a problem.

"I'm sorry I complained about the trip and didn't talk to her the whole way," he began. He really did feel bad. It was actually a pretty cool idea. Mountains, camping, flying. Why had he been so pouty?

She wasn't his dad. That's why. And it wasn't the spring break he'd been living for.

After such a crappy year, decade, life, it would have been nice to get a little downtime with the father he never saw. At first, he blamed it on her, but, deep down, he knew. His dad didn't want to spend time with him. His wrists started to throb and Tucker choked back a sob.

"I'm sorry, Mom. I'm sorry I was so irritated. You tried to do your best," Tucker gathered her under her arms again and heaved.

Her weight wasn't the problem; she really was light as a feather. It was the pain that shot through both wrists as he lifted her. He felt her coming to.

"Mom, are you okay?"

"Tucker, what's happening?" Catherine sounded groggy.

Tucker hurried back and retrieved the water bottle, but she was out cold when he returned.

"Mom? Mom!!" Tucker wondered if he should slap her, then realized maybe that only worked in the movies. He placed the water bottle on the ground beside them and sat for a while. The smoke was still thick, but it didn't seem to be wafting in their direction as much.

He looked toward the cave and visualized exactly how he would get her over there. She really did do a lot for him. He would do this for her, no matter what.

Again and with extreme effort, Tucker lifted Catherine up, got a good hold, and dragged her, step by trembling step, toward the incline. The pain in his wrists travelled up to his elbows and he wept as he pulled, whispering prayers just under his breath. When he felt the bottom of the hill, he let go and leaned back, feeling each vertebra realigning along his spine.

"Ooof," he said aloud, and held his wrists tenderly. He retrieved the water bottle and took a swig and almost another, then thought the better of it. "We might need this later," he said to no one.

Tucker considered the five feet or so up to the little ledge before the opening. "Drag her or push her? I guess I'll be lucky enough to try both."

His footing sound, Tucker heaved up with all his might until his mom was halfway up the small hill.

"Okay, this isn't going to work." Tucker leapt down to below where Catherine slouched and started pushing her up by her knees. Even worse, but he did gain a foot. Then she started sliding back down.

"No, no, no, no, NO!" Tucker wedged his shoulder against her belly to stop her from sliding all the way back down.

"Okay, God. You and me," he said and climbed above her and grabbed both her hands. He pulled slowly and gently for what felt like twenty minutes, finally collapsing beside her after pushing her onto the little ledge.

"Thank You," he breathed out, barely able to get enough air to say the words. He didn't even want to think about how he was going to get her inside. He wasn't mentally ready for that ordeal yet. And he needed to calm down.

Her lashes flickered and Tucker scurried down to get the water bottle and back up the incline. Then he held it up to her lips. She took a sip and then looked him over. "You okay, Tucker?"

"Yes, Mom. I'm all right." He tried to mask that his

breathing was coming faster. He didn't think she noticed.

Catherine stood, feeling shaky. She wobbled a little but steadied herself, reaching out for Tucker's shoulder. He was struggling to breathe.

Catherine looked toward the cave's opening. It was a wide, slender mail slot. Her traumatized brain found it funny. A moment ago, she had woken up to find her poor boy trying to drag her to the cave. To mail her home. But he hadn't gotten to pop her in. "Not enough postage." She giggled, then registered the sound of ragged breathing and sobered suddenly.

It dawned on her that he was fighting for air. "Wake up, Catherine," she ordered herself.

She kept an extra inhaler in her purse. Now where did she leave it?

The plane! A crash!

"Tucker!" He had gone back to the base of the tree to gather the bags.

"I'm...okay..." he said as he made his way back, fighting for air.

"No talking, T. Just breathe." Catherine took the bags and ushered him toward the hole, reaching in to pull out a few leaves and sticks to make him more comfortable.

Wind whistled around the mouth of the cave as they entered through the slot and huddled together. In the distance, Catherine and Tucker could hear howling. They looked at each other as Catherine reached out to take Tucker's hand. She wanted to reassure and comfort him, but she wasn't sure if she had the strength. "Just breathe, baby. Slowly. In and out."

Tucker laid back against the stones and closed his eyes. Catherine put her arm around his shoulders and he rested his head on hers. A few minutes later, he had calmed his breathing enough to be in control.

"That's my boy."

Catherine could hear the slightest wheezing and knew Tucker was willing his lungs to relax. She wondered how long she had been out cold by that tree and how long he had been struggling alone.

"Why should I bother?" He had been facing the same dilemma for almost two days. "The boy. The woman. That's what they were, after all. People. Like me. Not like me," he thought once again. "They are trouble." Yet he couldn't get their images out of his head.

When he chopped wood for his cooking fire, he thought, "They don't have wood for a fire." When he cut herbs near the mossy stump, he thought, "They don't have medicine. I bet they don't even have a knife." When he laid down on his over-sized bed and pulled the warm fur over him to escape the chill of the spring evening, he thought, "They don't have beds." The notion of their suffering grew in his head until he could barely stand it. The wolves stared at him, full of reproach.

"They should've known what they were getting themselves into," he spoke mainly to the light-colored one. The jet-black wolf let himself get distracted too easily. When she didn't answer, the man huffed.

"It's not my job. I've done my job. I'm done."

She sat patiently, watching the man begin to pace.

"They are trouble. You must have felt that too?"

Her attentive look made the man feel as though he was getting through.

"Fine, you take care of them."

Tucker and Catherine ached for days. They found that they had both sustained massive whiplash. It took several days to manifest in the most uncomfortable way. But most of their cuts were superficial and Catherine was grateful for that. And, so far, in the intervening days that had passed as they drifted in and out of consciousness, Tucker had not experienced another asthma attack. "Thank God for small miracles," Catherine thought to herself.

But their whole bodies, from their legs to their backs to their heads, had been traumatized. They barely moved the first two days and nights in the cave. Whenever Catherine slept at various points throughout the two days, Tucker would grab the empty water bottle. He knew she wouldn't approve of him wandering back to the stream without her, but she was in no shape to keep them hydrated. He quickly refilled the bottle half a dozen times during those first days, racing back and forth as quietly as he could. Who knew what was in these woods? He dared not venture out as the sun went down.

Catherine smiled at her brave son. Tucker sprawled out along the floor of their little space, fast asleep. She was glad he'd gone back to the plane and retrieved what they needed. They subsisted on the snacks Tucker had salvaged from the wreckage and the small pouch left by...who?

During the first long stretch of lucidity, Catherine had noticed a pouch made of animal skin among the things Tucker had pulled from the plane. She opened it tentatively and found it contained beautiful fresh red berries and what looked like beef jerky.

"This pouch," she had wondered. And then she remembered a man. "Did someone help us? Where was he? Why would he leave us?"

After what seemed like hours trying to comprehend why another human would leave them alone and injured, exhaustion eventually overcame her and Catherine slept fitfully.

It was less reason than instinct that told him to wait until the cover of night to approach the cave where the two were hiding. Each footfall was silent. No leaf or twig was disturbed as he came closer. The wolves stayed back, confused by the scent of the strange creatures in their territory. They shouldn't attack, unless he bid them to. They knew that. But the creatures were defenseless, wounded.

The man had lost the debate with himself. He gathered strips of cloth, the herbs he had cut, and an extra skin of water, as well as more jerky and berries from the cave. Then he set out into the darkness. His home was close enough that he could cover the distance to their hiding place easily and quickly, but far enough and so well hidden that he could never be followed or found. He was leery of leaving the pouch out in the open, but he would not risk revealing himself again. They weren't friends, which meant that they must be his enemies.

On the third morning, Catherine staggered outside to get the lay of the land, hoping a helicopter pad was just beyond the stand of trees.

"No luck," she said to herself, massaging her neck. She had slept better the night before, but she knew it would be several days until she could manage to take charge and get their butts back to civilization. It all just hurt too much.

She glanced down and found a large drawstring pouch. She looked around, expecting some specter to emerge from the dark woods, horror-movie style. Her curiosity got the better of her and she gingerly picked open the sides. "Clean cloth to bind our wounds," she said aloud. "Huh. How about that?" When she found the food and water beneath the shredded cloth, she felt her initial hope rise again. She dumped the green leaves and stems onto the ground and shook out the bag. "Must be like packing peanuts," she thought to herself, then she looked around again.

"Helloo?" Catherine stood up and called loudly.

"Mom! Stop!" Tucker's face appeared just inside the mouth of the cave.

"No, T, it's okay." She handed him the re-filled pouch and cupped her hands around her mouth again. "Hello! Anybody out there? Thank you!! Please, we need help! Please help us!" She repeated the call for many minutes, but there was no reply.

The rabbit wasn't giving up without a fight. It had pulled the snare taut and was twisting wildly, trying to get away. As the man approached, it wedged itself between two granite rocks. The man stroked its fur and broke its neck in a single motion. Then he untied the rabbit and added it to the brace. This would nourish the boy and woman in the cave quite nicely, he thought to himself. Two fat females, not too lean.

He had begun spending more time at their cave than his own, watching and listening. He noticed that the boy sneaked out occasionally to get water. The boy tried to be quiet, but his thrashing through the underbrush was so loud it could wake the man's ancestors. The man shook his head. It was hopeless. He would have to care for them until they could make it on their own. The jerky and berries wouldn't be enough. He hoped the rabbits would tide them over for a while.

It was well after sundown when he rounded the knoll and reached the entrance of the cave. He had waited for several hours until no murmurs or any other sounds could be heard. He debated about whether to skin and cook the rabbits for them. No, this would do. He needed to prepare dinner for the wolves and himself anyway. Hanging the brace on a protruding rock at the opening, the two would be sure to see the rabbits as soon as they looked outside in the morning.

Chapter 10

"You hear those coyotes? Or, um, wolves?" Tucker asked.

"Mmm hmmm. Just be quiet now." It was silent again outside the cave.

A loud roar, very close, echoed in their ears. They both instinctively edged as far back into the cave's recess as they could. It was almost completely black beyond the opening.

They heard the sound of snapping, snarling, squealing. Tucker flinched when he thought he heard the sound of flesh tearing and bones cracking. He must be mistaken. He looked at his mom, who he could only just make out in the darkness. He could see the whites of her eyes and he thought he must look as frightened as she did.

Catherine fished around in her pocket. She didn't have her purse, but she remembered she'd put her phone in her pants pocket before take-off. She held it up and the screen glowed, but no signal. No wonder, she thought. No cell towers within miles. She had a feeling of déjà vu and realized she'd tried two days ago.

Minutes later, the sounds outside the cave stopped abruptly. But it took several hours for them to calm down. Tucker spread the blanket across them and they held onto each other in their hovel. For days, they'd eaten sparingly from the damaged bag of trail mix, and he had drunk his fill from the water bottle. The water skin rested against her bruised thigh. She took a few sips, but it was almost empty.

They didn't dare go to investigate. After a while, she sensed Tucker's head starting to droop. She would make a plan in the morning.

The man watched the wolves as they settled down just beyond the heat of the small fire that night. Akasha looked exactly like her great-grandmother, with wisps of white around her muzzle and ears that made her look almost angelic, or at least regal. Blue looked nothing like the wolves he had befriended so many years ago. He was dark as night, with fur so black that it looked midnight blue in the moonlight. The man was glad the two got along so well. If not for Akasha's halo, he might lose both in the darkness when they were only a few feet away.

The man built small fires for cooking on the trail and always beneath the densest, most layered canopy of leaves he could find. In this part of the woods, the trees grew tight together, but he still worried that the smoke would lift away through the highest limbs and be visible from the air. That smoke from the fire by the crick… The wind had been strong. If it had reached the treetops, it would've blown away quickly. And he had doused it after pulling out those…people? He wanted to make sure nothing more could be seen from above. He'd nearly been seen carrying the water when the young one went back to the plane.

People. He still couldn't be sure. After so many years, he had forgotten. He began to recall his first years out here. Like tonight, he would stare into the firelight, dazed, disconnected. Flashbacks of the wars, too many people. The isolation so soon after leaving the dark cell of his prison played tricks on him then. He had been prone to seeing and hearing things that weren't really there. He worried that it was starting again.

"Imprisonment in a dark cell can have extreme mental effects on the human mind," Dr. Weber had told him in Landstuhl, just a few days before he'd been transported stateside. But Weber had told him the same thing, again and again, when he was trimming the meat off a deer, or washing his tools in the stream, or just walking in the woods. He would turn a corner and Weber or Dr. Jeff from Walter Reed would be sitting there, behind a desk set right on a bed of pine needles. In the early days, he'd press his palms against his eyes, willing them to go away. But they were right there, in Idaho, lecturing him.

"Solitary confinement and total darkness can cause delusions, create invisible friends, and cause one to yield to the captors' commands. What you Americans call PTSD is one of the effects of isolation. The mental strength of the individual can lessen the effects or cause social withdrawal. The dreams you're suffering from, Sergeant, are your mind's attempt to eliminate or blank out negative memories of your imprisonment."

The man had accepted the doctors' words, each and every time, but nothing they said had fixed anything. They had watched him closely in the hospital, even as he slept. When he could eventually hold a fork and spoon, despite his broken wrists, Weber encouraged him to play cards and chess with the other soldiers. They never left him alone for too long. It wasn't until Diane and Dr. Jeff at Walter Reed broke through that he had begun to reconnect. But all that work had unraveled when he'd gone underground.

In the first several years out here, he would often hear his mother calling him in to dinner while he played outside. He would wander around outside his cave, calling for her, then he would slump down against a tree, his head in his hands, and the tears would come.

"Pull yourself together," he would growl, wiping them away. Sometimes he didn't hear anything at all. So he would talk and yell and call and shout just to hear another human voice. No one answered then. He had wondered if he had lost his mind.

Anger sometimes came over him and he wished he had not run away. Maybe he could have survived prison for a few years, he thought to himself. It was self-defense, after all. He never imagined he would be confused and lonely. Despair nearly consumed him at those times.

Some nights when there was no moon, he would see spirits in the firelight. Ghostly images had glided before his eyes. Sometimes something dark and menacing would glare back at him from the flickering embers.

"Get out of here," he would yell. "I know who you are and what you want. You want me, but I'm not going with you." He would be convinced he was being watched. Something—or someone—lingered in his peripheral vision. He would turn suddenly, expecting to catch them out.

"I'll kill you," he would cry. "Like Afghanistan." The elusive specter skipped just beyond his grasp each time. Often, and this was the worst, he was convinced he was back in the thick of combat. He would call out for his team to get their locations, sure he heard them clear as day. He darted among the trees, keeping to the shadows, conveying his own location into a radio that wasn't there.

"Roger that," he would respond. Sometimes it would go on for hours. His comrades just out of his eyeline, but he'd call each one's name to make sure they were okay. Most of the time they responded, or he'd thought they had. Sometimes they didn't. And he knew they were gone.

He didn't fear dying. Never did and never would. He didn't fear anything, not snakes, spiders, or large, furry predators. He didn't care enough; he was becoming all animal in those early years, surviving on instinct and routine. He tried to build up walls to repel his fears and demons.

But now those memories were fading. The wolves had claimed him, and he them. Months and years went by. A new generation of wolves replaced the one that passed on. His heart broke each time one of his family members died. He said words over their graves, while the younger wolves howled, mourning the same loss. After they trotted away, he would bow his head in silent prayer for his dead comrades.

Akasha whimpered in her sleep. He looked at her, her muzzle tinted red from the coyote's blood and the faint glow of the fire. He recalled another time, a better time. It was still long ago, ever since time became more fluid here in the woods.

One evening when he was eating a rabbit that he had skinned and roasted over a similar fire, he had a waking dream. Through his blurred vision, he had seen four eyes staring back at him across the firelight. He panicked, but then he saw two dogs. No, young wolves. They had come close and growled, baring their teeth and challenging him. In his stupor, he tossed pieces of meat to them. At first, the wolves growled another warning, but then they ate eagerly. Just as quickly as they'd come, they were gone again. It took him a few moments to realize just how much danger he had been in.

The next night, they returned. Again, he gave them bits of meat, talking to them in whispers. For what seemed like weeks, the wolves came every night and disappeared as soon as they had gotten what they'd come for.

Then something changed. The wolves started hanging around from a distance even during the day. He began carrying around a leather pouch filled with cooked meat scraps. When they did something he wanted, like walk alongside him or sit, he voiced a command, tossed the treat, and praised them. They were young, so he was reasonably sure they were trainable. Every time he saw them, he worked hard to calm his breathing and adopt an alpha-male attitude. It wasn't too tricky. He was half-wild by then anyway.

After a few weeks, they started running alongside him as he chased down prey. He started feeding them out of his hand and teaching more advanced commands and whistles. Sometimes they would bring their kills to the entrance of his cave. When he hunted and fished, they tagged along, curious to see what this strange creature had in store for them each day. Eventually they stayed with him all the time, sleeping by his make-shift bed, getting rubbed behind the ears, rising with him each morning, and, in their own way, communicating with him.

He no longer felt isolated then. The hallucinations came less and less frequently. He didn't see movement in the corner of his eye, he didn't think he was being watched, and he didn't hear voices in the wind. The furry wolves laid on his bearskin bedding for comfort and to protect him. His nightmares ended. His sleep became dreamless.

The man was part of their family now, their pack. Or they were part of his. Akasha's grandmother had pups and he was never lonely again.

"Don't let yourself get lonely, sir." Am I dreaming? He looked around the campfire but saw no one. He was sure he had heard one of the orderlies at Walter Reed speak to him. This isn't good, he thought to himself. This can't be happening again.

But it made him recall what the orderly had been trying to get across. He had been at Walter Reed only two weeks and he had refused to interact with the other patients at dinnertime, growing angry when they tried to insist. "You stay by yourself and you'll get suspicious of everyone," the orderly had said. "Even those that wanna help you."

His paranoia had returned. He couldn't be sure whether the intruders were real or one of his waking nightmares coming back to haunt him. The boy and the woman felt real enough as he had lifted them from the burning plane and left them by the tree. He could hear their voices from the cave near the spruce. They took his pouches and ate his food. His pack had stalked the coyote that had smelled the blood too and had come to investigate. Blue made short work of the coyote, with a blazing assist from Akasha. Yet he didn't hear anything more from the cave. Had he imagined them?

Chapter 11

Quietly, Catherine straightened the blanket around Tucker's shoulders and knees so he was completely covered before she ventured out. She held the empty bottle and waterskin in one hand as she began to pull herself through, when the fingers of her other grasped something wet and furry. She quickly stifled a scream when she saw the two rabbits hanging across the entrance of the cave. It took her a moment to recover without alerting Tucker. Then she stood up on the slope to examine the "gift" and survey their location, scanning the area for immediate danger. Her head was still fuzzy, but she was starting to figure out which way was east and which way was west from the location of the sun.

She started to make her way down when she nearly tripped on the leg of a wolf or a coyote. Looking around, she saw the half-eaten carcass—not large enough to be a wolf, she thought—strewn around below the entrance to their cave. The severed and mauled head lay not far off, and she shuddered as she edged around it to climb down the rocks.

"Mom!"

"It's okay, honey, I'm just going to find us some water."

"This is a House of Horrors," she thought to herself.

"Don't leave me!" Tucker's face appeared at the mouth of the cave, his eyes widening when he saw the dead hanging rabbits.

"Yeah, you're right. Maybe we should try to cook these, eh?"

Tucker stepped out of the cave, still wrapped in the blanket. He shivered when he saw the coyote's carcass. The two glanced at each other. They had tried many times to get their benefactor's attention, but to no avail. And they had decided it was best not to attract unwanted attention.

Tucker figured the dead animal on the ground had been attracted to the rabbits and something had gotten to it first. He gave it a wide berth as he began to gather sticks for the fire.

Within the hour, Tucker had managed to build them a decent fire, after a few false starts. First, he had forgotten the kindling and moss, then he didn't blow on it when the first sparks had come to life. He was out of breath from all the effort. Catherine helped and together they sat back and warmed their hands at their first mother-son fire.

"Okay, what's next?" she asked.

"What do you mean?"

"What do we do with the rabbits?"

"I dunno. I thought you knew."

"Hmm. Okay. Well, maybe it's like roasting corn on the grill." Catherine tossed one of the rabbits onto the small fire. The fur instantly blazed up and gave off a sulfurous odor.

"What were you thinking!?" Tucker cried, leaping up and away, covering his nose with the edge of the blanket. In minutes, the entire animal was charred to a crisp.

"You leave the husk on!" Catherine started to laugh. Her exhaustion and hunger and pain made her punchy.

"What are we going to do?"

"I am not skinning that other one," Catherine said, gasping for air.

"Me neither."

They both sat back down by their charred meal and contemplated what could possibly happen next.

Akasha and Blue sat licking their chops as the three watched the boy and woman pull one of the rabbits off the string. The man and wolves were hidden many yards away.

When the fire finally got going, the man sat back on his heels and gave the wolves a little rub behind the ears.

"See, they got the fire going," he whispered and smiled. "It took them five tries, but they figured it out. They'll be fine out here."

But when the rabbit went up in plume of flame, the man's optimism crashed. The wolves and he backed out of the blind and made their way back to the cave.

"We'll keep an eye on them, guys," he told them. "This may be more than we expected. Hope they leave soon."

"T, I'm coming right back," Catherine said, standing on the ledge by the cave. "The stream isn't too far off. You gave me good directions." Catherine gave her son a reassuring smile and he nodded, withdrawing back into the cave. It was later the same day, after the Rabbit Fiasco, as they had begun calling it. Tucker didn't want her to go out in the woods where there could be a crazy, rabbit-killing, coyote-mauling person lurking. He had called to his mom as she headed across the open area near the knoll. She promised she would be quick.

Following the sloping forest floor to the creek, Catherine caught a glimpse of the gleaming white hulk of the ruined Piper Arrow.

"Oh, no." She stood and gaped at the damage. It took her several minutes to pick her way through the underbrush and rocky terrain to reach the plane. She walked around to the back and saw that the wings and tail had been torn off. She looked back along the "landing strip." Plane debris and the limbs of trees, many of which were broken nearer the crash site, littered the creek bed. When she looked up toward the sky, it was almost completely blocked by the canopy of the huge trees. I'm lucky I saw this spot at all, she thought to herself. She turned and had the sense that she was being watched. She looked in all directions, but couldn't find any movement. "I better move," she thought.

She made her way to the passenger door and looked inside. The entire instrument panel was fried. She reached behind her seat and found the medical kit. She also found a little bag marked "Survival Kit." Inside, she counted a metal spork, compass/whistle combo, Swiss Army Knife, three lighters, a box of matches, and a flashlight. No batteries.

"Handy," she said aloud as she retrieved it too and backed out of the plane.

She went upstream of the wreck and bent down to fill the water bottle, then splashed the freezing water on her face and neck. As she did, she thought she heard a twig snap back near where she had come from, but the sound of the water made it impossible to be sure. She continued cleaning off the blood from around her eye and felt that it didn't feel quite as tender as last night. The painkiller in the med kit would help.

As she looked up, she found herself staring straight into the eyes of a large grey wolf about ten paces away. Crouching and backing up slowly, Catherine tried not to panic.

"Hi there. It's okay…" she said, stuffing the med kit and water bottle in the back of her pants and putting her hands in front of her. A rustling sound behind her caused her to glance around. Another grey wolf stood fewer than five feet away.

"This is not okay," she said, pivoting so her back was toward the direction of the cave. Both wolves began stalking her, herding her into a stand of enormous pines grown very closely together. She bumped into one of them, but it didn't feel like a tree.

She spun and came face to face with a tall, bearded man with a mat of thick, black hair. Her first thought was that she had found the original Mountain Man.

Stumbling back, Catherine saw nothing menacing about the man and hoped he knew how to save her from the wolves. Then she thought that maybe they had been stalking him.

"Don't move. They won't attack unless they think you're a threat," she said, turning so that all three were in front of her. She worried about Tucker and hoped he wasn't getting scared of being alone.

The mountain man stared at her without moving a muscle. He didn't seem at all concerned about the wolves. She looked him over and saw that his clothing was made of rough-stitched animal hides: a buckskin shirt with toggle buttons, buckskin leggings, a fur coat that looked like brown bear. Small leather pouches, like the one containing the jerky and berries, hung from his belt, as well as a large hunting knife.

"You probably know that already," she said. One of the wolves moved closer and snarled. Catherine yelped and backed into a tree. The mountain man gave a quick, sharp whistle and both wolves loped to either side of him.

"They're your…pets?"

Ignoring her, the man walked past with the wolves fanning out. She watched as they disappeared into the forest.

"Hey, wait! Do you live around here?" No response.

"Wait! My son needs help. Do you know where I can find a phone, or…?"

She marveled at the sudden feeling of complete aloneness. He had covered the ground back into the dark of the forest so effortlessly, she wondered if she'd seen a ghost.

Chapter 12

Catherine tripped on a root as she tried to pick her way through the underbrush to the exact spot where she last saw the mountain man's back. Tumbling, she recovered quickly. He could be their only hope.

"You're going the wrong way," she called out, panic rising that she wouldn't be able to find her way back if she followed him much farther.

Furious that he wasn't slowing down, turning around, or even answering, Catherine pursued him. The wolves were no longer a threat. She burst through the brush and finally saw him ahead of her, heading toward a little slope with a familiar-looking cave.

"Huh," she said to herself, looking around and realizing where she was. "He must know these woods," she thought.

Inside the cave, Tucker could make out his mom's voice. Was she calling to him? Somehow it didn't seem like it. He tilted his head and licked his dry, chapped lips. He could hear her coming up the rocks, but quickly. He pulled his knees up and rested his head on them, waiting, relief washing over him.

The light from outside dimmed as a figure, much larger than his mother, knelt by the cave and glanced in. Tucker let his eyes adjust to the new vision before him and could see the silhouette of a man...

"Mom, is that...?" Two wolves' heads peeked in through the brush. Tucker's eyes widened in fear and he tried to swallow, but found he couldn't. Too weak to scream, Tucker squeezed his eyes shut, awaiting the attack.

He felt something land on his foot and looked down to see a waterskin. He lifted the stopper and guzzled the water. He could hear his mom scrambling up the side of the rocky slope, cursing as she lost her footing and had to start again.

When he was finished, he looked and the man was gone, but he could tell he was just outside the cave. Tucker crab-walked to the opening and peeked out. His mom bent down and touched his cheek.

"Tucker, baby, are you okay?"

Tucker nodded and they both looked at the mountain man in front of them. After a few long moments, Tucker said, "He saved us from the plane."

Catherine thought she noticed a flicker of acknowledgment in the man's eyes, but she couldn't be sure. Her frustration dissipated; she suddenly felt deep gratitude.

"Thank you."

The man looked at her, unable to process her expression. He whistled and started down the small hill, wolves by his side. Catherine and Tucker exchanged looks.

"Wait here, Tucker," she said and began following him. She could hear Tucker rustling around in the cave and then pull himself out of its mouth to follow her. She turned to focus on the quickly retreating back of the massive mountain man.

"Excuse me! Could you at least point us in the right direction before you leave us here? We won't survive for very long on our own!"

Catherine and Tucker staggered after the mountain man, who was almost always out of shouting distance, but just close enough to see.

"What's wrong with this guy?" she asked. "Does he not speak English?"

"If he wanted to lose us, he could," Tucker offered.

"How about showing us a way to get the hell out of here?"

Tucker watched as the man headed up a slope. "Maybe that's what he's doing."

Wrestling with whether she could afford not to follow, Catherine looked after the man and accelerated her pace. Either stay and wait for rescue near the crash site, with limited food and water, or follow a person who clearly could survive out here. It really wasn't a choice.

The wolves and the mountain man led the ascent along a path that became a ridgeline. Tucker and Catherine, stiff and aching, lagged farther and farther behind.

"You think he's trying to help us?" Catherine asked Tucker after what seemed like half an hour.

Tucker shrugged and kept following.

They found themselves distracted by the beauty of the land around them. Snow-capped peaks rose above them and, to the east, rocks converged into a narrow pass. They had a decent view of the forest below them as they hiked the ridgeline. They admired the dainty early columbine and ferns peeking up through the brush along either side of their trail. The day was cloudless, unlike the day before, but they could see trouble brewing far off to the west. Catherine checked the sky often, wishing she had at least pocketed the compass before she'd left the Survival Kit, yet she still couldn't get a good sense of exactly where they were. The crash and her head injury had left her befuddled. She just knew they had to keep moving and hoped this mountain man would be their salvation.

When they struggled to keep up, the man slowed imperceptibly so he was just beyond shouting distance. Tucker wondered if he even knew they were still behind him. As he stepped over a log, he glanced down and saw a huge paw print in the mud. And two little pads, each with five prominent claw marks. *Bear*, thought Tucker. He'd been one in Cub Scouts. He knew the prints.

Tucker looked behind him. His mom had stopped again and was holding her iPhone above her head, shielding her eyes with her other hand, and searching for a signal.

"Hey, Mom, you gotta keep up," he called back, imagining Mama Bear charging her from somewhere beneath the brush.

"Yeah, yeah. I'm coming." She sounded irritated. They hadn't stopped now for nearly an hour and he was feeling fatigued. She must be too. The mountain man had started descending the path and heading back into the implacable darkness of the forest. "As long as those wolves stay up there with him," Tucker thought, "we will be okay."

They were getting close to the river, but the man still couldn't hear it yet. But he could smell it. The wolves could too. His dad had brought him to the river when he was young. He could remember that. It wasn't an illusion or a trick of his memory. Where they were headed wasn't the same part of the river, but it was a branch that had Chinook and Steelhead.

"Your granddad brought me out here many times," he recalled his father telling him as they sat by the fire after a day of fishing. "When I was about ten, same age as you, he taught me how to catch the salmon with my bare hands in the shallows. Showed me how to filet it and roast it over the fire." His dad had taught him all the same ways. Old ways of the Crow.

He remembered how they'd slept up in a tree under the stars that night, safe from prowlers below, their bellies full of fresh fish. He looked back at the boy in the bulky sweatshirt who looked like he'd never slept out under the stars in his life. He wondered if the boy would like to learn to catch salmon with his bare hands.

The forest felt secretive and nothing stirred around them as they walked along its floor. Soon the sound of water reached their ears and the wolves took off in its direction. They reached it a few minutes later. It was a narrow river, maybe twenty feet across, but the flow was noisy. The mountain man stood out on the highest rock, looking up and down the river to plot their crossing. Catherine knelt by the water's edge to gulp handfuls of water and rinse her arms and face. She was jerked to her feet a moment later.

"Hey! I don't know how you do things out here, but where I come from…" she began, wresting herself free of the man's grasp. Tucker shook his head quickly and she followed his eyes to bear prints near her foot.

"Are those…fresh?" she asked. The lighter-colored wolf with the fluffy ears howled and Catherine was very glad the wolves were on their side.

"Right. Let's cross first."

The mountain man strode over to Tucker, picked him off the ground, and slung him over one shoulder like a sack of potatoes. Tucker was surprised, but smiled back at his mom and saluted as the man leaped from rock to rock across the river. When there were no more rocks, he stepped in, waist deep, and waded to the other side.

"This man has no boundaries," Catherine thought. Even though she still felt very weak, she wouldn't wait. She followed as closely as she could, but his legs were longer and she had trouble judging the distances. "One, two, three...four," she kept going until she had reached the next to last rock before she would have to wade in. She wobbled and looked up to see where they were. The man and Tucker watched her from the bank. She felt shaky from the hike and leaping from stone to stone, but she was determined. She jumped and heard Tucker yell "Mom!" She had leapt farther than she had meant to.

Catherine tumbled head-first into the stream. In a cat-like move, the mountain man grabbed an enormously long branch and speared it into the river, ahead of the current. Flailing, Catherine reached it almost by accident. She grabbed the branch, but the current started to pull her away. A moment later, she was standing on the bank. The man had lifted her out of the water and placed her next to Tucker. She coughed and gasped for breath, then turned to the man.

"I'm sorry...I," she began, but he wasn't looking at her. He reached into a pouch and pulled out something black. He tossed it to her and then another to Tucker. Two more pieces to the wolves. The wolves snatched them out of the air and swallowed them in a single gulp. Catherine and Tucker watched, mouths agape, as the man found a spot on a flat rock in the sun, stretched out, and fell asleep.

Shivering, Catherine tried to process everything that had just happened. She looked at Tucker for an answer, but he was examining his piece of dog food and sniffing it. He nibbled a bit, gagged a little, then bit off another piece, and began chewing hard.

"Slow down," Catherine said, looking at her own piece. She pulled off her soaking jacket and sat down in a warm spot by the bank and began to eat, revolted at first, then forced herself to finish it. Tucker took off his hoodie and handed it to her. Smiling at him, she put it on and they both glanced toward the mountain man as a low snore reached their ears.

"What if the bear comes after us?" she asked, pulling off her wet shirt from under the hoodie and wringing it out.

"Crossing the river broke the scent. Now she can't follow us."

"You have a wilderness survival game on your phone I don't know about?"

"Cub Scouts," Tucker said, shrugging.

"You hated Cub Scouts," she said.

"I hated the other kids in Cub Scouts. The nature stuff was okay."

Catherine hung her jacket, shirt, and jeans on a nearby branch. Even at 13, Tucker was already so tall his hoodie covered her nearly to her knees. As she slung her jeans over the limb, she felt for her iPhone and pulled it out of her pocket. Drenched with a cracked screen, the phone was even more useless.

Sitting side by side in the midday sun, finally alert after so many days in a pain-riddled fog, Catherine and Tucker tried to make sense of all that had happened.

"How come there haven't been any planes looking for us?" Tucker asked.

"I don't think they can see us. Even at the crash site. This is deep woods. They definitely know we're missing by now. It's…Thursday, right? Only a matter of time," she replied, but she wasn't so sure. The last text that had gone through was to Lewis, telling him that she may not be in touch until Tuesday, but now that was two days ago. She had flooded her outbox with S.O.S. messages to everyone she could think of. All were undeliverable. But she couldn't tell Tucker that. He had to have hope.

The pair huddled together, the warm sun heating their skin. After a few minutes, she felt Tucker slouch heavily against her and she knew he was out. As she began to drift off, she glimpsed their sleeping guide, more animal than man, wild and untrustworthy. She dozed off hoping she was wrong.

"No cell towers, no signal," the park ranger said. Lewis had been on the phone with him for nearly half an hour. It was the same refrain.

"I still don't understand how you can't know what's going on in your forest," he said. He'd begun to feel uneasy around midday three days ago. Catherine had always been good about checking in, even when she was in a remote location. When he was getting ready to head out for the day, he had searched for the number of the RV park. "I'll just make sure she's okay," he had told himself. "She's used to me checking in too." When he'd gotten no answer, he looked up the number for the regional airport.

The manager answered on the first ring. After Lewis explained, the manager told him he thought she had taken off early Monday morning, but he didn't really think so. The manager got there around seven on weekdays and he hadn't seen anyone. He had seen the truck and figured it was hers. But it was way too early to fly without being seen.

Lewis tried to reassure himself. He knew Catherine. She was cool-headed, a time-tested pilot who knew her way around almost any kind of small aircraft. And she wouldn't leave Tucker alone for long. "I'll bet the manager just missed her and maybe she landed somewhere else," he thought to himself. "Took Tucker with her." When he started worrying again before dinnertime on Tuesday, he had made his first call to the nearby ranger station.

"It's simple. We monitor by satellite, watch from towers, and follow a variety of routes to inspect sectors. But there's thousands of acres out there. And you said she was in touch by text, right?" Lewis knew where this line of questioning was going to lead.

"Right, but…"

"I'm sorry, sir. I promise that I'll take a look around when I can. I have your number, e-mail address, and assistant's number. I'll be in touch." With that, the ranger hung up and Lewis hadn't felt one iota better about Catherine's whereabouts. Every attempt since then had been met with similar responses. No one had seen them. No one knew where she was.

Chapter 13

Splash.

Catherine's eyes flew open, expecting to see a bear swimming across the river toward them. Instead, she saw the mountain man's naked backside as he dove into a deep, relatively calm part of the river.

She turned away, careful not to move too much and wake Tucker. Shadow had fallen over them, but she checked that her hanging clothes were still in full sun. Compelled to take another glimpse, Catherine took a furtive look at the water. His back was to her and she marveled at the sculpted, powerful body, pale from neck to waist. He was washing, splashing at the wolves that ran back and forth along the riverbank. She fought the urge to laugh aloud as she saw them biting at the droplets. When he started to turn around, she closed her eyes and tried to look exhausted. But her mind was fully awake.

After hearing him shake off the excess water and dress, she noticed that he had walked over to stand near where Tucker and she were sleeping. She could hear the wolves panting and she wondered how close they were. She dared not open her eyes. It felt like ten minutes that he stood there. If he wanted to kill us, he could've done it a thousand times already, she thought. And he carried Tucker across the river and likely would've carried me. He saved us both, me twice, fed us, brought us to water. And, Lord willing, he's going to lead us back to civilization.

Catherine cautiously opened her eyes, but the man and wolves were gone. She looked around and found them by the riverbank.

"Tucker, it's time to go, honey." Tucker lifted his head, wiped away the drool on the side of his cheek, and straightened up. Catherine gingerly stepped over to her jeans. "Damp. It'll have to do." Her jacket was heavy with wet and still dripping a bit, but her top was nearly dry. And warm.

"Are you warm enough?" she asked Tucker. He seemed to be shivering.

"Yeah, Mom, I've got my coat. You keep the hoodie 'til your jacket dries off," he replied, giving her a reassuring smile. "Besides, we're roughing it, right? This is what you'd planned."

"Ha! Far from my plan," she laughed. The two walked over to the mountain man, staying far from the wolves.

"So, what's the plan?" she asked him. "Are we going toward a nearby town, or some kind of road?"

The mountain man stopped petting the black wolf and started toward the dark forest beyond the riverbank. Catherine and Tucker looked at each other and Tucker began to follow as quickly as he could limp behind the wolves. Catherine stood, debating with herself. She surrendered and tried to keep up.

After what felt like another fifteen minutes, Catherine's patience had nearly run out. Tucker could sense his mother's ire building. Ever the peacemaker, Tucker caught up with the mountain man.

"Wow, this part of the country is really beautiful," Tucker began. "Do you know what it's called?"

No response. Tucker followed a little closer, stumbling to keep up.

"Mom and me were just taking a Sunday flight to look at trees. Never thought I'd see 'em up close like this. Do you know about how much farther to the airport? That's where our truck is parked."

No response. Tucker glanced back at his mom. She raised her eyebrows. As she started to pass him to catch up to the mountain man, he put out his hand to hold her back.

"Mom, what are you going to do?"

"T, we can't keep traipsing through the entire western part of the United States. I have to get us home, or at least to a hospital. I need to find out if he's really helping us. He has to answer some way." As she finished her rant, the two emerged from the forest into a narrow valley. Boulders, interspersed with trees, rose on one side. The wolves were making their way on a nearly invisible path toward an outcropping dense with trees and underbrush. Tucker's face lit up.

"We're here."

"What? Where?" Catherine scanned the area and didn't see anything different about this valley from all the other hills, valleys, and forests they had slogged through.

They approached the area cautiously. Tucker thought his eyes were playing tricks on him when the man pulled away tree branches halfway up a rocky slope. He watched the man follow the wolves and disappear into…a hole? A moment later, he came back out and started building a fire by the entrance. The system of branches and brush obscured the front of a cave, making it impossible to see in the compactness of its surroundings.

"Now let's just be careful," Catherine whispered to Tucker as she looked up through the canopy. "If you were flying over, you'd see nothing but trees."

Something near their feet suddenly lunged. Catherine screamed and jumped back, while Tucker kneeled down to inspect it. A rabbit caught in a trap was trying to make its escape. The mountain man, mallet in hand, strode over quickly and retrieved the rabbit, laid it against a flat rock nearby, and smashed the rabbit's head.

Just as quickly, he sliced off the head and turned the body upside down to drain the blood. Catherine stood immobile, but Tucker was fascinated and followed the man toward a wood pile where he drew out an enormous old hunting knife and started to sharpen it against a stone.

"You need help with that?" Tucker asked, sitting down next to him.

"Tucker…" Catherine said. Her eyes wandered to the tanning racks nearby.

"You think he brought us all this way to hurt us?" Tucker turned to the mountain man. "No offense. She thinks all men are evil."

Catherine gave Tucker a scolding look, but she could see the mountain man wasn't bothered by their presence. They watched as he cut a gash down the rabbit's back and reached into the fur. He pulled in opposite directions and the hide slid off, revealing flesh and entrails.

Catherine looked away, swallowing her dread. The man gestured to a crude bucket by Tucker's foot. He handed it to him and watched him spill the entrails into it. Slop. Catherine began walking around the outside of the cave, her skin crawling.

He watched as the woman wandered away, looking around. He was still worried about leading them back to his sanctuary. Would anyone be looking for them? Would they lead anyone to him? He had camouflaged his cave well by arranging limbs and branches with materials he had at hand. It wasn't just proximity to fresh water that made his cave ideal. He had scouted the perfect location for a man who never wanted to be exposed again—the deepest, darkest part of the forest he could find.

"The boy seems okay, though, he thought to himself. Inquisitive, but who wasn't at that age? Especially if this was all new to him. Not everyone could grow up in the traditions of the Crow Nation. And the U.S. Military." The man glanced at the boy, who was watching his hands with interest. A thought came back to him, one he hadn't considered in nearly ten years.

"I blew it. I had fixed myself…mostly. My relationship with Valerie was behind me…mostly. I had done my duty to my country. I had paid my dues and the dues of the guy next to me. I was out and ready for the next chapter. I was ready for a normal life. Everyone else got one. Hell, I'd fought to ensure everyone else got one. I was on my way to a regular job, maybe a girl…a family." The feeling of defeat almost overwhelmed him again as he stood there efficiently cleaning the rabbit. "All hope was gone," he reminded himself. "Never forget that."

She noticed hand-made traps hanging to the side of the cave's entrance. A little farther on, she nearly missed what looked to be a smokehouse, with some cured deer meat high up on a line strung among a very compact stand of old-growth pines. Nearby, there was an outdoor toilet, enclosed and with a deep hole. She thought it actually looked safe and maybe even comfortable. Walking back toward the food prep area, she watched the smoke from the fire spread as it reached the bottom layer of leaves and tree limbs. It dissipated before it could be seen from the air. "Ingenious," she thought.

Tucker was examining the rabbit and asking rapid-fire questions while the man cleaned and put up his tools. He seemed to be ignoring Tucker. "…And how do you cook it? I mean, do you just throw it on the fire? I didn't even know you had to skin it. That was cool." The man finished with his work and started to walk away. Tucker followed him, carrying the rabbit and continuing the stream of queries. Catherine watched their host pause and thought maybe he was reconsidering.

The mountain man turned around and snatched the rabbit from Tucker's hand. He headed to the firepit and waited until Tucker had caught up with him. The man showed him how to put it onto the spit. A flicker of a smile crossed Catherine's face, but she remembered where she was and what she was after. The smile died and she pulled aside the giant bear hide covering the cave's entrance, hoping she wouldn't find bodies stacked up inside.

Framed by felled trees and lined with fur, the mountain man's wide bed stretched along one arching wall of the cavernous space. Tufts of black, brown, and white fur in two indentations by the bed told her that the two wolves always slept next to it.

On the other side of the space, she found a damp little room. She examined the pulleys and was genuinely impressed when she understood the complex engineering of the tiny space. When he wanted water for cooking, she thought, he pulled a rope on a pulley that lifted a small door above a bucket. She looked up and saw light filtering through a hole in the rock above. Rain and snow supplied water for his shower, which was built from some sturdy fabric and pine needles on a tall wooden frame. "Gravity does the rest," she marveled out loud.

The thought of leaving Tucker alone for too long prompted her to go outside and check on things. The rabbit was roasting on the spit and Tucker was turning it slowly, his face aglow in the firelight.

"Smells good," she said.

"I'm starving. It's almost done," Tucker replied, glancing up at her. The wolves laid near him, just beyond the heat of the small fire. The man placed simple, well-used utensils across a wooden board. As they ate, Catherine decided to try again.

"So…how far is it back to civilization?"

A shadow crossed the man's face. Tucker looked at his mom, his brows furrowed. He shook his head.

"I work for a big company. They'll be looking for us. We should probably be somewhere they can find us," she let the last part of her sentence die out as one of the wolves started to howl. The other wolf got up and walked out to the edge of the circle, then paced back. The mountain man rose and walked into the forest with the wolves.

Mother and son exchanged a glance and waited. When it was clear the man wasn't returning, they decided not to let the meal get cold. After they had eaten and saved scraps for the wolves, Catherine and Tucker cleaned up the cook site. They chatted easily about the beauty of all they had seen and wondered again how close they were to getting home. Tucker seemed hopeful and was in better spirits than Catherine had seen him in a long time. They had both taken the painkillers in the med kit and their bellies were full. Tucker kept pointing out the bright side: they had found someone—or, rather, he had found them—who knew the terrain and might take them out of here.

"But I don't feel like we should rush it, Mom," Tucker added. "I'm not feeling great, especially after that hike today. And your head looks pretty messed up."

"We'll take it easy, T," she agreed. "Don't want to re-injure ourselves. I'm sure a search party will be along within a day or two. We're not far from the crash site."

Tucker nodded and started to turn away. Catherine reached out her hand to touch his arm. When he had turned back to look at her, she said quietly, "Let's just make good choices while we're here, okay?"

As they were finishing, the wolves returned, followed by their guide. Without a word, the mountain man made sure that all evidence of the meal was completely removed. He gestured for the two to go inside and take his large bed. Catherine resisted at first, but the look of sheer exhaustion on Tucker's face made her relent.

After they had covered themselves with the animal skins, Tucker fell into a deep sleep almost immediately. The man came to check on them and stood framed in the doorway, the glow of the last embers silhouetting his large form. Catherine fought the urge to run, but Tucker felt safe, so she thought she should try to trust their host. He hadn't led them astray yet, after all. "And besides," she thought, "I'm so tired I'd prefer a slow death to hiking one more miserable mile."

"Thank you for dinner," she said. "It was delicious."

"You're welcome." He turned and let the flap fall across the doorway, engulfing the room in complete darkness.

"He speaks," Catherine whispered.

Chapter 14

"Sure," the park ranger said. "As I was saying, we filed your report and have a general idea of where Ms. Esquivel may be flying or may have flown in the western quadrant, up near a branch of the Snake." Lewis listened intently.

"We normally don't do more than a satellite surveillance, but, because of your call, we drove out to check it out. The ranger I sent didn't see anything from the track. If we get any more reports like yours, we'll let you know. And we'll keep an eye on that sector."

"Maybe you could fly over it?" Lewis's nerves were shot. He had been unable to shake the uneasy feeling. His assistant, Rufus, leaned against the office door, listening to the ranger on the speaker phone, his face etched with concern too.

"Well, they're not missing, sir. I'm not authorized to use those resources unless we get a report from the state police or local sheriff's office."

Rufus was about to jump into the conversation when Lewis piped in, "Okay, thanks. We'll keep trying to find her on our end and we'll let you and the local sheriff know if we learn anything that leads us to think they are truly missing. We really appreciate your help with this. You have our number." Lewis pressed the "end" button on the cell phone.

"Lewis, man, I don't think they're doing enough. Maybe we could convince the rangers to hike into the woods."

"Yeah, maybe," Lewis ran his fingers through his graying hair. "These guys are doing all they can reasonably do right now. There's no cell service. Let's give it until after lunch. Maybe she's been out surveying and got caught up in it. Or maybe they're just having fun taking in the sights."

As light filtered around the enormous bear hide blocking the eight-foot entrance to the mountain man's cave home, Tucker blinked and opened his eyes. It took a moment to adjust to his surroundings. They had spent the past few days trying to revive from their ordeal. The fresh, prepared meals and the man's healing poultices had done wonders, but Tucker's neck, shoulders, and arms still ached, though with less intensity.

His mom was worse off. After she had fallen asleep that first night, the man had cleaned the cuts around her head, some of them deeper than Tucker had thought, and put some kind of green gunk on them before bandaging them with gauze and tape from the first aid kit. The man looked after them every few hours as they slept and ate and slept some more. Tucker hadn't felt like doing much else. His mom had slept the entire first day through and barely woke long enough the second day to eat a little.

But now Tucker was eager to explore. He could tell he was wedged against the curve of a rock wall on the large bed, his mom's back to him. She had insisted that he take the inside so she could defend him if the strange man tried to hurt them.

The thought made him smile. "Poor Mom. Always having to be strong and brave."

Quietly, Tucker rose and stepped over his mom onto the deerskin covering the floor near the low make-shift bed. He could stand to his full height here and stretch his arms over his head because the rock ceiling was so high. It felt like a regular room, except no right angles and no windows.

He actually felt well-rested. There was just enough light for Tucker to find and put on his shoes, then he took a look around. Skins, tools, and handmade gadgets hung on the walls around the room.

A wooden Y near the head of the bed caught Tucker's eye. It had a leather thong attached to the points of the Y and it looked as though someone had pressed the letter "J" into the thickest part of the leather. Tucker had remembered using a leather stamp on a belt in Cub Scouts. He still had that old belt somewhere in his climate-controlled bedroom, with the soft sheets, plush carpet, and gaming system. He shook the thought from his mind and wondered at how different this world was. Yet maybe this mountain man had been a Scout too.

Tucker pulled the slingshot off its peg and went outside. As he lifted the flap, he thought he heard his mom stir. He didn't look back, but searched around the compound, looking for their host. He was about to turn back when he noticed the man watching him from near the smokehouse. The wolves were nowhere to be seen.

"This is a cool slingshot," Tucker held it up and smiled.

"You know how to use it?" The man's voice was deep and startled Tucker.

"Uh, no."

"'Bout time then." The man walked deeper into the woods and Tucker followed. He watched him bend down and scoop a handful of small pebbles into a pouch on his belt.

He led the boy to the little glade. As they walked, he thought about the restless night he had had. He couldn't get comfortable. And he was a little stiff from the night before too. He was still worried that his insanity was returning. Externally, he could look normal. Fishing, gathering berries and roots, cooking a rabbit. Normal. Yet, internally, he had struggled all those years ago. He thought now about his Ranger buddies, then his mom and dad, his granddad, then Diane. The conversations he had thought they had had when he had first retreated here. He recalled the one-sided debates and how he had yelled at the trees.

But over time, he had blocked out events that he couldn't change and let go of the conflict within himself. He had filled his time with projects, like the shower, or digging the trench from the creek to the cave, making brushes from stems, roots, and leaves to clean his body and his teeth. His memories, before he had turned into whatever he was now, began to threaten him again as he led the boy into the forest.

He stretched and shook his head to clear it for the day. The boy—she called him Tucker—wouldn't stop with the questions. Questions that had the simplest answers if the boy would just be still enough to think. He had thought about how today would be more of the same. He would have to take matters into his own hands.

Catherine stretched in the cozy bed and let the remnants of a dream slip away. She had dreamed she was wandering in the greenest forest she had ever seen and, even though she saw drifts of white snow here and there, she felt warm and safe. She couldn't remember a time she'd ever felt safer. Tucker walked ahead of her, but never turned around. He was always just a little out of reach. An enormous black bear rose up in front of him and he disappeared into its fur.

Catherine's eyes opened wide and she looked around. She squinted toward the door, which she recognized as the bear hide from her dream, and saw light streaming around its sides. She turned back in the bed and saw that Tucker was gone. Had he gone outside?

Catherine wobbled a bit as she tried to sit up. Her head began to throb and she quickly laid back down. She tried again, much more slowly this time. She celebrated as she pulled on her boots and checked to see if her jacket was dry. "Of course," she thought to herself, "it's been days. We've been here days because I haven't been able to stay awake." She thought about how glad she was that Tucker seemed to be recovering much better.

Pulling on her jacket, she made her way outside and studied the landscape. She looked around and gasped at the proximity of the snow-capped mountains, the beauty of the forest. She admired how well-positioned the cave was. "How different everything looks from three days ago when I felt so groggy," she thought to herself.

It seemed as though the sun was already high in the sky. The sunlight streamed through the high canopy, its light dappling the new shoots coming out of the ground. She looked out deeper into the glade. Tucker and the mountain man stood near a large tree and Tucker was using a slingshot. Catherine smiled as she saw that Tucker and the mountain man seemed to be getting along so well.

The man pointed at some spot on the tree and said something to Tucker, then handed him a rock. Tucker's attempt flew off two feet to the left. The man pointed at the slingshot and Tucker made an adjustment to the way he held it. After several more tries, Tucker got the hang of it. A thin smile peeked through the man's thick beard as he glanced back at Catherine, then he quickly looked away. She watched for a few more minutes, felt that things were under control, and went back inside to close her eyes again, just for a little while.

When she emerged again, the two men and two wolves were gathered around the firepit. Tucker had spread out the last of their food and the man had set out jerky, nuts, and berries. It felt like lunchtime.

"What is your name?" Tucker asked, offering his mom a handful of berries. The mountain man sipped water from his waterskin and looked up into the trees.

"I'm Tucker. This is my mom, Catherine."

The man remained silent. Impatient, Catherine opened her mouth to speak, but Tucker signaled her to wait. A few moments later, the man spoke.

"Jackson." Tucker and Catherine both smiled.

"What are their names?" Tucker asked, nodding to the wolves, which were gnawing on sections of large bones.

"Akasha. Blue."

"Nice to meet you all," Tucker said. Catherine smiled at her son. She was proud that he had drawn out the mountain man—Jackson—when she couldn't.

Tucker and Jackson had spent all morning and much of the afternoon at target practice. They had traipsed all through the forest, setting up targets until Tucker could shoot them down with consistency. She had lost sight of them sometime after lunch. Her calls went unanswered and she started to become alarmed.

By the time the late-afternoon chill had returned to the glade, Catherine had worn a trough in the hard-packed earth near the entrance to the cave. She had begun pacing frantically, worried about Tucker. When she heard their voices and Tucker's laughter, she stopped. Relief washed over her as soon as she saw his smiling face and the quail he was carrying.

"Can you believe I actually shot this one out of the sky?" Tucker asked, holding it up by its feet. "I never thought I could hit one. But this one. Whoa!"

Catherine patted Tucker's shoulder and smiled at Jackson, who ignored her and walked past them.

"Jackson showed me how to track rabbits and birds and all kinds of animals," Tucker could barely contain his enthusiasm. "It took me a while to realize that if I just watch him, I'll learn. If you make any noise at all in the forest, they can hear you. They can even sense the vibration along the ground as you walk, so you have to be really, really quiet and slow. But he told me a bunch too. Like how to sight a covey of quails' flight through the sky after they take off. I shot right in the middle of the covey and hit one. It was kind of by accident, but it fell."

"That's incredible, T," she said, but still had a look of concern.

"Is everything okay?"

"Yeah, yes, of course," she lied. "I was just getting worried. I have been so out of it for...what? A week now? I'm feeling better now, though." She looked toward Jackson, who had taken the quail and was removing its feathers on the wooden table.

"Thank you for teaching him."

When he didn't respond, Catherine turned back to Tucker.

"How are you feeling? Do you think you would be up for getting out of here pretty soon?"

Tucker looked from his mom to Jackson and back again. He felt confused about what to do. He didn't want to leave.

"Well, the thing is, is that while we were out there tracking the quail, I tripped a little and I may have re-twisted my ankle." Tucker leaned down and made a display of rubbing his right leg.

"I thought you'd hurt your left foot," Catherine said, raising her eyebrow.

"Yeah, I did, but I think I did something to this one too. I think we should really try to take it easy. Plus, your head is still bandaged and we wouldn't want to risk anything so far from safety." Catherine had the sense of being played, but she couldn't fault her son for trying to keep them here. It was tranquil and the man seemed to be no threat to either of them. And her son was getting more of a spring break than she could have imagined.

Chapter 15

After returning from the outhouse the next morning, Catherine heard the sound of an axe striking a tree trunk. She followed the sound until she found Tucker swinging the axe at a young tree, nearing its tipping point. Jackson stood aside, holding a rope lassoed to the top of the tree and judging the direction of the fall. Tucker's smile grew bigger and bigger as he hacked away. He looked at Jackson for reassurance and the man nodded his head. Three more strokes and the tree made a distinct "crack" in the quiet forest. Tucker stopped, suddenly wary. Jackson gestured for Tucker to keep going. Another whack and a massive cracking sound reverberated through the woods. The tree toppled over as Tucker raised the axe above his head and let out a yell. He turned to see his mom and gave her a big smile.

"Did you see that?!" he called. Jackson stiffened slightly and kept his back to Catherine. He walked his hands along the rope to the top of the tree, now resting on the ground.

"Wow, honey! That was amazing," she called back. "Your first harvest."

Tucker swung the axe over one shoulder and looked back at the tall, thin tree laying along the forest floor, a shadow crossing his face. Jackson went to work stripping the thinnest top branches with his large hunting knife. After they had hacked the branches from the fallen tree with the axe, he showed Tucker how to make walking sticks, one for each of them.

Leaving the two to their task, Catherine wandered back toward the cave. At first undecided, she looked around the inside, picking up and examining tools and other odds 'n ends, mostly whittled by Jackson's hand. She marveled at the delicacy of some of the pieces, images of wolves, birds of prey, and bears mostly. Then she glanced back out and heard them still working away at the limbs of the tree with the axe and realized she had an opportunity to get the measure of the man who was helping them.

The night before, she had noticed an old backpack hanging in a crevice at the foot of the bed. She lifted it carefully from its hook and unzipped each of its pockets before looking in. She wanted to be thorough. In the largest pocket, she found an old Army jacket with a Rangers' patch and some others she didn't recognize. In one of the smaller ones, a few medals, including a Purple Heart and what looked like the Bronze Star. Since she'd never been around anyone in the military, she couldn't be sure.

As she reached into a side pocket, her fingers grasped a small piece of slick paper and a larger sheet of note stock. She pulled them out. "Dear J," the writing on the large sheet began. It was a "Dear John" letter, signed by someone named "Valerie." The smaller paper was a photograph, well-worn on the edges, but still clear. A stunning woman was laughing in the photo. She was on the lap of a handsome, dark-haired man, clean-shaven, very young, his arms holding her while she leaned forward, laughing at something out of the frame. He was grinning at the camera.

"Jackson," Catherine said aloud, with a hint of reverence and a little sadness in her voice. Her fingers touched the image of his face. Then she put the items back in the pack, zipped it up, and hung it on the hook. She didn't know why she felt sympathy for someone who didn't seem to need anything, or anyone.

It was after midday when the two men, for that is how Tucker appeared with Jackson, strode up to the cave, covered in sawdust and with twigs and a few leaves in their hair.

"What time is it?" Catherine asked.

"Does it matter out here?" Tucker said. Tucker gave her a big smile and came over for a hug. Catherine laughed and patted him on the back, then gave his ear a tug. Jackson looked away toward the wolves and started shaking the leaves out of his hair and beard.

Jackson knew he needed to get away. As much as the boy had grown on him, he needed a break. He grabbed his fishing trap after they had gone into the cave to nap and he headed out with Akasha and Blue. He considered leaving one of the wolves to stand guard, but he didn't think they would get into too much trouble on their own. And nothing would bother the two if they stayed in the cave.

He thought about how much more the boy would need to learn in order to fend for themselves. He was a quick learner, but still asked too many questions. Jackson was not accustomed to conversation and he grew weary from the barrage. "I need them to be on their own," he thought. "I need life to get back to normal." But the realness of the boy had begun to dispel Jackson's fear of his own impending madness. Or maybe reality was just getting skewed again. He couldn't tell.

One thing he did know: They seemed to be recovering well. He could tell they had been in good health before the crash. And the boy had no trouble breathing now. Blue had started following the boy around a bit too. "It's okay for them stay a little longer," he thought, "but then they would have to go and live on their own."

Catherine woke with a start and realized it was after dark. With no clock, she had begun to lose track of the days and nights. She thought it was the same day, but she couldn't be sure. She followed the scent of cooking fish to the firepit outside. Tucker and Jackson were finishing up their dinners and handed her a small plank of wood with a beautifully garnished grilled salmon across it.

"This looks and smells delicious," she said and savored her first bite.

"And it's brain food," Tucker laughed. "So that should help." Catherine laughed at the joke and tucked into the salmon. Every bite was as scrumptious as the last. She ate the entire fish without uttering a word. Tucker and Jackson cleaned up the cooking area and Jackson went into the cave. A few minutes later, they heard the sound of the water splashing in the W.C.

"I think he's getting a little tired of us," Catherine said.

Tucker shook his head. "I sure hope not. I do feel bad we've taken his only bed, but he seems like the kind of guy who is comfortable sleeping anywhere."

"You are really learning a lot, T," she said.

"Yeah, can you believe it? This is the opposite from Mickey, Minions, and the Millennium Falcon in Orlando."

"I know. I'm just glad we're both alive and relatively safe."

"Not relatively, Ma. We *are* safe. Jackson is a good guy. Nothing's going to hurt us."

It took Catherine a long time to fall asleep that night. The only lingering sign of Tucker's breathing condition was a persistent snore, which kept her up for a while. But his breathing was stronger and clearer than she ever could recall, and he seemed healthier, too. He wasn't some sick kid she had to coddle anymore. She thought that Tucker was adjusting to this life a little too well.

But still her mind raced. She began worrying about Lewis and work, wondering what Richard must be thinking, hoping everything was being handled back home. Here they were stranded in the middle of nowhere and she didn't know how she was going to get them back home. She drifted off when she realized it was all out of her control, for now.

"What's good for breakfast besides nuts and berries around here?" Tucker asked the next morning when he found Jackson whittling on a stump overlooking the glade.

Jackson went to one of the outbuildings without a word and returned with one of the most impressive-looking hunting bows Tucker had ever seen. He had slung a quiver of aluminum arrows over his shoulder. Not everything around here is handmade, Tucker thought to himself. Jackson tossed a bag of berries at Tucker and said, "Let's go find it."

"I'm not sure it's a great idea for a green teenager like me to handle deadly weapons," Tucker said and smiled.

"I handle," Jackson replied. "You watch."

Tucker smiled again and fell in behind Jackson, who was already halfway down the slope. The wolves followed Tucker closely and he couldn't help but feel a little sense of pride.

A young buck lowered its head, grazing for a few moments. He lifted his head and looked around. A hundred yards away, Jackson signaled to Tucker, waiting for the buck to dip his head back into the winter grasses and newly sprouting nutrients of spring. When the buck went back to grazing, Jackson glided forward, his feet barely touching the ground. Tucker followed close behind him. As Jackson stopped, Tucker stumbled on the root of a tree. The back of his shoe came off and he scraped his heel on some lichen. Paying no mind to the blood, Tucker shoved his heel back into the shoe and darted to keep up with Jackson, on the move again.

Now fifty yards away, Jackson paused as the buck lifted its head, and Tucker stopped just behind him.

"Do what I do," the mountain man whispered without turning his head. Tucker nodded.

Lazily, the buck returned to his meal. Jackson powered forward another fifteen yards, freezing just before the buck lifted his head again. Tucker wondered if Jackson could read the deer's mind. It still didn't seem to be able to see them.

In one swift movement, Jackson nocked the arrow and pulled the bowstring taut. Tucker stopped breathing as Jackson crouched motionless. A moment later, a small bird landed on Jackson's quiver and in that instant, he let go and a muffled "thwack" echoed back at them. The bird took flight as Jackson ran toward their prey. Tucker watched as the buck jumped, then staggered a few paces and fell over, dead.

After checking that the buck was truly dead, Jackson removed the arrow, wiped it off, and replaced it in his quiver, which he handed, along with the bow, to Tucker. In a single motion, he lifted the young buck and slung it over his shoulders. The wolves had stayed far back, but fell in line with Jackson as he walked past, back toward the cave. Tucker gauged it had taken a couple of hours to reach this spot. He couldn't imagine Jackson would be able to carry the buck the whole way back.

"You want me to help with that?" Tucker asked. The man didn't answer, so Tucker popped in his Air Pods, then realized they couldn't connect to his phone. He left them in and ran through his playlist, using his imagination. After about an hour, Jackson paused to rest and drink some water.

"That's for music?"

"Yeah, but they don't work. Need wifi," Tucker said, pulling the buds out of his ears and holding them out. Jackson took them and looked them over. The mountain man handed the earbuds back without comment, pulled the deer over his shoulders, and kept walking.

"How long you been out here, anyway?" Tucker called after him. Even without carrying a heavy buck, Tucker was going a lot slower now and struggling to keep up. Jackson didn't answer and seemed to go even faster.

His heel had begun to really ache and he promised himself he would clean it out as soon as they got back. Tucker took a deep breath in and heard not even the faintest wheezing sound, which was usually a clue that an attack was imminent. He couldn't recall a time when his lungs had felt so clear. He shook off the pain in his foot and loped to keep up.

Jackson felt his sense of reality was sliding off into a crevasse. Since revealing himself to the woman and her son, he had walked a tightrope between compassion and high alert. They were like infants out here. He still knew he had to help them. But they could be trouble. The best-case scenario was that they would bring trouble.

He had never felt so vulnerable. When he was at war, he was on someone else's land. Foreign soil. Boots on the ground. Not his land, his ground. His ancestors' ancient hunting grounds that he knew like no one else. After the murder, they must have come looking for him, but they never could. No one ever tracked him, even from the air, even with infrared. The cave ceiling and walls were six inches thick at their thinnest. And he was careful to use fire only when he needed it. He never left tracks. Always scrubbed the area of any hint a human had been there. Now, by accident, this family had plopped down right into the middle of his life. Akasha and Blue had accepted them, even seemed to like them. And now he was about to barbecue a buck. This was risky. Why was he taking such a risk?

The boy.

Tucker was his age when he had learned to live in the forest by himself for days on end. He had absorbed all the lessons from his grandfather and father by then. There was nothing he couldn't handle. He could've survived for weeks, if he'd wanted to. Yet this boy, this Tucker, was like a little lamb. He had no training, no strength. But he seemed willing. And he had courage. He'd saved his mom by getting her into the cave. He'd gone back to the smoking husk of their plane for supplies. "Yes," Jackson thought, "I see something in Tucker that's so much like me. I want to show him how to survive out here. All he needs is a little help."

Akasha looked up at Jackson just then. She seemed to sense his conflict. "Help," he thought. She tilted her head a touch and he was reminded of another time.

It was a severe blizzard that hit sometime around his eighth year out here. Snow fell for days, with icy blasts of air breaking up the monotony. The sky began to rain half a day after the first snowstorm had passed. Overnight, the rain had frozen to ice. It covered every rock, limb, and trunk in the forest. The cracking sounds echoed through the trees for most of the early morning. Limbs fell from the weight of the ice.

Jackson recalled having seen a big buck near the glade just before the storm had really begun to rage. He remembered thinking it might be a good time to stalk him through the snow.

The wolves wore their warm winter coats naturally, but Jackson piled on extra-warm skins before opening the hide covering. A light snow had begun to fall. The wolves slowly rose from beside the indoor firepit, none too happy to leave its cozy warmth.

"Sorry, guys. Game is going to be lean, so we need to get while the gettin's good." He had held the hide open as the wolves slinked through.

As Jackson walked into the glade, he could feel the wind biting through his extra layers. The wolves looked just as miserable, but he forged ahead. With his bow and quiver full of arrows, Jackson moved in the direction he saw the buck heading. The cracking and popping of the tree limbs above their heads sounded even louder in the icy air, here out in the open. Blue stopped to listen and Jackson stopped with him.

They had made it about a hundred yards from the cave's

entrance. Suddenly a mighty crack sounded and a limb fell from a big ash. It hit Jackson's right shoulder and then caught him on his leg, knocking him down. A branch of the limb caught Blue on his hind hip. The wolf yipped and fell.

Pinned to the ground, Jackson lay stunned for several minutes. Akasha moved between her two den mates, sniffing their faces and legs for signs of injury. She began to whimper.

"Oh, great," Jackson said aloud, masking the deep pain he felt in his leg. He managed to dig around the limb until he could finally pull out his leg. He carefully checked to see if it was broken. "It's cut and beginning to swell," he thought to himself. "But it appears not to be broken. It's really going to bruise, though."

Akasha began to dig around Blue. In a moment, Blue was free, but limping.

"At least he can stand," thought Jackson.

The pain in his leg was excruciating. He could hardly put any weight on it. Broken branches were strewn around him, so Jackson found a small limb to use as a crutch. He took out his hunting knife and pruned enough sticks from it to make a brace. Slowly, the two limped back to the cave, Akasha in the lead, picking the easiest route through the snow and icy rocks.

They had crawled back into the cave, where Jackson put more wood on the fire, checked Blue's leg for cuts, and flopped onto the bed. Blue was not as seriously hurt and managed to crawl into bed with Jackson. Akasha paced back and forth and then hopped in on Jackson's other side.

"I'll clean it after a rest," Jackson thought as his eyes slid shut.

He remembered waking after a bit, cleaning his cuts, and

pressing snow onto the swelling. It had begun to storm again in earnest and the icy blasts made them think the renewed blizzard could last for days.

"This is the biggest one I've seen in all the years I've been here," Jackson thought.

He calculated the amount of food and figured out how well it would last. They took meager amounts from the stockpile in the cave's pantry and Jackson gave up on the idea of stalking the big buck. The pain and swelling were much too bad and lingered for many days. The wolves seemed to move even less than Jackson during that time.

One day, Jackson woke to find Akasha standing by the bed, a dead rabbit dripping blood in her jaws.

"Atta girl," Jackson said, taking it from her and limping to the firepit to clean and cook. The sun had come out that morning. Jackson checked Blue's leg again and found they could both move around the cave a bit. Blue continued to keep his leg off the ground and Jackson knew neither of them would be going hunting any time soon. He pulled the hide aside to look outside the cave entrance. The snow was several feet high.

"We aren't going anywhere for a few days, Blue," Jackson said. "I wish I'd brought a shovel." Akasha looked at the wall of snow and back at Jackson. Then he noticed that she had made a path to get in and out. "Smart wolf," Jackson thought.

The wood supply dwindled at an alarming rate, thanks to the bitter cold. Jackson knew they needed to restock from the pile outside. Despite his frugality, food was also getting low.

"I better head out before we're past the point of no return," Jackson said as he struggled into an extra layer of buckskins, wincing at the pain in his leg. Hungry and weak, Jackson gathered up his backpack and pushed through Akasha's tunnel until he got to the ledge. The snow wasn't as deep here. He paused and shook his head, then forced himself to scale down the icy bluff. Akasha tried to join him, but he left her to mind Blue. Limping and still in considerable pain, Jackson went as far as he could beyond the glade to set his traps. When he was close to passing out, he turned back to rest. Akasha retrieved the trapped prey for the next week until Jackson was completely back on his feet. "No man can do it alone," he thought to himself. The thought confused him. He had to stick to the plan.

After resting, Jackson repositioned the buck on his shoulders and picked up the pace. He wanted to get the venison ready and cooked before it got dark, so that no one looking for his new housemates could spot a fire. In this, at least, he wouldn't be reckless.

Was that the only reason he was hurrying? It was just the boy, wasn't it? Jackson shook his head and let out a little growl. Akasha looked up at him, then scanned out in front of her, ready for whatever he had spotted up ahead.

It took less time to return than it had taken to find the buck. They had meandered on their outbound journey. No stream, rock pile, hill, or deadfall blocked Jackson's passage back. He paused several times to let Tucker catch up and take a breather. When they were almost home, he slowed so that Tucker could take the lead. The boy hadn't seemed particularly concerned about falling behind. Jackson figured the landscape distracted him. "Teenagers never change," Jackson thought. The thought made him smile.

Catherine was sure she'd heard an airplane engine, but, when she'd pulled back the bearskin flap and looked up into the clear sky, she couldn't see anything. The sound had disappeared too. "I must have dreamed it," she thought. The late-night worry session had knocked her out until mid-morning. She could tell it was well past dawn from the way the shorter shadows fell across the woodpile by the side of the cave.

She called out for Tucker, then Jackson, then Akasha and Blue. No one responded, not even a howl.

"Another day," she thought to herself. "How are we ever going to get back if we keep lingering here? I have to make a plan."

Catherine decided to use the time to think and clean up. At first, she headed for the stream, but the water was frigid. She thought she would start a fire and heat up the water from the contraption in the cave's damp room. When she lifted the pulley to allow water into the bucket, she found it was steamy. So she tried the other rope. Water came through the top of the shower and it was luxuriously hot. She quickly stripped off her clothes and stepped into the shower, letting the warmth reach all the way into her bones. She grabbed her socks and underclothes and washed them off too.

After she'd dried off the best she could, she hung her laundry outside in the only direct sun she could find, on a large, flat rock. She spent an hour fluffing out her hair and trying to get it to dry in the cool spring air. Then she wandered around the site again, investigating the space, seeing how the water came out hot for the shower, and again marveling at the ingenuity of the hermit.

Chapter 16

Catherine had gathered kindling and small logs for a substantial fire. She figured that they must be going for big game if they were gone for so long. Rabbits, small rodents, and all kinds of birds were in abundance all around the little valley.

She watched as Tucker, bow in hand and quiver over his shoulder, emerged from the darkest section of the forest, a look on his face that she had never seen before. Something was there now that had been missing. He glanced over at Jackson, who emerged a few feet behind him, carrying an entire deer over his broad shoulders.

Catherine felt like she was observing some pre-historic scene of men returning from the hunt to the fire tended by the woman. She eyed the slain buck, but didn't feel the revulsion she'd felt the day she had watched Jackson bash the bunny's head in. There was no violence now. She met Jackson's eyes with a new openness.

He returned the gaze. But he didn't see the strange creature he had seen just a few days ago. His feelings were unlocking classified files his mind had shut away to protect him years before.

"She is attractive," he thought. "She's wearing her hair down and it's pretty like that." He made his face a mask so she couldn't read his thoughts.

Catherine saw that they were heading for the large table near the smokehouse. She brushed away slim twigs and leaves that had fallen there before Jackson unburdened himself of the buck. Ka-THUNK. Both mother and son looked at one another. It must've been heavier than it looked.

Together the three field-dressed, skinned, and cut up the buck. Tucker seemed eager to get his hands dirty, identifying organs as Jackson cut them and pulled them out, and holding pieces aside to assist Jackson with the cutting. He watched intently as Jackson separated the sinew from the loin, gently cutting the tenderloin off and moving his blade with keen precision. He sliced the thick meat down the middle to create a butterfly effect on the steaks.

Catherine took the meat to the cooking area by the firepit to season it, using the herbs she'd found earlier in the pantry of Jackson's cave. She had had to sniff every one; nothing was labeled. She had blended the seasonings until she had tasted a particularly savory combination. Humming to herself now with the venison, she enjoyed the process and knew just what to do after having watched Jackson with the rabbit.

Placing a little gristle from the buck in a shallow pan—the only one she could find—she added pine nuts and began heating them over the fire. She turned the venison on the grill as Tucker and Jackson came up and Jackson went inside. A few minutes later, they heard the water running in his makeshift shower. Without letting his mom see, Tucker examined the cut on his heel.

"Nature calls," he said sheepishly to his mom and headed off toward the stream. "T, the outhouse is that way," Catherine said and pointed behind her.

"Oh, yeah. Right," Tucker went to the outhouse and figured he would sneak around her to rinse off his heel. While he was gone, Jackson emerged in clean buckskin, his beard and hair slick with water.

"Am I doing this right?" Catherine asked, gesturing to the steaks. Jackson nodded, but didn't say anything. He looked around as if he'd lost something, then started to go back inside the cave, the wolves following him.

"Hey, wait. The steaks are almost done. I may need some help," Catherine said. Jackson turned and watched her as she expertly turned the steaks and then took the pan of pine nuts off the fire. He retrieved the clean board and pulled out his hunting knife to carve up the steaks into smaller pieces.

"So, how'd you happen to be so close to the crash?" she asked. She had learned from Tucker to be patient with Jackson, so she waited.

"Felt like taking a walk."

"Lucky for us."

"If luck's what you believe in," he replied, turning slightly to look at her.

Something glinted on his chest and caught Catherine's eye. She saw a small gold ring hanging from a cord. Unconsciously, she touched the silver cross around her own neck.

"I appreciate your sharing your space with us," she said.

"It's not mine."

"Well, you were the only one here. Until we came along," she said and looked around. "Don't you get lonely out here?"

"People get lonely around other people. Not on their own." He didn't mean it, but it felt like the right thing to say to bring the conversation to an end. He began retrieving the steaks from the grill over the fire and placing them on the board.

"I just can't imagine a whole life without loved ones. I'd never make it through the day without Tucker."

He stopped cutting and looked directly into her eyes. She felt like they were piercing right into her soul. She held the look, then looked down at the ring.

"There must be something you miss."

It looked as though Jackson was about to speak when Tucker returned a moment later.

"Aw, man, I'm starved!" Tucker said, popping a piece of venison into his mouth. "All that tracking and hunting made me hungry!"

Catherine laughed as juice dripped down her son's face. She started eating too and let the juice slide down her chin. The three ate with gusto for a while, not speaking, but Tucker and Catherine pointed at the mess the other was making and laughed. Jackson turned to Catherine. She sobered and stopped chewing. Tucker stopped laughing too.

"I miss…bread."

She burst out, laughing even harder and letting the tension pour out of her. Jackson chuckled too and Tucker looked between the two of them, confused.

Akasha and Blue gazed up at the sky the next instant. Jackson followed their sightline and was on his feet, scanning the sky through the treetops. Catherine stopped laughing and heard the barest whine of a plane engine. She bolted down the rocky incline and out into the meadow, waving her arms to a plane she couldn't yet see.

"Hey! We're down here!" she called at the top of her voice. "Help us!"

The tallest trees let the late-day sun reach the glade, but Catherine couldn't see above their overarching limbs into any full section of the sky. "Stop! Stop!"

She turned to Tucker, who was still standing by the firepit and watching her.

"They're looking for us! Wave your arms! Grab a stick from the fire!" she yelled, incredulous that he wasn't already down here with her. The sound of the engine faded. Catherine looked at them both in disbelief.

"It's gone, Mom," Tucker said. Catherine sensed relief in his tone. She marched back up to the firepit, skidding to a stop not far from Blue and looking straight at Jackson. His defiant look told her all she needed to know.

"You don't want them to find us, do you?" she asked, catching her breath. "Because then they'll find you."

Jackson looked away. He didn't want to hurt them, but he couldn't help them. Not in the way she wanted. He wondered what the boy wanted. The day had been a good one for them both.

"They won't find you here," Jackson finally said.

"Then what are we supposed to do? Stay with you?" she spat the last few words. Blue rose slowly and stood directly in front of her, then looked back at Jackson.

"Well?"

Jackson considered her question. "Until you can survive on your own."

Livid, Catherine started toward Jackson, but Blue growled and Akasha came up beside him. Undaunted, she brushed them aside and yelled, "Are you crazy? Survive on our own? Like you? Tucker has school. I have a job. We have lives. That may not mean anything to you, but it does to us." She looked at Tucker, but he remained still, neutral. Her eyes narrowed.

"They're not coming here," Jackson spoke quietly, but with an edge of menace. His tone sounded like a threat.

"How are you going to stop them?" Catherine asked. The man and woman stared at one another until she retreated inside the cave, shaking her head. Tucker looked at Jackson and shrugged, apologetic. He followed his mom inside.

"What are you doing, Mom?" Tucker watched just inside the doorway as his mom rifled through Jackson's tools and supplies.

"We need this stuff to survive."

"It's not ours."

"Doesn't matter in the wild," she replied, looking over her shoulder at him.

She pulled the old pack off the hook and started going through the main pouch. She remembered seeing a small flashlight in there.

"Stop." Jackson held open the flap and the light behind him made his features inscrutable. Catherine kept looking through the pack. He grabbed her by the arm and pulled the pack away, placing it back on the hook. She yanked her arm back and stood up to him, ready to fight.

"I'm not stupid. I know you're not out here because you thought living alone in the woods would be fun. You did something. And now you are hiding. I don't trust you," she shouted just inches from his face.

"You shouldn't," he replied calmly.

"Mom, just leave him alone," Tucker whined. She looked at him and backed away, realizing that Jackson taught Tucker more in a few days than his father had in his lifetime.

"First thing tomorrow, we're leaving," she said firmly to Tucker.

"You'll die," said Jackson.

Catherine turned back to Jackson and paused, regaining her composure. She smoothed her hair and said, "We have to try."

Chapter 17

Since the mother and son had come to his little glade and taken over his cave and bed, Jackson bedded down across the meadow, on a thick bed of pine needles under a small rock outcropping. Layers of buckskin covered him completely. And the wolves slept beside him each night, keeping him warm against the chill. He had a clear sightline to the mouth of the cave in case anything tried to wander in. Or out.

After the trauma of the crash and the stress of caring for his intruders…er, houseguests, Jackson was glad to have a space of his own where he could think without interruption. As he watched the bear hide for any sign of movement, he thought about the direction the two would take in the morning. Any direction they headed offered danger. There was no good way out and back to safety. On purpose. The waterfalls blocked one path, the deep forest another. The canyon walls up to the mesa, yet another. "That might be a possibility," he considered. If they had climbing gear and knew how to navigate a sheer cliff face, it might be the fastest way back to a town. Jackson rolled over on his back and stared up at the rock just inches from his face. It was much later in the evening until he finally fell asleep.

It was still dark when Catherine rose the next morning. Trying not to wake Tucker, she gathered what little they had. She raked her fingers through her hair, pulled on her boots, and donned her warm jacket. Zipping it as she pushed through the heavy hide, the frigid morning air coupled with the oppressive darkness almost made her turn around and crawl back into bed.

She planned their journey until her brain stopped whirring and let her rest last night. They would head back the way they came, perhaps finding a narrower spot in the river to ford. She replayed the trek over and over until she felt she had it down. She must get Tucker back. With no asthma medicine, she was borrowing time.

It took her several minutes to walk into the glade and find a patch of sky through the darkness. A few stars peeked down on her and she let God's spirit fill her, prepare her for the most difficult journey she would ever have to make.

"Please..." Her breath was a prayer and the mist hung in the air a moment until it wafted toward the heavens. She was still and resolute. She told herself she had nothing to fear. With God's help, she would get them through this.

As she turned back and headed up the slope to wake Tucker and get him ready, she saw Jackson standing near the woodpile, watching her. She couldn't make out his features, but she sensed he'd been there the whole time. She stopped in front of him and stared into his eyes. He looked into hers for a long moment, until she finally broke off her gaze and started toward the cave's entrance. She saw there what she missed before.

Jackson stacked a pile of leather sacks by the doorway. Catherine stooped to open each one and was relieved when she found all the provisions they would need, and then some.

"Thank you," she said, quietly. Jackson nodded and turned. The two wolves followed him into the darkness. She stood and went inside, suddenly conflicted again about the path that seemed so clear just a moment ago.

Tucker was already up and sitting on the side of the bed when Catherine came through the flap. He quickly pulled his bloody sock back onto his heel and gingerly pushed his foot into his hiking boot.

"Maybe this isn't such a good idea," he said, hoping she hadn't seen.

"Everyone thinks we're dead. I can't imagine what everyone at work is thinking."

"I guess that's fine for you, but I don't have anything to go back to."

"Oh, honey, don't say that," Catherine sat down beside Tucker and brushed the hair away from his forehead. "You're thirteen. Things will get better, I promise."

"Whenever someone wants to help us out, you always pick a fight, and then we're just stuck on our own. I shouldn't even be here! I should be at Dad's!" Tucker couldn't hold it in any longer. He'd tried to keep his complaining on the drive to Idaho and in the RV to a minimum. The plane ride was the highlight of his spring break...until it wasn't. Now, when he was finally seeing nature up close, experiencing it like he'd always wanted to, learning new things, and, well, simply surviving, his mom wanted to trade it all in for desks, phones, and, ugh, responsibilities.

"Tucker, if you knew your father…" she stopped. "Honey, I have to trust God is going to help us through this."

"What if we don't?" Catherine looked at her son and didn't remember the last time he looked so vulnerable. She held up his chin so she could look him in the eye.

"We will. Remember? I can do anything," she smiled at him and he did his best to assure her he believed her.

They headed out through the opening and found Jackson sitting on a rock overlooking the little glade. Tucker stopped a moment to marvel at the bird emerging from the small piece of wood Jackson was whittling. Catherine picked up the pouches and was heading down the slope.

"Bye," Tucker said, then turned and picked up the remaining ones, slinging their leather strings over his shoulders. He looked back, but the mountain man didn't look up or turn his way. Tucker followed his mother.

Jackson watched the backs of the two babes in the woods as they retreated into the morning fog. He shook his head and tried not to give them another thought.

Instead, he turned the bird over in his hand. He remembered one day not long ago when Akasha and Blue were out hunting. The perfect piece of whittling wood was laying on the kindling pile for nearly a week. Jackson finally carved out enough time to begin working with it the way his granddad taught him.

Years earlier, his granddad shown him carvings he'd made and explained each object's significance to the Crow people, their stories and legends. Symbols of birds were always Jackson's favorites growing up and he'd gotten quite good as a boy at creating majestic eagles and other birds from the most unassuming pieces of pine and cedar.

His granddad would gather fallen limbs throughout the day as they hiked deeper into the woods on hunting or fishing trips. As they sat around the campfire each night, his granddad would relay Native American myths, like how the robin got his red breast or how the crow became the symbol of their tribe. Jackson marveled at the bravery and cleverness of the creatures.

On the day Akasha and Blue went hunting, Jackson recalled looking up from his work to see his wolves trotting toward him, with another wolf following closely behind them. He stopped halfway through the glade while Akasha and Blue loped right up to Jackson to nuzzle their greeting. The wolf approached cautiously, stopped a few paces from Jackson, who was still seated on the cave's ledge near the fire pit, and growled menacingly. He bared his teeth and immediately Blue put himself between Jackson and the wild wolf. He backed away, but stayed close. It occurred to Jackson that the new wolf wanted to be a part of the pack. They saw the wolf circling around the glade for several days. But Akasha and Blue paid it no mind and eventually Jackson forgot about it too.

As Jackson walked back from the stream a few days later, however, the wolf blocked his path to the cave. Akasha stepped in front of Jackson and growled at the wild wolf. Jackson realized that the new wolf didn't want to just be in the pack. He wanted to lead the pack. In a moment, the wild one attacked and Akasha fought back, biting him so viciously that the wild wolf fell back to the edge of the bluff. She stalked him, growling the entire time, until he gave over and leaped down the side of the bluff and out of sight.

Instinctively, the wolves didn't bring stragglers back to the glade after that. Jackson was relieved; the pack was just the right size.

Jackson regarded the bird that emerged from his handiwork. He looked back at the spot where Tucker and Catherine disappeared among the trees. He thought about whom he made it for. Of the oral tradition he'd hoped to bestow.

Jackson tucked the bird into his belt and walked back into the cave.

Within half an hour, Catherine shut off the flashlight to save the battery. Tucker tapped off his cell phone light, which cast a shorter beam, but shone much brighter than the decades-old flashlight. The dawn broke brilliantly now along a ridge with only a smattering of trees. Catherine stopped a moment to drink a little water and take in the view.

"The fog makes it look like a dream, doesn't it?" she said, mostly to herself.

"Yeah, pretty impressive," Tucker responded, then looked back and around, munching on some nuts from his pouch. "Um, you sure this is right? I thought we'd head back toward the plane, since we know kinda where we were when we crash-landed..."

"My thinking exactly."

"Huh, so, you think this is the right way?"

Catherine turned to look at Tucker, then surveyed the land in a full circle. "Yes, don't you?"

Tucker just shrugged. They continued hiking and Tucker imagined his music to pass the time.

Lewis zoomed into the area where he thought Catherine and Tucker might have flown. He tapped a few keys on his keyboard and the resolution improved. Roseburg's proprietary mapping program was the most sophisticated in the world. He could view the quadrant using ten different aspects, from topographical to hydro-sensitive, even down to the types and densities of trees one could expect to find growing there. But nothing he was looking at showed him people in infrared. Too much wildlife, some bigger than humans.

Rufus set a cup of tea in front of him and sat down in the chair across from his desk, sipping his coffee.

"I dunno, boss. I'm starting to get a bad feeling," Rufus said.

Lewis sat back and rubbed his eyes. Yesterday was tough. Tuesday. A full week since the day Catherine said she'd call. Text. Email. Anything.

"Starting to feel the same way. Spring break is over. No way Catherine would let Tucker skip school. And she's always prompt with her field reports," Lewis said and took a sip. Always too hot.

"I still don't understand why it took them this long to put a search plane in the air," Rufus said. Lewis shrugged and blew on his tea. He took a tentative sip.

"The sheriff told me they had to be sure. When they finally reached that good-for-nothing campground manager, they discovered Catherine and Tucker hadn't returned since leaving early Sunday morning, more than a week ago. Might've been nice if he'd mentioned it to someone."

"Now what?"

"Now," Lewis shook his head, contemplating all manner of possibilities and unwilling to accept any of them. "Now, they keep looking."

The sun was approaching midday when Catherine swung around, her eyes searching the trees in every direction. Tucker kept quiet through most of the morning. What seemed like familiar landmarks always fell short of being quite right. It didn't help that every tree looked like every other tree.

"I just need to think for a minute," Catherine said. Tucker hadn't said anything. He sensed her indecision. "We're lost." He finally resigned himself to the truth.

"Maybe we could retrace our steps back to Jackson's place," he said. He felt like a traitor, but it was the only way he imagined they would survive.

His mother's gaze fixed on something close by. "Oh, please, don't let it be a bear," he thought. Reluctantly, he followed her gaze and saw a wolf standing twenty paces away. She held out her arm, gesturing for Tucker to stay back or stay still, he couldn't figure out which.

"If it attacks me, run for it. Don't stop," she said, taking a step between the wolf and her son.

"Akasha."

Tucker recognized the fluffy white tufts of fur around her ears. He smiled and held out his hand as Blue circled up from behind them. Tucker turned and grinned. "Hey, Blue, what are you doing here?"

The wolves loped toward mother and son and let themselves be rubbed thoroughly around the ears. Catherine looked around. Jackson stood not far off, his face betraying no emotion.

"You better come back to the cave."

Catherine gave Jackson an embarrassed smile and said nothing. He turned and the group followed.

It took the small party much less time to return to Jackson's glade than it did on the way out, but it was still a struggle. Catherine felt defeated and had trouble willing her feet to keep pace. Tucker, on the other hand, was deeply relieved to know he would be under the mountain man's protection at least another night and could sleep in the oversized bed again.

No words were spoken during a dinner of berries and smoked meat from Jackson's stores. Distracted by the pain in his heel and exhausted from the meandering early morning trek, Tucker ate quickly, then retired to the giant bed and fell fast asleep. Catherine cleaned up as Jackson sat by the fire overlooking the meadow, deep in thought.

"What did I get into?" he thought to himself. "I've been invaded by this woman and her son. The kid's got the makings of a good man. But the mom has been trouble from the start."

Jackson cocked his head to listen as she threw out the dirty pan water, then watched as she went into the cave. He turned back to stare into the fire. His thoughts from the morning completely dissipated.

"Wow, she can really get in your face, though. Lord, why me?" Jackson looked up toward the tops of the trees. "Why do I want to help them? I could get caught."

Jackson shivered despite the heat of the fire. He didn't want to even form the next thought: "And put in jail. I'd rather be dead. But that boy needs a fighting chance. Maybe I can take them close to that old mining road and they can find the rest of the way..."

Catherine appeared next to him and sat down by the fire. She felt completely humiliated. She looked into its flames and kept quiet. After a few minutes, she looked at Jackson.

"I know I'm being a pain and I seem ungrateful," she began. Jackson didn't stir. She rested her upturned hands on the tops of her knees.

"I'm sorry!" she burst out. "I'm really sorry to cause you this trouble, but I am so worried about T. If I don't get him back, he'll miss so much by being away from friends and family." She choked out "...and his future" as she began to sob.

"He's 13 and has a full life ahead of him," she finished, then her expression changed to anger. "Are you hearing me? I'm sorry I tried to go on my own and got lost." Tears flowed freely down Catherine's face and she brought her hands in to hug her ribcage.

Jackson turned to Catherine.

"I'll take you back," Jackson said. Catherine could barely believe her ears. Her eyebrows shot up and she wiped the tears from her face.

"You will?! Oh, thank you thank you thank you!" She was so relieved that she put her arm around Jackson and tried to hug him. Jackson remained rigid and turned his head back to face the firelight.

Catherine pulled away, feeling a little sheepish, but beyond grateful. The idea of home flooded her senses and she felt at peace for the first time in...weeks.

Sitting next to her, Jackson felt a...tingle? The warmth from the first hug he

had since Diane welcomed him home had a dramatic effect. He was overcome with tenderness.

"I think your son is a fine boy," he said softly. "He'll be a good man."

Catherine smiled, dropped her head, and said, "He sure likes you. You've been more of a father...er, more like a father-figure than he's ever had. Thank you for that." They sat in silence for a while, watching the embers glow.

"You said once that I was hiding from something," he said after a bit. "I am." Catherine adjusted her place on the log so she could listen more carefully. It took Jackson a while to say the next. She sensed an internal struggle.

"I was a POW once. I was held in a dark pit. The torture was severe. I'd given up hope. I thought it was the end. I couldn't let it happen again. I can't be in a confined space."

"I'm so sorry," Catherine replied. "I understand, Jackson. I understand you will be risking your way of life and safety here by helping us."

"It's a fair trade for Tucker. The boy needs to get his life back."

Tears welled up again in Catherine's eyes. She didn't fight them back. Jackson rose. "I need to figure out what we're going to need for the trip back. We better get some rest."

Chapter 18

It took a full day to gather all the supplies they would need for the weeklong trek out of the wilderness and a second day to seal up the cave and make the area invisible.

At daybreak on the third day, Tucker and Catherine stood in the sun-dappled glade, their boots wet with condensation, as they watched Jackson move about the cave's entrance. He moved all the firepit seating and tools into the cave. Then he brought branches he cut from trees deep in the forest and covered the ground, and followed this by littering it with leaves. He already covered the tools hanging on the side of the outside of the cave by pulling evergreen branches from a rooted tree down and securing them so they would continue to grow and thrive. The cave, outbuildings, and any sign of human activity or habitation completely disappeared from view. The boy and his mother gripped their hiking sticks and looked at each other, dumbstruck. Then they followed the mountain man as he set off, trailed by the wolves, without a single glance back.

It took most of the morning for them to see it, but it became clear to Tucker and Catherine that they were on the wrong path from the beginning. Heading away from the mountains toward a valley with steep, vertical canyons, the five hiked with real purpose. Jackson led with Catherine close behind. Tucker, his heel chafing from the injury and becoming more inflamed from the certain infection, tried to hide the limp that was becoming more and more pronounced as the day wore on. He stopped occasionally to watch a hawk flying overhead or a small herd of deer grazing in a distant field. Though he was genuinely interested, he needed any excuse to take a break. Catherine watched everything in front of Jackson and seemed careful of Jackson himself. "She still doesn't trust him," Tucker thought, grimacing slightly and trying to catch up. He hadn't seen their fireside exchange a few nights ago.

"How long have you been out here?" Catherine asked. No response.

"You can count the seasons, right?" she tried again.

"Can. Don't."

They picked their way among rocks and fallen trees. She decided to shift the conversation.

"For all this time out here alone, you're still a person with a good heart," she ventured, but Jackson didn't respond. "I'm trying to thank you. Like I said, I'm grateful that you came and found Tucker and me. I know he wanted to stay."

"I've done enough I'm not proud of without adding you and your boy starving to death. Don't think I'm a good person. You might be wrong," Jackson lunged forward, leaving Catherine to scramble to catch up. When it was clear he wanted to walk ahead, she slowed to allow Tucker to walk alongside her.

"You're limping. Why are you limping?" she looked down at Tucker's leg and then into his face. Tucker walked on.

"I dunno. I think I scratched my heel when we were hunting. No big deal."

Catherine let Tucker hike ahead so she could observe his gait. No big deal! Catherine could tell Tucker was suffering. She called to Jackson to stop. The wolves, which fanned out on either side of Tucker, closed ranks around him and looked to Jackson as he strode back to them.

"Sit here, honey, and take off your shoe and sock," Catherine said, holding Tucker's arm as he eased himself onto a low rock. As he pulled off his shoe, Catherine gasped at the sight of the red sock, soaked through the heel. She knelt and peeled back the sock. Tucker grunted in pain as Jackson knelt down for a closer look.

"Oh, no. What did you cut it on?" Catherine examined his ankle and heel, covered in dried blood and pus. It was hot and red and swollen.

"A rock covered with some kind of moss…?" Tucker replied.

Jackson grabbed Tucker's calf and pulled it out of Catherine's grasp. He inspected the wound carefully. Tucker and Catherine studied Jackson's face. They'd not seen this level of concern from him before.

"Sphagnum."

Catherine doused Tucker's heel with water from the waterskin and cast about looking for a clean piece of cloth. Jackson wandered a few yards away and was picking leaves from a plant.

"Tucker, this is so basic. Why didn't you tell me? You must've been in pain for hours."

"Sorry." Tucker looked defeated and Catherine gave him a hug. Jackson's shadow enveloped them both. As Catherine pulled away, Jackson pushed the shredded leaves into Tucker's mouth.

"Chew."

"What is that?" Catherine demanded. "How do you know that'll work? What if Tucker has a reaction?"

Tucker looked at Jackson and began to chew. Jackson pulled a small pouch free of his camping frame, then set the frame on the ground near Tucker. He waded into the underbrush, searching for something. A few minutes later, he came out holding a variety of herbs in one hand and a makeshift rock pestle in the other. He ground them together then emptied the compound into a worn, but clean, handkerchief. He knelt by Tucker's foot and looked at him.

"Do I swallow this stuff?" Tucker asked around a mouthful of crushed herbs.

"Yes. Listen, Tucker, I'm going to clean your wound with this cloth filled with herbs. Catherine, pour a little more water here and here." She did it immediately, then stood back as Jackson tenderly cleaned Tucker's heel. She was moved. Reaching out, she rested her hand on Jackson's shoulder and said, "I keep doubting you. I'm sorry."

Jackson looked at her fingers on his shoulder. Her words and, most especially, her touch, had an instant, almost electric, effect on him. He went back to work on Tucker's heel, methodically cleaning the deepest part of the cut. It took several minutes for his breathing to return to normal.

Catherine stepped back again. She didn't want to crowd. She also needed to regain her composure and focus on her son. She offered the waterskin to Tucker for a drink and then stoppered it when he was finished. She used the remaining water to rinse off his sock and wipe out his shoe with a damp corner of her shirt. Clouds covered the sky and the dropping temperature signaled snow. Catherine wrung out the sock the best that she could.

When Jackson was finished, he propped Tucker's foot up on a clean part of the low rock. He went back to the pack and pulled out a sock-shaped piece of animal skin. He started to slide it over Tucker's heel. Catherine came closer to watch.

"Moose-hock shoe," Jackson said, noting their curiosity and deciding not to wait for the inevitable questions. "The lower leg of a moose. Makes for a good poultice." Tucker thought it looked like an elastic ankle brace.

"Did you come out here and just figure all this out on your own?" Tucker asked, rolling his ankle in the shoe to get a feel for it. Jackson packed herbs between the animal skin and the wound.

"My granddad was Crow. Taught me."

"You're lucky. I didn't have anyone to teach me that stuff. Just what I learned from Mr. Caldwell, my den leader in Cub Scouts."

"Your mom seems to know a lot." Jackson looked over his shoulder. Catherine

wandered into the woods, out of sight.

"She tries making up for my dad...too hard sometimes."

"It is hard being different. But there are ways you can use it."

"Like what?" Tucker leaned forward, grasping his ankle. It was feeling better already. Jackson looked him in the eye.

"I was quiet at your age. Liked trees better than most people, so I spent my time with them. Learned to survive on my own." Jackson paused. Tucker stayed quiet.

"That's how I became a Green Beret." Jackson draped the pouch of remaining herbs over Tucker's head and brought it down around his neck.

"Chew. It will help the pain."

"What's a Green Beret?"

"Army. Special Forces."

"Cool. Did you ever kill anybody?"

Jackson looked Tucker full in the face and narrowed his eyes. For an instant, he heard the single gunshot. A woman's scream. Tucker's smile faded as he realized he made a faux pas. Just then, Catherine emerged from the woods.

"I don't care how long you've been out here. Don't pretend you don't miss toilet paper," she said and hoisted her pouches over her shoulders. Flakes of snow settled on her hair and shoulders. Tucker looked up and let a snowflake fall on his tongue.

He looked back to Jackson, but he was already pulling on the pack frame. "Get your shoe on. It's still a long way till we camp."

After a meager dinner and restless night, the group rose early, re-bandaged Tucker's foot, and set off again. Jackson led with the wolves flanking him far out on either side. Tucker followed a short distance behind, with Catherine taking up the rear. Walking through the brush over uneven, rocky ground would have been slow going already, but Tucker's limping gait kept progress to a snail's pace.

About three hours in, Jackson stopped suddenly. Tucker, concentrating hard on not stumbling, almost ran into him, with Catherine close behind.

"Don't move. Don't bend or move your heads. Listen," Jackson said. Then Tucker and Catherine heard it too.

A rattle.

Jackson pointed his walking stick at a huge rattlesnake coiled and ready to strike three feet from them in some brush by a fallen tree. He started to step away from the snake, but the snake followed his movements. The snake struck at Jackson. The motion was so fast Catherine saw only a blur of brown.

Tucker swung his walking stick and struck the snake in midair, knocking it back to the ground.

Jackson used his walking stick to hold the snake down, then pulled out his hunting knife to cut off its head. Catherine and Jackson looked at Tucker and were surprised to see him smiling.

"You see, these walking sticks are good for more than one thing."

"That was amazing! My hero son!" Catherine exclaimed. Jackson smiled at Tucker and said, "You can cut trees with me anytime."

Jackson cut the rattle from the Diamondback and held it out to Tucker.

"That was a big snake. Look at the size of the rattle," he said.

"Ugh," Catherine said, and leaned away. Tucker took the rattle and admired it, then threw it back into the brush.

"Time to move," Jackson said, after they'd each taken a drink from their water skins.

Jackson continued to watch the ground for danger and the horizon for landmarks. During his trip in fifteen years ago, he'd made mental notes of all the landmarks so he could always find his way back, no matter season or weather. No route was going to be easy and this time he'd decided to take them a slightly different way. It would be faster. And more dangerous, particularly at one point. But the path would serve to get the boy to care sooner.

Over time, land shifted, new forests had grown up, and deadfalls blocked paths, but he knew he was going in the right general direction. The day's excitement behind them, Jackson stopped often to give the kid a chance to rest. An hour before sundown, they found themselves at a shaded clearing and decided to stop for the night.

"I met a rattler once before. Not a pretty sight," Jackson began, as the three cleared off a space for the tent, while the wolves laid down nearby and watched them. Catherine and Tucker waited for more to the story, but they were soon disappointed. Jackson continued kicking pebbles off the dirt to make a smooth surface. But they could tell he was deep in thought.

He glanced at the wolves and smiled. He remembered one morning years ago, when they started out to hunt for game. The wolves fanned out around him. They knew their roles well. As Jackson walked through the forest, he tripped over the root of a tree. Catching his balance, his foot landed off the trail. Right next to a rattle snake, just inches from his foot. The snake struck him on the outer calf of his right leg.

The wolves were upon it instantly and killed the snake. Jackson sat down by a tree and immediately took off his deerskin boot. He saw where the snake's fangs penetrated the leather. Drawing his knife, he started to feel the effects of the poison. He quickly made a cut a quarter inch deep up and across the bite to drain the poison. Then he found some leaves to pull it out. He compressed them, put on his boot, and headed back to the cave.

Dizzy and weak on arrival, Jackson chewed some leaves for strength and to fight the effects of the poison. He began sweating profusely and could no longer stand. He laid down on his bed and took off his boots and clothes.

Sleep overtook him immediately. Blue and Akasha stayed by his bedside constantly and watched him toss and moan. All the trauma from combat and torture came flooding back. He was overseas, fighting, fighting for his life. Again.

Somehow, even now, Jackson could remember pieces of his delirium. He saw the wolves, but their watching eyes turned into the eyes of his brothers. He felt Akasha nudging him, trying to make him wake up, and it felt like he was being pushed into a foxhole by Lance or Paul.

"I cried out," he thought, as Catherine and Tucker shook out the tent and began arranging it for pitching. He wondered if mother and son would've been as attentive as Akasha and Blue, had he been bitten today.

His leg swelled up to twice its size. His mouth was dry. Jackson felt the dryness even now. "I think I slipped into a coma," Jackson thought. "It's a miracle I survived."

As Catherine and Tucker prepared to bed down, Jackson strode over and scratched Akasha between the ears. She looked up at him with a contented look.

"Thank you, girl," he said. Catherine and Tucker straightened up and looked over at one another but said nothing.

He awakened to the feeling of the wolves licking his wound. Nudging him from time to time to try to get him up. When he'd fully gained consciousness, he was certain that at least three days and nights passed. On the fourth morning, Jackson recalled getting out of bed very slowly. Weak from lack of food and water, he put his boots on and stumbled to the stream. The wolves continued licking his leg. He could still picture them wagging their tails and pressing against him for recognition. Their leader was going to live.

It took nearly a week for Jackson to recuperate by eating whatever was in his stores and resting all the time. When he started to get his life back, he was still weak, so he settled for trapping rabbits and easy prey. "None of us has a week to hang out here and recuperate," he thought to himself. "It's a good thing Tucker dispatched that rattler so neatly. But his injury could present an even bigger problem."

As the party picked their way among huge boulders along the canyon floor the next morning, Catherine pulling up the rear to keep an eye on Tucker, the steep walls felt like they were closing in. Catherine felt a chill despite the physical effort. The only time they stopped was for Jackson to change the poultice on Tucker's heel after a few hours. It was still red and swollen and it looked as though the infection started up his calf. She hoped they would find the road soon.

She watched as Akasha and Blue stayed close to him, scanning out and then looking him over, coming up to sniff him from time to time. They lifted Tucker's spirits and made Catherine feel safer.

Up ahead, Jackson signaled a stop. The wolves and then mother and son saw what he'd seen and stopped suddenly. A mountain lion lay crouched, watching them from a ledge along the rock face. Jackson glanced around slowly, looking down on the ground close to the lion, then motioned for the group to give the predator a wide berth.

"Don't limp," he called back to Tucker. Tucker straightened up, grimaced, and followed Jackson into the cover of the trees. Jackson looked back at her and said, "Don't run." Catherine drew herself up to her full height and walked as casually and quickly as she could along the new path.

When they were clear of the mountain lion, they found the terrain even more challenging. The floor of the canyon was littered with jagged rocks dusted with snow. Jackson climbed, sure-footed, looking for openings, but the large frame of the backpack hindered his progress. Catherine stayed close to Tucker, offering him a hand or a shoulder. The slippery rocks made their way particularly treacherous. He could barely put weight on his leg.

Jackson looked back and then up at the sky. He had to get over that cliff. It would take too long to find a pass. He looked back at Tucker, his arm around his mother's shoulder, hers around his waist, both looking down, cautiously choosing their footing. The wolves came up to stand beside Jackson as he debated with himself.

When the pair joined him, Jackson saw that Tucker's face was pale with droplets of sweat covering his forehead. Catherine was flushed, but not out of breath. A look of concern was etched on her face.

"Wait here. I'll take the pack to our campsite and come back to get you."

Catherine nodded and found a spot for Tucker to rest.

"How long will you be?"

"Not long," Jackson replied. He vanished over the next rock, both wolves trailing him.

"Don't forget about us!" Catherine called after him.

Tucker smiled weakly and she offered him water. Feeling his forehead as he drank, she sensed he was a little feverish. She applied a damp cloth to his head and pulled him closer so he could rest it on her shoulder. He pinched a few more leaves in his pouch and put them into his mouth.

"Did I tell you what these taste like?" Tucker asked, snuggling against her neck.

"No, what?" Catherine relaxed against a rock.

"Imagine boiled cabbage, dipped in deer brains, then coated with used motor oil."

"Mmm. Yum. Got any extra?" Tucker pulled back and opened his mouth to show her the chewed-up leaves. Catherine laughed, disgusted, then regarded him seriously for a moment. He was not the boy he was just days ago.

"How come I never realized how strong and brave you are?"

Tucker shook her shoulders playfully.

"Mom, it's me. Tucker! The wilderness is making you delirious!"

"Nope. I'm saner than ever. And the past few weeks have just proven that I raised an amazing young man."

Tucker rested his head against her shoulder again and she patted his arm. He felt a little embarrassed, but, deep down, it was exactly what he needed to hear.

Chapter 19

Sometime later, the group descended into a relatively flat, open space perfect for a campsite. A rocky overhang would give them ample protection for the night. Catherine took in a sharp breath, looking up at the sheer looming face of the cliff rising hundreds of feet high in the swirling snow.

"We're going to climb that?"

When Jackson didn't respond immediately, she looked at him. His face affirmed it.

"We should make camp," he said.

Within minutes, the pair set up the tent, gathered wood, and started a small fire in front of it. Tucker sat helpless at the tent's entrance as Jackson and Catherine worked quickly to make him comfortable. Jackson gave Tucker the job of keeping the fire going. He placed a stack of kindling by him, along with a piece of sturdy hardwood to poke the fire.

The rocky shelter kept the light snow off the small tent so that it was actually cozy as Tucker climbed inside not long after dinner. The day took everything out of him and he fell asleep instantly, while there was still a bit of light outside.

Catherine stood and scanned the sky again, hoping to catch sight of a plane below the cloud cover. Still nothing.

While Akasha and Blue stayed close to the tent, Jackson scouted along the base of the cliff, looking up for a logical point to ascend. There weren't a lot of options.

He walked back into the brush to get a better vantage point of the top. A lone oak leaned out from the top more than 200 feet above him, as if extending a helping hand. "That'll work." Jackson turned and headed back to the campsite.

After he returned, Catherine decided to freshen up and walked between the rocks away from the campsite, keeping it in view. She didn't want a run-in with the mountain lion. This mountain man was risking everything for Tucker. And for her. She resolved to do everything she could to be helpful to him. "Even if it's against your better judgment?" she asked herself. "I sure hope so."

She returned to find Jackson bedding down between Akasha and Blue in front of the fire.

"You can't sleep there."

Jackson looked up at her, confused.

"It's snowing. You'll be covered by morning."

When Jackson didn't say anything, Catherine unzipped the tent flap and opened it. She climbed inside and held it open for him, then closed it after he pulled his bedroll in with him. As she zipped it up, she called out, "Goodnight, Akasha. Goodnight, Blue. Thank you. Keep an eye out for that mountain lion."

The tent was too small for three, even two really, and Tucker was wedged, sweating but asleep, between them. Turning to get comfortable, Jackson laid his arm out above Tucker's head and gently brushed her cheek with his finger. He moved it above her head immediately, but Catherine smiled to herself. Her own hand rested on Tucker's stomach, just a few inches from Jackson's chest. "We just have to make it home," she reminded herself. "Nothing else matters."

When Catherine and Tucker arose the next morning, Jackson was already up and preparing for the climb. The spring snow hadn't stuck, and any ice wouldn't last long. The clouds dissipated, and it looked like it would be a marvelous sunny day.

Jackson spread much of the contents of his pack out on the wet rocks. He was uncoiling part of a thinner rope. The thousand-foot climbing rope, a heavy-duty pulley, and a climbing belt with a loop full of carabiners lay by the cold logs of last night's fire.

Catherine folded up the tent and shoved it back into its bag, along with its spikes and folding poles. Tucker tried to roll up the bedding, but the pain was too great. Catherine had him rest nearby while she finished striking the camp. The wolves snuggled against him for warmth.

After everything was packed up, Catherine stood back from the site and looked up the towering rock face.

"We have a climbing wall at my health club."

Having no idea what she was talking about, Jackson remained silent.

"Never mind. Tell me."

He gestured for the two to follow him to the spot just below the oak tree.

"We take these to the top," he said, gripping the rope and pulley. "Drop the rope down to your boy." He pointed to the harness he made on the backpack.

"He ties on here. Signals. Then I tie on as a counterweight. Drop back down the cliff, lifting him up to you."

Catherine was silent, imagining it.

"Then I fix the rope up there, and you climb back to meet us?"

Jackson nodded. She continued to stare at the top of the cliff.

"What if you get stuck? Or Tucker?"

Jackson picked up some small loops of rope and handed a part of the rope to hold taut.

"This is a Prusset knot." He showed her how to attach it to the rope.

"You tie on, step your foot in the loop, and jump down. Or pull." He demonstrated how the knot slid up and down the rope. "Move the knot. Pull again."

He untied it and handed the loop to Catherine as if to say, "your turn." She tried the knot and struggled. Then she felt Jackson's hands over hers, guiding them to the proper place to secure the Prusset. She let him linger there for a moment, then untied it and did it herself.

"Don't worry. I can handle it," she said, handing the rope back to him.

"On the cliff, you obey me."

Catherine was caught off-guard. She looked him in the eye but decided against challenging him. She nodded.

Jackson cleaned Tucker's foot again and prepared fresh herbs for the moose-hock sock poultice, then slipped it on. Catherine noted the red line of infection creeping up Tucker's calf but didn't comment as she helped him on with his sock and shoes. They both looked over as Jackson held up the chair he fashioned from the pack and frame for Tucker to sit in.

"Three tugs means I have the rope. Three more means I've locked the carabiner," Tucker said, studying the chair. He slipped the knotted end of the big rope through a carabiner and locked it. Jackson nodded and handed him a pair of thick leather climbing gloves.

"Push off with these as you hit the wall."

Jackson placed another waterskin by the chair. "Drink it all before you go up."

He gestured for Catherine to turn toward him and held his climbing belt near her feet for her to step in. As he pulled the belt around her hips and cinched it tight, her eyebrows went up and she grinned. He glanced at her but didn't break a smile. His taciturn expression made Catherine's grin grow even bigger. He tied her with another rope to his own waist.

Sober again, Catherine hugged Tucker tightly.

"I will see you at the top. Okay?" she said firmly.

"Bye, Mom."

"Enjoy the ride, T."

Tracking old goat trails that crisscrossed the mountain, Jackson led them expertly up the face, carrying the long, coiled rope over one shoulder. Catherine followed, tethered behind. She tugged on the safety rope whenever she couldn't find the next hold. Part way up, Jackson sat down in a shallow crevice and body belayed her up to where he stopped. From a small pouch, he sprinkled natural talc onto her hands and then his own. Catherine looked at the talc on her hands and looked up to where he was now moving. *Just don't look down,* she reminded herself.

Jackson moved smoothly sideways under the ridges as they rose. She tried not to fixate on his sleek form as it defied gravity to save her son, but she caught herself staring a time or two. The ascent was slow, but she was in the zone. All her concentration focused on this climb.

She guessed they were nearly seventy to seventy-five feet up. He secured himself at regular intervals, then signaled for her to go. He watched her intently, surprised to see that she could climb so skillfully. It was taking less time than he anticipated because she followed so quickly. When she reached her next mark, he unlocked, turned, and continued up and around a bulge in the cliff. She waited for the signal. It didn't come.

"Jackson." No answer.

"Jackson!" she called again and tugged the safety line. It was hung up on something. She spotted a hold beyond the bulge where she could see farther up the face.

Catherine hesitated, then committed to make the climb blind. She moved quickly up toward the bulge. As she rounded it, her handhold disappeared. She inched out, dug in a toehold, and squeezed up another foot. She reached toward the next crevice and gripped it tightly, her arm shaking. Taking a deep breath, she pulled her entire body up into the clear sightline.

Jackson was above her, still climbing. Unsecured.

She realized her mistake. Trying to hold her place, she struggled and began to sweat. The talc on her hands was dissolving. She gave the safety line a quick, desperate tug.

Jackson wedged his foot and looked over his shoulder. She registered the shock on his face and they both looked around him, realizing there was nowhere for him to sit securely.

"Don't move." He scanned around again for his own safe place and found a spot about ten feet away.

"I can't hold it..." she called. He studied her position from above.

"Kick your left leg out. There's a little ledge."

She looked around and saw it but couldn't bring herself to move. Her hands began to shake from the tension. She could sense that Jackson was moving toward his secure spot as he talked her through it.

"Relax your body. Let the tension go. Rest on the wall."

Catherine closed her eyes, willing her hands to relax. She kicked out her leg and reached for the ledge, her toe finding it, then slipping off. She began to slide off the wall and she screamed as she dropped. Her safety line snapped taut a second after Jackson wedged his arm around a rock. The force of her fall nearly pulled his arm out of its socket, but he held on.

Far below, Tucker watched his mother swing back and forth as if on a pendulum.

"Mom..."

Catherine bumped against the wall, scraping her arms and hands. She looked up to see Jackson straining to pull himself onto an outcropping, bearing all of her weight too. He pushed himself up and came to a rest, then waited for her to stop swaying.

"Jackson..." Catherine was so relieved he was okay, she didn't give her own predicament a thought. She watched him shift position and then pull her up, hand over hand, his biceps bulging from the effort.

Spinning on the end of the rope, she looked down and could see Tucker, far down on the ground, looking up at her. She looked up and began to reach for the ledge. She could just grip it with her fingers. Jackson pulled her up the rest of the way.

They shared a ledge barely wide enough for one. Catherine looked down to see her arm bleeding. She sensed Jackson's anger as he huffed to regain his steady breathing.

"I'm sorry. I couldn't see you."

She could see disappointment flash across his face before he looked up at the vertical in front of them.

"We climb side by side from here."

Chapter 20

Tucker lifted the waterskin to his lips and took a long drink. He squeezed some out into Blue's mouth. The beautiful black wolf licked and lapped playfully.

"Thataboy."

Tucker tilted back his head to see his mom and Jackson moving almost imperceptibly, their arms and legs spread out like spiders. Above them, red sandstone chimneys rose like drapes all the way to the top of the canyon.

One hundred and fifty feet up, Catherine found a rhythm. Revived, she stopped for a moment and took in the spectacular view. She could see the whole length of the canyon and beyond. Above her, Jackson was admiring the view too, waiting for her to reach his position. When she did, he went a little sideways, then up toward the pillars near the top of their climb.

Climbing to the flute of a nearby chimney, he squeezed into one of the folds. He looked up at his next obstacle and studied the three-sided tunnel. When Catherine joined him, he showed her how to wedge her body between the walls and ascend, using her hands and feet on one side and her back and shoulders on the other.

"If you get tired, rest."

She got the hang of it right away. The pair scrunched their way straight up like two hamsters in a tube. Twenty feet up, the chimney widened. They each extended their arms and legs, forming a deeper "L."

Fifteen feet farther up, the flute expanded into a small chasm, maybe five feet wide.

"What do we do now?" Catherine asked.

Jackson found a hand hold on one side and signaled for Catherine to climb up even with him and do the same. They each faced the opposite side of the chimney, their backs to each other, separated by a two-foot gap.

"Lean back against me."

Catherine looked down at the 200-foot drop and hesitated.

"I'll fall."

"Do it." Jackson arched his back, narrowing the gap. She let out a little cry, then did the same. Their bodies met in the middle, forming a wedge that filled the chasm.

"Relax against me," Jackson said, opening his arms so they could lock elbows.

"What if I slip?"

"I'm your chair."

They pressed against each other, letting their heads touch as well.

"Lean your head back," he said, and Catherine rested her head on his shoulder. Jackson did the same. Their temples touched and Catherine stared straight up into the tunnel.

"Ready?"

"Let's go," Catherine said.

In fits and starts, they began to climb. They found a rhythm soon, completely trusting each other. If either faltered, they would both fall. But they rose instead in harmony, bridging the gap between them.

The crown of the chimney in sight, they both hesitated when they saw how it widened dramatically. Jackson paused, pushing against Catherine's back and shoulders, savoring this connection. Still contrite from the fall, Catherine waited for his next instruction. She, too, didn't want to break the connection, but had no idea that's why he stopped. He took a deep breath and closed his eyes for one more moment. Then he opened them again and looked at the wall above them.

"Find a hand hold."

Catherine gripped her side of the tunnel and prepared to drop her back out of the wedge.

"Ready."

He nodded and gripped his side of the wall. Simultaneously, they dropped their legs and he found toeholds, then quickly free-climbed to the lip. Pulling himself up and over, he turned and pulled Catherine into his arms.

Relaxing for the first time in hours, Catherine let herself be held. They looked out at a mesa that stretched for miles.

"Which way are we going?"

Jackson pointed east. No civilization was in sight. No planes. Just sky. She turned to see the old oak tree jutting out over the lip of the cliff. A flash of fear gripped her when she realized that Tucker would have to come up, but her trust of Jackson grown so completely over the last several days that she just as quickly dismissed it from her thoughts. She smiled at him as he unclipped her and uncinched the climbing belt, holding her hand as she stepped out of it. He picked it up and, after a few adjustments, stepped into it and cinched it up.

While she took a big drink from the waterskin, she watched him clamber out onto the limb of the tree with the rope and pulley. Fixing the pulley with a piece of webbing, he threaded through the rope and tied one end to his belt. He pitched the heavy coil over the side of the cliff toward Tucker.

Hundreds of feet below, the wolves perked up as the rope dropped in front of them. Akasha picked up the end of the rope and brought it over to Tucker, but he did not respond. He passed out, rivulets of sweat running down his face.

Blue licked Tucker's face. He awoke with a start and saw the rope in Akasha's mouth. Taking it, he gave it three quick tugs with as much power as he could muster. Then he stood up, nearly falling from the weight of the backpack and the pain in his leg. He gripped the gate of the carabiner and tried to open it. No luck. He felt too weak. He looked desperately at the wolves. They sat obediently watching him.

After several tries, the carabiner clicked into place. Remembering the gloves, he looked around where he'd been laying and found them. He pulled them on and gave three tugs again. The wolves continued to watch him intently. Blue leaned over and nuzzled his bad leg.

"Bye, guys," he said, rubbing Blue's furry head. Tucker was jerked off his feet and began rising into the air.

On the mesa above, his mom watched as the rope moved quickly through the pulley. She ventured over to the lip to see Jackson repelling down the sandstone sides of the chimney. With each kick off the wall, he dropped down ten to twenty feet.

"Beats coming up," she said aloud.

She watched as Tucker swung out and up as he was lifted skyward. Then he smacked against the cliff, but the backpack cushioned the blow. Spinning slowly, Tucker squinted up the face as it whirled around above him. He felt a little short of breath. He took deep draughts of air, slowly inhaling and exhaling, until he felt steady. He didn't want to ruin the ride with an asthma attack. He'd been doing so well.

Halfway up, he made out Jackson's legs dropping toward him. Smack! He hit the cliff again, but this time with his injured heel. Tucker screamed in pain.

One more tug on the Prusset and Jackson dropped to just below the dangling boy. Tucker fought back tears as Jackson found a hold on the cliff face and climbed up and over to Tucker. He clipped his carabiner to the backpack harness.

"You okay?"

Tucker bit his lip and pushed through the pain. He tried to control his breathing too. *Don't panic,* he thought to himself. He looked down and saw the canyon spread out below him.

"Nice view, huh?" But Jackson didn't answer. He opened the tent bag secured to the frame and was pulling out the tent poles. In a moment, he fashioned a splint around Tucker's wounded leg.

"Your mom can climb," he finally said.

"Yeah, she can do pretty much anything. What's annoying is she knows it."

Jackson smiled as he finished his task, wrapping and tying the blanket Tucker brought from home around the splint for padding and cushioning Tucker's heel from the wall.

Next, he cinched the harness to keep it from spinning. Then he put his hand on Tucker's shoulder.

"She's waiting for you."

He secured another Prusset loop on his end of the rope and stepped into it like a stirrup. Then he kicked himself away from the wall and stomped down, sending Tucker skyward.

Feeling safer and spinning less, Tucker allowed himself to enjoy the rest of the ride. A snow-topped range to the east, the dusky canyon below, blue rivers, green forests everywhere else. No one is going to ever believe this, he thought to himself.

Rising higher, he looked up and spotted his mom by the ledge. She waited until he was above the ridge line, then threw him a rope and pulled him to solid ground.

"Hey, T," she said pulling him into a fierce hug and kiss on the cheek.

"Thanks, Mom," he said, hugging her back. They uncinched him and removed the backpack. She helped him sit down and admired the leg brace that Jackson crafted hundreds of feet in the air.

"You, okay?"

"Yeah, you go ahead." She examined his face, holding it and turning it this way and that. When she was satisfied, she gave him a quick peck on the forehead. Tucker smiled and closed his eyes.

Catherine ran to the oak tree and tugged on the taut rope three times, then looped and knotted it around the trunk the way Jackson taught her. She pulled on it several times to make sure it wasn't going anywhere.

"How's Jackson going to get back up?" Tucker asked.

Catherine turned and gave him a big smile.

"Fly."

Chapter 21

At the base of the canyon wall, with a rucksack on his back, Jackson was tied on and ready to go.

Akasha and Blue sat side by side, staring up at the leader of their pack.

Jackson looked into their woeful eyes, then up at the cliff. He looked back at his forlorn companions.

Above, Tucker and Catherine found a bit of shade against the late-day sun and sat beside one another, taking sips from a waterskin and watching the rope. Catherine let the warmth seep into her skin as she closed her eyes. She had checked on Tucker's leg, and it seemed stable, for now. Tucker was alert, scanning the plateau and keeping a vigil for Jackson.

Suddenly, a hand appeared. Then another, working the Prusset handles up the fixed line. Jackson's head popped up above the edge...and two others. Akasha and Blue were strapped over each of Jackson's shoulders.

Tucker laughed and looked at his mom, who was covering her mouth and sighing with relief. They both rose and she helped Jackson gain his footing and unstrap the wolves.

Tucker leaned in and hugged Jackson. Jackson hugged him back, hard.

"Tucker! Do you need me?" Catherine called into the darkness. Tucker limped off to find a place to do his business. She feared he might fall into a chasm. But the mesa was mostly flat, with no trees, and there was a full moon to light the way.

"I'm fine, Mom!" came the semi-distant reply. Blue followed Tucker, while Akasha remained curled by the tent after they'd eaten. Since there was no wood for a fire, they laid the bedding outside the tent to look up at the sky.

Jackson crouched nearby as Catherine propped her head on her hand, laying sideways in front of the tent. She regarded him for a moment.

"I've spent a lot of my life taking orders from men," she said. "I think I've built up a resistance to it." A cold breeze blew over the mesa, then stilled.

"Me too."

Catherine grinned, then laughed. After a few minutes of silence again, she said, "Sometimes I miss having someone tell me what the hell I'm supposed to do, though. Tucker's father was a jerk, but he had a really convincing way of telling me everything would work out."

She curled up on her side, turned and stared at the moon.

"You ever going to tell me more about why you're out here on your own?"

"Well…" then he smiled at her and said no more. She waited a moment, then offered: "Whatever happened, it seems like you've made up for it. What you've sacrificed, the way you live…I think I'm starting to get it."

Jackson looked at her, then stretched out on his back next to her, leaving a couple of inches between them. A bank of clouds glided over the moon, making their mesa just a little more secret.

"I killed a lawman who was attacking my sister."

Catherine waited.

"I was protecting her from being raped." He paused again.

Catherine considered for a moment. There was more to the story than he told back at his cave.

"So, you were helping your sister?"

"Yes, it seems as though the bouncer at this club had his mind set on taking advantage of her. I happened to be walking up to meet her for a party. She was being attacked in the parking lot when I showed up. He was an off-duty deputy and I just let all my training kick in. After a struggle, he pulled his gun. We wrestled, and the gun went off...I had to get out of there because I couldn't stand to be put in a cell again."

"Oh, Jackson, I'm so sorry," Catherine said and put her arm around him.

"I never was like other people. But after that...it was best to get away."

"From everyone."

"Me. What was inside," he paused again, and Catherine sensed he had more to say. "Taking lives got easy."

It made sense. Catherine suspected when they stayed in the cave that Jackson must have had an extreme life to choose such an extreme form of isolation. She nestled against him, to his surprise. She felt him tense, then relax.

"So much time has passed. And it wasn't your fault."

"No witnesses to say that."

She touched his hand and said, "What about now?"

Jackson didn't respond. He debated about whether he should put his arm around her and pull her close.

"Any way you would change your mind and come with us?" she asked. "I could help you for a change."

"I will get you where you need to go," he said, solemnly. "But that life is…gone." He turned to look at her.

Catherine was quiet. After a moment, she looked him in the eye, their faces only inches apart. They both felt a kiss looming. Jackson put his arm around her. Catherine pulled away.

"I can't. Not if I'm just going to lose you."

He nodded and turned back to look at the sky. She propped herself up again and noticed the ring around his neck. She reached out and touched it. The intimate gesture sent electricity radiating from his chest through his arms. His fingertips twitched.

"Do you think anyone's still looking for you?" She thought of the letter and the picture of the beautiful young woman laughing. She didn't know if they were the same person.

It took him a moment, but then he nodded.

"I don't know."

Catherine realized that her question could be taken two ways.

"I won't tell them where you are."

Jackson turned his head to look at her and his eyes expressed the gratitude he felt. He put his hand on her leg in an unspoken "thanks" and she placed her hand over his.

"It's the least I can do," she said. There was a long silence.

"You might be surprised how much less people can do," he finally said. She locked her hand with his and brought it up to her chest.

"Trust me. I wouldn't be."

Tucker dozed fitfully. He was alone in the tent, its flap open. The night before had felt so close. He complained that he couldn't even roll over as they got ready to bed down for the night. Catherine and Jackson agreed that he needed to be comfortable. Tucker stuck his heel out into the cool air to lessen the pain from the heat and swelling.

But now his poultice was leaking blood and his entire leg was throbbing. He was too exhausted to care, and he nearly ran out of herbs. The few single packs of painkillers from the med kit were consumed two days ago. Just outside, Catherine and Jackson slept, nestled against one another in the wee hours of the cold spring morning. The wolves lay beside Jackson in a single ball of fur.

Akasha's ears pricked up. She raised her entire head out of the pile, sensing…something. She looked around, then rested her head on Blue's back, keeping her eyes open and her ears straight up.

A mountain lion pounced, coming through the air straight at Tucker's leg. Akasha leapt up and collided mid-air with the ferocious animal, its fangs bared, both snapping and snarling. Blue joined the attack from behind and the creature fell away from the tent. Jackson jumped up, knife in hand.

Catherine threw herself in front of Tucker and they both watched horrified at the scene unfolding in front of them. Blue sunk his teeth into the lion's hindquarter. It spun with terrific force, throwing Blue into the air. Jackson looked for an opening while Akasha counterattacked and got swatted by a thick paw. She rolled dangerously close to the edge of the canyon. A red slash formed on her front leg but did not deter her. Both wolves leapt in to circle their adversary.

Jackson faced off against the lion.

"Get in the tent!" he yelled, keeping his eyes on the predator as it stalked forward.

"But..."

"Do it!" he yelled. Catherine pulled Tucker all the way into the tent and huddled with him as far from the action as she could.

"It's okay," she said, holding Tucker tightly. "It'll be okay..."

They heard a snarl and snapping sounds. Then the sound of a bite and a whine. She ventured closer to the flap and peeked out. Akasha was laying close to the tent, struggling to rise. She did, but Catherine noted a little limp as she rejoined the fight. Catherine could barely see Blue, teeth bared near the oak tree. The mountain lion backed Jackson up to the lip of the canyon. The wolves drew close, snarling and snapping to distract the lion, but they were no match for the cat's power.

Out of space, Jackson feinted with the knife, then rushed the big cat, stabbing its shoulder. The lion screamed and attacked. The two wrestled on the ground, rolling over and over...off the edge of the cliff.

"No!" Catherine screamed. It echoed for a moment. Then, silence.

Catherine burst out of the tent, her face white with panic. She ran to the edge and froze as she heard a thud. She couldn't bring herself to look.

She dropped to her knees, shaking, trying to will herself to crawl the last six inches to the edge. Beside her, Tucker came up and began crawling to see what happened. Sobbing, he looked over the edge. She crawled up to join him and put her arm around his shaking shoulders.

Chapter 22

They looked down, both crying now, as they looked over the cliff. Jackson, less than four feet below, was gripping a limb jutting out into the abyss.

"Oh, thank God," she exhaled, crying now for relief. Tucker reached down to give Jackson a hand and Catherine and he helped pull him up. He reached up slowly. The rocks were illuminated by the brightness of the moon, which shone in the now cloudless sky.

Jackson stood on the limb and was almost near the top. Within a few minutes, he'd thrown an arm and then a leg over the lip. Tucker and Catherine, still holding on, grabbed his jacket and pants and rolled him over onto the mesa. She laughed as he caught his breath, amazed that he survived. He looked at her a moment, then started laughing too. Neither could quite believe he lived through that ordeal. Tucker offered Jackson water, which he drank long and slow. Together they cleaned and mended the wolves' cuts. Catherine insisted that Tucker go back to bed after they fixed up his poultice so he could rest. She gave Jackson first aid for the gash on his forearm.

He watched her clean the wound and tie it up in a clean cloth. He looked at the curve of her face and the brilliance of her hair in the moonlight. Tomorrow we will say goodbye, he thought to himself. This woman and this boy who mean so much, suddenly. And, just as suddenly, they'll be gone. Jackson sat quietly, contemplating the next 24 hours, while she worked. She sensed that he wanted peace, so she bit her tongue, even though she wanted to ask him how badly it hurt, if the dressing was too tight, or if he really, really had to leave them. A million questions swirled in her head.

They lingered in each other's arms in front of the tent as the sun rose higher above them. As long as Tucker is sleeping, I'm not moving, Catherine told herself. She was sore from the hike and the scrapes from her fall. If she was honest with herself, she was still aching from the crash. The big bed in Jackson's cave had done wonders, but the pain in her head and neck was making a dull comeback.

Beside her, Jackson felt like he landed at the bottom of that canyon and broken into a thousand pieces. His arm began aching from the swipe from the mountain lion's sharp claws. His shoulder was puffy and tender from nearly being pulled apart to save Catherine. Two climbs—one free-handed and one with two adult wolves—and one descent after a full day of hiking and a full night on watch…"What am I doing?" he asked himself.

Then he turned his head slightly and saw the sun's rays glint against her cheek, and he remembered. A smile crossed his face as he thought about Tucker, so brave, hiking without complaint for miles before they realized he was injured, then bearing up, a kid in the middle of nowhere, trusting him to get him back home.

And her. Jackson almost couldn't express what he was feeling. The only way he'd been able to cope the first few years out here had been by shutting out everything. He'd gone from the loss of his first and only love, to imprisonment and brutality, to a night of horrors in the space of just a few months. The extreme isolation of the wilderness after these harrowing, life-changing experiences enhanced his trauma, had fed his paranoia. But now the woods were his backyard, the cave was his home, and Akasha and Blue were his family. He neither needed nor wanted anything else. Everything outside the world he'd built was suspicious.

But here they were. Embracing him. Asking him to be a part of their world—*the* world—again. But it was impossible. He could feel his heart turning, actually considering a different future than the one he'd mapped out all those years ago. Even as he did, he knew that, logically, a civilized life wouldn't turn out the way he was permitting himself to imagine. He'd have to answer for the death of the deputy.

The sun's heat on their backs eased the strain of the sledge. The cold of the past few days added to the tension in their muscles, but now the heat felt good. After several miles witnessing Jackson's quiet determination, Catherine insisted on pulling her share. Tucker could no longer walk. Despite a new poultice that seemed to lessen the swelling for a little while, the infection spread up his calf to his knee. When Jackson saw that he could barely stand, he crafted a stretcher from the tent and poles, with wooden skids at the bottom to cushion the bumps along the mesa floor.

"It's better if I pull by myself," Jackson responded. "And you need to keep an eye on Tucker, make sure he is okay." She acquiesced and now walked silently behind Tucker, watching his face for any sign of discomfort. They lightened the backpack before they left. The thousand-foot coil of rope was placed under a large stone at the base of the old oak tree, along with the pulley and other climbing gear. Tucker wrapped them in the blanket he'd carried from the plane. Jackson assured them they would be going downhill and wouldn't need to climb any more.

Tucker developed a steady fever after the attack. Catherine gave him water and the few herbs when he was conscious. Despite the weight of the sledge, Catherine struggled to keep up. The wolves trotted behind her, nudging her with their soft noses, stopping and standing with her whenever she took a break. Jackson kept a brisk pace. But it looked like they were going nowhere.

For miles all around, Catherine could see only a few scrub pines and rock outcroppings. No birds in the sky. Just the desolate, lifeless landscape. Around late afternoon, they spotted fingers of stone rising up from the plateau. Jackson directed their journey toward them and, within a few hours, they reached their base. Now carrying Tucker on the stretcher between them, Jackson in front and Catherine behind, the convoy paused for a breath. Jackson looked up at the sky and wiped the sweat away from his brow. The clouds rolled in and were now getting thicker and darker.

"We better stop."

Catherine nodded and looked after Tucker while Jackson pitched the tent. As they sat in the opening and shared jerky and nuts, Jackson and Catherine watched flashes of lightning streak across the sky far off near the horizon. They heard the faint thunder nearly 30 seconds later. Catherine looked over her shoulder, where Tucker was stretched out on the sleeping bag, resting peacefully for the first time all day.

"It's lucky we found this gorge. We're protected here once the wind and rain come," she said.

"I think it'll wait until tomorrow."

Catherine looked doubtful, then shrugged and climbed into the tent. She fell asleep instantly.

Jackson kept his gaze fixed on the clouds until well after sunset. The storm kept up, but didn't move toward them. He propped himself against a smooth rock by the tent and eventually closed his eyes. Akasha trotted over, circled once, and laid down against him. Blue stretched out across his lower legs, huffed, and drifted off too.

Catherine could see sheets of rain in the distance when she peeked out of the tent the next morning, but the storm wasn't any closer. The sky directly above them was a brilliant blue and gave her hope for a better day. Tucker roused slightly as she splashed water on his face and hands, but she could tell he wouldn't be able to walk today either.

"Do you think we'll get to a town today?" she asked Jackson. He looked out at the rainy horizon and said, "Not if we don't beat that."

Jackson struck the campsite and packed their gear quickly, then positioned himself at Tucker's head on the stretcher. He looked back at Catherine, who nodded as she finished drinking from the waterskin, and they hefted the stretcher.

The climb through the stone pillars took longer than the entire hike across the flatland. Straining under Tucker's weight, Catherine remained focused and silent, willing her muscles to work and not give out. She envied the wolves their four legs and agility as they leapt from rock to rock and found narrow, straight pathways where Jackson and she went around outcroppings with the stretcher.

Through it all, Tucker stayed quiet, drifting in and out of consciousness. Occasionally, Catherine asked Tucker questions to keep him alert, questions only he would know the answer to.

"What was the name of that pitcher on your Twins Little League team?"

"David?"

"No, the one with the pigtails."

"Oh, yeah. Um…Abby."

"Do you remember that time we went to that comic book convention downtown? How old were you?"

"Eight, Mom."

"Yeah, that's right. And which superhero had the longest line? We must've waited for hours."

"Iron Man."

They took only two breaks as they progressed through the columns: one for lunch and one to make sure Tucker hadn't slipped into a coma when he didn't answer with the name of his sixth-grade science teacher's name. It was late afternoon and the shadows of the stone pillars lengthened across the ground. He finally woke up when Blue licked him on both cheeks and across his nose.

The rain began on the down slope in the early evening. Stopping for the night, the stretcher bearers let the fresh rain wash over them, cooling their aching muscles. Catherine examined the callouses on her hands and pulled clean cloths around them, trying not to show her weariness.

She held the last of the full waterskins up to Tucker's lips. After he drank, she brushed the wet hair away from his face and held her cheek against his. She nearly wept when she felt how hot it was. But she remained calm, unzipped his jacket, and whispered in his ear that they were almost home. Jackson watched her, wishing it was true. She caught him staring and he gave her a reassuring smile.

"How much farther?" she asked, sitting down on a rock and wiping her forehead with the back of her wrist. Jackson looked east and scanned the sky.

"A few hours once we get moving again tomorrow morning. If the weather holds." He handed her some jerky and fed the wolves, then took a bite for himself.

"What do you mean 'grounded'?" Lewis hadn't shaved in days. Rufus thought he was wearing the same shirt from yesterday but couldn't be sure. Lewis wasn't adventurous in the fashion department and pretty much wore blue shirts with similar ties every day, crisis or no.

Lewis was on the phone with the local sheriff's department and the park rangers in Idaho almost non-stop for weeks. When the search finally went airborne, the office returned to some semblance of regular business, expecting good news any minute. But then reporters started to call for a quote and PR needed to put together a hasty press release on Roseburg's concern for one of their top employee's safe return. Now this.

"But you haven't even found the plane yet. You can't give up when we don't even know if they're..." Lewis's voice trailed off. Rufus lingered in the doorway, shooing away people who stopped by to check on him. As Lewis hung up, Rufus asked, "Are they quitting already?"

"Yeah," Lewis sat back in his chair and rubbed his eyes with the heels of his palms. He took a deep breath, sat up, and looked at Rufus. "Thunderstorms are rolling in. They could fly when it was snowing, but warm air has come in from California and the Pacific. They don't want anyone to know, though, because some fool civilians have been out looking on their own. They don't want more people stranded in the wilderness who they have to rescue. So, we're not going to say anything and hope that they start up again."

"You think they'd stop completely?" Rufus couldn't grasp the idea of no more Catherine. She was tough as nails, a solid worker. And she was always pleasant to him. They made each other laugh.

Lewis didn't look him in the eye and turned back to the computer screen. He looked over the search area, now a grid marked with dates and times.

"Not sure what else anyone can do," he replied, sounding defeated.

The rain was steady all night long. The persistent shower against the tent fabric kept Catherine awake. She finally drifted off just before dawn. When she woke, she felt disoriented and it took her a while to remember where she was and what she was supposed to be doing. Jackson patiently waited as she helped Tucker get ready for the day. He was a little more alert and his smile gave them courage to sally forth against the pouring rain.

After the first hour of their trek, it felt like a forced march. Jackson was used to it, but Catherine was not. She pooled all her strength and energy, focusing on his back. The relentless slogging through the mud almost made her laugh at the incredible situation. "As if things couldn't have gotten worse.

Of course, they could. A plane crash, a mystery man, wolves!"
She shook her head, incredulous. She went down the list.
"Killing our own food, sleeping in caves, missing our chance
at a rescue…the climb, a mountain lion attack… Snow, rain…
my poor, sick boy." The gravity of it all felt like rocks in her
pockets, pulling her into the earth. The pole started to slip out
of her hand. She caught it before Jackson noticed or Tucker fell
out of the stretcher.

"Are we close?" she asked, trying not to sound a little
panicked. A lightning bolt splintered across the sky, followed
almost immediately by cracking thunder. She jumped and
started to slip, but again regained her composure and focused
on his back.

"There's an old mining road." She squinted to see where
he was looking and saw the thin band of a trail emerge. It
became harder to see the horizon as the clouds pressed down.
It felt more like midnight than mid-morning.

Jackson slowed to a crawl and looked back at Catherine.
She shook her head vigorously and called over the sound of
thunder, "We can't stop! Keep going!"

They soldiered on. Another hour passed. Catherine felt and
looked drunk. Her legs splayed out to each side as she tried to
gain traction in the muck. Correcting course, she headed too
far to the right and slipped and fell backwards into the mud.
The stretcher bounced to the ground and Tucker slid half-off,
his body a jumble.

Catherine crawled to her knees. She looked down and
was coated in red-black mud, then she looked up and let the
rain wash over her. "I don't even have the energy to cry," she
thought. "Help me, God," she prayed, and put her head back

down. Droplets of water splashed against her bare neck and formed rivulets down her cheeks, neck, and back. She felt a hand on her shoulder.

When she looked up, Jackson stood beside her, his hand out. He secured Tucker back onto the stretcher. The wolves stood beside him, covered from head to paw in mud.

She held up her hand. He pulled her up, then looked down at her hands as they rested, palms up, in his. The cloths were wet with blood. He furrowed his brow and looked into her eyes.

"I'm okay," she said, softly. He didn't speak, but just stood there for a long moment, processing the next step in their journey, or praying. Catherine couldn't tell which.

Akasha let out a mighty howl. It felt as though she was punctuating Catherine's despair. But Jackson looked around and listened. He knew that howl. Akasha was alerting him. A moment later, Catherine heard something too. A mechanical whine rose and fell through the downpour. She dropped her hands and ran toward it.

Chapter 23

Just before Catherine emerged from the dense forest by the road, Jackson overtook her. He pulled her back against a wide elm, his hands gripping her upper arms.

"What are you doing?!" she cried.

"Let me go. I'll make sure it's safe," he said, dropping his hands from her arms. Her look of alarm turned to one of gratitude. She nodded.

"Yes, of course. I'll go check on Tucker. See if he can walk."

As she ran back to Tucker, still strapped to the stretcher and shaking his hair in the rain, she hoped and prayed Jackson would be safe. And as good as his word.

"We're going home, baby," she said, wiping Tucker's face with her hand. He gave her a wan smile and let her unfasten him and pull him to his feet. The wolves nudged him into a standing position and strode behind him until they reached the edge of the forest.

The Chevy pick-up's wheels spun in the mud. One side was listing a little in the ditch and a spray of brown muck flew into the air, then abruptly stopped. A man in a green ball cap and brown hunting jacket leapt onto a patch of grass with a jack in his hand. He stopped in his tracks when he saw Jackson approaching him. Before Jackson walked five steps, the older man, wisps of gray peeking from under his hat, tossed the jack back into the cab and pulled out a rifle.

"Wait, wait!" Jackson called. "We need help!" Jackson realized his appearance didn't help matters. Covered in muddy deerskin, with a full beard and long hair, he must've looked like Sasquatch emerging from the woods.

"Don't come any closer," the man warned. Jackson pleaded again for help, but the man raised his rifle and pointed it at Jackson.

"Please, we have a sick boy. We need to get him to a hospital!"

The man cocked his head, considering, then looked around, suspicious of a trick or trap of some kind.

"Stay back!" the man called out and Jackson took a hesitant step backwards. Behind him, Catherine and Tucker limped into view and came up to stand beside Jackson. The man immediately put his rifle back on its cab rack and grabbed the jack from the front seat.

"Help me get this jacked up. We need to stuff some of that brush underneath the wheel," he said, pointing at Jackson, "then I'll get you to the hospital." Jackson helped Tucker into the cab while Catherine thanked the man as he found solid ground to jack up the tire. She went to help Tucker stretch out his leg and lean against the door when Jackson returned to help. It would be a tight fit in the cab for just Tucker, she thought. Tucker needed all the space to prop up his leg.

The man hopped into the cab a few minutes later, put it into drive, and said, "Hold on, everybody. Here we go!" Then he hit the accelerator. The truck rolled forward over a few bumps and the man put the truck into park.

Catherine came around the side of the truck as Jackson handed the man his jack. The man took it and held out his hand. "Name's Pickett."

"Thank you, Mr. Pickett. I'm...very grateful to you," Jackson said, shaking the man's hand.

"I am too, Mr. Pickett. My name is Catherine and that's my son, Tucker. He injured his leg , which is terribly infected. If you could get us to the hospital, we would be so thankful."

"Sure, hop in. Closest one is in Charleston, about twenty miles thataway." He got a cloth to wipe off the jack. Catherine and Jackson looked at each other, hesitating. She could see the conflict on his face. She walked to the passenger side to squeeze in next to Tucker. Jackson followed her, then reached out and pulled her back toward the truck bed. Then he turned and whistled.

Akasha and Blue ran out of the forest and stopped in front of him. He bent down and scratched behind their ears, then whispered something. The wolves hesitated, then raced back into the woods.

Jackson helped Catherine into the truck bed and, taking a look around, followed her to sit near the back window. The rain was just misting by then and Catherine finally allowed herself to relax for the first time in hours. She leaned against Jackson, who looked back into the cab at Tucker. He was slumped against the window. She looked up at the concern etched on Jackson's face.

"He doesn't look good, does he?"

"He's a strong boy," Jackson said, giving her a reassuring smile.

The forest flashed by, and the cold wind felt refreshing to them both. They were finally going home, Catherine thought. But the thought was bittersweet. She closed her eyes and snuggled against Jackson.

Pickett bumped onto a paved road and fishtailed down the highway, joining traffic. He laid on the horn, speeding past a slower vehicle. As they passed, a little girl in the backseat of an SUV gawked at the two strange creatures in the back of the pick-up truck. Jackson instinctively touched the chain around his neck. A reminder of the world he was coming back to.

Catherine noticed and put her hand in his.

"It's been so long. They can't still be looking for you…" But Jackson didn't respond. He looked out at the rain-slick road and passing cars, betraying no emotion.

"Hey," she tried again. "You've taken a huge risk bringing us back. And at no small peril to yourself. It's going to work out, all right?"

Jackson gave a single nod. After a few moments, he said, "I could be arrested, Catherine."

"If they catch you, and that's a big if, I will do everything in my power to fight the charges," she said, turning to look at him. "I've never met anyone like you. I want…" but she couldn't finish her thought. She needed to stay focused on her son. Sensing this, Jackson looked back through the windscreen at Tucker.

Catherine shifted in her seat so she could get a better look at Tucker. She grew alarmed when she saw that the color drained almost entirely out of his cheeks.

"He's going to die," she said, starting to cry. "After everything we've been through and he's going to die on his way to..." She started to sob. Jackson pulled her chin around so she was looking directly into his eyes. Strength and resolve exuded from his warm brown eyes. Catherine snuffled once and stopped crying.

He glanced back at Tucker, saw the traffic light reflected in the window, and looked around. Suddenly, they were in civilization. He studied the stores, gas stations, and stoplights. Yes, he recognized Charleston. Probably twenty, twenty-five miles from Arapaho Glades.

"We're back," Catherine whispered to herself.

Within minutes, Pickett bounced up to the emergency room doors and screeched to a halt. He leaned on the horn while Jackson and Catherine jumped out of the bed and started to help Tucker, who was unconscious again.

"Let's move it, sunshine!" he yelled at the paramedic who peeked out to see what was happening. A moment later, two paramedics brought out a gurney and helped Tucker onto it. Jackson nodded at Pickett who returned the look of thanks with a warm smile.

"You did a great thing, bringing those folks outta there," Pickett said, walking over to Jackson as Catherine followed the paramedics through the bay doors. "The good Lord won't forget what you've done."

Jackson's face darkened, thinking of what he'd done long ago. Guilt washed over him, and he stood debating about what to do next. Pickett sensed Jackson's indecision.

"Aren't you going to go in?" Pickett asked. Jackson looked at him, uncertain.

"Tell you what. I'll go park and join you in the waiting room. Make sure the boy's okay." Jackson nodded and headed inside.

Pickett had never seen anything like it. A hermit with two wolves for pets helping a mother and son. The good Lord certainly did put some interesting people in his path. He felt compelled to see it through. He wanted to be sure the boy was okay. Quite frankly, he wondered about how the man and the woman were going to manage as well. He needed to be here for these people, in whatever way the Lord wanted him to be. Hunting could wait. Wasn't great weather for it anyway.

"We're down here," Catherine called, coming back around a corner. Jackson blinked as he entered the hospital, his eyes unused to the fluorescent lights, his mind trying to process the beeps, the buzzes, and all the people. The walls and ceiling felt unnatural. Too close. She beckoned to him, and he picked up the pace.

"He cut himself maybe a week ago, out in the woods," Catherine was telling an intern as Jackson rounded the corner and stood in the doorway of an open exam room. Tucker lay on a gurney, receiving an IV. His clothes were being cut off him, starting with his boots. A medic—a doctor, a nurse, Jackson couldn't be sure—was starting to clean off the mud. Another called out his vitals.

"We need to get him cleaned off so the doctor can examine him, Mrs..."

"Esquivel. Catherine Esquivel. That's Tucker, my son," she answered.

"And you are..." It took Jackson a moment to realize that the woman in scrubs was addressing him.

"I'll go wait in the waiting room," Jackson said stepping back into the hallway. He could feel Catherine looking at him as he slowly made his way down the hall toward a sign stating, "Waiting Room." Gurneys and wheelchairs—some occupied, some not—lined the hallway. He saw a young man, tattoos around his neck and down his arms, his ears, lips, and nose filled with piercings, lounging in a wheelchair with his arm in a brand-new cast. As he passed by the ER bay doors, two police officers rushed by, holding up a man who looked like he'd been shot. One of the officers looked Jackson up and down, but then rushed past.

Jackson pushed through the waiting room doors and was immediately assaulted by a cacophony of sounds, louder than in the ER. And everyone's heads swiveled to look at him. Two boys, their attention locked on a loud video game on a small tablet, looked up as he passed. TVs mounted in two corners of the large room showed boxes of people all talking at the same time. People filled every corner of the room. Jackson began to panic.

Then he saw Pickett, sitting in a quiet corner near a window, waving him over. Jackson made his way to the old man and stood against the wall next to him.

"You're going to be okay, son," Pickett said.

"It's Tucker I'm worried about," Jackson replied.

"I get that. But we need to be worrying about you too. I suspect you haven't been out much in a while."

Jackson looked down at the man and let a brief smile cross his face at the euphemism. "No, it's been a while." He looked around and found the exit.

Pickett caught the look. "You best get comfortable, son."

When Jackson looked at him, the old man just nodded and sat back in his chair, propping his gimme cap forward to cover his eyes as he closed them.

"Sorry, ma'am. Can't go in there."

"I am looking for the doctor. It's been hours," Catherine said, whirling around near a Restricted Area sign. "My son is finally asleep, but we need an answer about his foot and leg. I need a doctor!"

"Ma'am, if you can't calm down," the orderly became stern. Catherine could see where this was going. She forced herself to be calm and the orderly started to walk away. She grabbed him by the arm.

"You are not going to lose him. Understand?" The orderly looked down at her hand until she released him, then met her gaze with a steely one of his own. He disappeared through the doors to the operating area. She stood there, alone, worried and exhausted. Then she looked around, searching the hallway for Jackson.

After working her way back through the halls, she found the waiting room and stepped through its doors to find it full of people. It took her a moment, but she caught sight of Jackson and Pickett returning her hopeful gaze. She rushed over to them.

"Your boy going to be okay?" Pickett asked.

"I don't know. They cleaned his wound and are running some blood tests. I signed off on some pretty serious painkillers. I stayed with him until he drifted off to sleep," she answered, then looked into Jackson's eyes. "One of the nurses said he could lose his leg." Tears welled in Catherine's eyes and Jackson stepped forward to embrace her. After a few minutes,

Catherine pulled away and gave them both the best smile she could muster.

"Thank you, Mr. Pickett, for staying," she said. "You didn't have to."

"Oh, I know. But it felt like the thing to do."

Catherine sat beside Pickett and Jackson stood nearby, looking down and avoiding curious glances. Pickett studied Jackson a moment, then said, "Here's $60. There's a Walmart down the street. Go buy some clothes, shoes, whatever you need, and clean up in the restroom."

"Thanks," Jackson said, taking the three twenties from Pickett and relieved to get outside for a while.

Jackson took Catherine's hand and led her to the doors leading to the hospital parking lot.

"Listen, Catherine. You're safe now. But I'll be back," he said. Before she could respond, he stepped through the automatic doors as they slid open.

Chapter 24

Catherine called after him, but he was already halfway down the block and turning out of sight. She debated with herself. She couldn't leave Tucker. Her gaze sought the mountains beyond the town, hoping he was sincere.

She returned to sit beside Pickett in one of the molded plastic chairs.

"He'll be back," Pickett said and patted her knee. She gave him a weak smile. They sat silently together for a few minutes. Pickett glanced at Catherine's hands, still covered in bloody strips of cloths. The woman at the admitting desk called out "Esquivel" and Catherine approached her.

"Yes? I'm Catherine Esquivel, Tucker's mom."

"Mrs. Esquivel. I just need to get some information." Catherine took the chair opposite the woman in the lavender blouse and matching glasses. She answered her questions, first the easy ones—her address, Tucker's birth date—but struggled when the woman asked her to provide insurance and other information for the admitting forms. She was glad the woman filled out most of the form. Her hands were still bandaged in the bloody rags and Catherine didn't think she could hold a pen. The woman handed her the clipboard and propped the pen in her right hand.

"Take your time while I make a quick call to your insurance provider," the woman said and turned toward the phone on a desk behind her.

Catherine tried to recall other details besides the name of her health insurance, then scrawled her name on several signature lines and passed the clipboard back to the administrator.

"I did the best I could from memory," she said. "I'm afraid I didn't bring my purse."

The woman chuckled. Then she looked over the form and told her she had all the information she needed. She paused to study Catherine in her tattered, mud-streaked clothes.

"You might feel better if you freshened up a bit. The restrooms are down that hall. Here, let me give you some clean towels." The woman returned a moment later and handed Catherine two hospital-white towels and a washcloth. Catherine thanked the administrator and headed down the hall. After she cleaned up, she brought the woman the towels.

"Do you need someone to look at your hands?" she asked.

"No, thank you," Catherine said. She didn't want to get tied up if the doctor needed to see her about Tucker. "I appreciate your help."

"Really, a resident is right here. I'll call her." A few minutes later, a friendly looking, red-headed young woman ushered Catherine into a curtained examining room. She cleaned and bandaged her hands quickly, then examined her other cuts and bruises from her month-long ordeal. By the end of the half hour, she gave Catherine a fairly extensive once-over. The resident handed Catherine a sample ointment and some extra bandages.

"Is your Tetanus up to date?" she asked as Catherine pulled her jacket back on.

"Yes, two years ago."

"Well, you're all set then. Try to get some rest."

Catherine thanked the doctor and returned to the desk to thank the administrator.

"I feel much better now. Um, could you tell me who will be looking after Tucker?"

The administrator looked on her computer screen and nodded.

"Looks like they are recommending surgery, but Dr. Flores really needs to be the one to talk to you."

"Is he in?"

"Not for a bit."

"Thank you," Catherine said and started to turn away.

"How 'bout some coffee then?" the woman asked. "We got a machine right down the hall."

"I'm guessing that takes money?" The woman handed over a few bills from her top drawer.

"On the house," she said, smiling. Catherine returned the smile and headed down the hall. She glanced at Pickett, still sleeping in the chairs, and figured she could afford to get him one too.

The sun was out and nearly directly overhead as Jackson loped through the streets, drawing attention from drivers and pedestrians heading to lunch and errands. The busy street, with all the noises and colors, confused him. He turned around at several corners, trying to get his bearings. He streaked across the main drag and ran straight into the path of a small car. It swerved, narrowly missing him. Jackson stood frozen in the road as the driver in the next car slammed on her brakes, coming to a screeching halt just feet from him. He stood unsure of where to turn.

Another car honked and Jackson was jolted from his trance. He looked around and then at himself. Everyone seemed to be looking at him. Some were starting to pull out their cell phones.

Jackson spotted a bright sign in a parking lot and walked quickly toward it. Keeping his head low, he made it through the crowded lot and the sliding doors, where a greeter awaited him.

"Welcome to Walmart," the man said. Jackson nodded and moved through, looking for the section he needed. He overshot it and found himself in Electronics. A bank of the biggest television sets he'd ever seen showed images of the world he purposefully left. He was drawn toward one screen that was giving an account of Navy SEALs killed recently in Afghanistan. *Afghanistan.* Still.

As he passed with his eyes on the screen, he bumped into the corner of a case containing wireless electronics of some kind. He looked down and couldn't even comprehend what they were for. Then he returned his gaze to the screen, his mouth open in disbelief. He gripped the three twenty-dollar bills from Pickett tightly in his fist.

Jackson blinked several times and moved along the bank of TVs. Demonstrators lined up and faced off against police, protests, mobs, tear gas, rubber bullets, talking heads yelling at one another. "A pandemic?" He was dumbfounded. "Who would want to live in this world?" He thought about Akasha and Blue, who he missed already. His constant companions. They stayed by him, even when he developed a fever, and they didn't leave his side for three solid days. Akasha on his right side and Blue on his left, pinning him into the bed and keeping him safe and warm.

His thoughts turned to Catherine and Tucker, then to Diane… and the night he accidentally shot the deputy who was attacking her. Dark thoughts clouded Jackson's head as he remembered being a prisoner. He quickly moved away from the TVs.

In the clothing department, he found a sweatshirt and checked the price. He pulled the items he needed off the racks and shelves, holding them up to avoid stares. As he came around a corner, a familiar face caught his eye.

Jackson watched the woman with a kid in the cart and three more lagging behind. The oldest looked to be about Tucker's age. His calves and wrists were covered with tattoos.

She looked beleaguered. Hair in a messy knot on top of her head, with gray streaks shooting through what was once beautiful blonde, she looked like someone who needed a make-over, like the shows he remembered from years ago. Her skinny jeans didn't hide the bulges of fat pressing against the rail of the cart as she wandered along, picking longingly at dresses in the petite section.

Jackson stepped back and watched her through a row of work shirts hanging on his side of the aisle. Beads of sweat stood out on his forehead. He had the sensation of a near-miss when he was in the forest and he spotted a giant bear before it saw him. The child sitting in the cart's seat kept kicking her.

"If you don't stop that right now, I'm gonna…" the woman started to yell. A few teenagers shopping in the next aisle looked over.

The little kid, whose cheeks were covered with some kind of red goo, stuck his tongue out at her and kicked her again. Jackson had seen enough and started backing toward the pharmacy to pick up a few items. When he was sure he was in the clear, he veered over to the check-out area, ignoring the stares, and then took his purchases into the restroom.

That was Valerie. Valerie!

"Wow. I can't believe it. That's who I wanted…

"Dodged that bullet," he thought to himself. "Valerie… thank you, Lord."

As he entered the men's room, an older man came out and did a double take. Then he looked Jackson up and down, tsked, and walked away. Jackson felt confused by the man's reaction, until he looked in the mirror.

Flushing the urinal a few moments later, he couldn't get over the strangeness of using an indoor restroom again. As he began changing out of the muddy clothes, a father and his seven-year old son came in. The boy took one look at Jackson and started to back out, but his dad held his hand and tried to push him into the crowded restroom.

"Bigfoot!" the boy screamed and ran out, followed by the dad.

Jackson got into his new duds quickly, then stood at the counter and marveled at the water flow into the tiny little sink. He looked again in the mirror and a shock went through him. A stranger looked back at his face. He touched it and the stranger touched his face too. He pulled on his beard. Then he fingered the gold ring hanging from the rawhide cord. The ring meant something different now, for some reason. He quickly trimmed his beard and hair and stuffed it into the trash bin.

Washing his hands methodically for several minutes, Jackson never took his eyes off his face in the mirror. Every emotion crossed his face as he became reacquainted with the man he once knew. After suffering much guilt and regret, he felt renewed. And he escaped a life with Valerie.

As he finished, a teenager in a cowboy hat entered and barely glanced at him as he headed toward the wall mounts, then turned slowly and looked at him.

"Is it okay if I use this?" the boy asked, carefully watching Jackson.

Jackson nodded, then looked back at his own reflection. Suddenly unsure, the young man backed out through the door and said, "I'll just come back later."

A sense of peace came over Jackson. "Whatever happened next would be okay. Maybe Catherine was right."

But when he came out of the restroom, he noticed several people standing nearby whispering. They pointed at the men's room door and at Jackson in particular. He walked past them without another glance.

"Do you think he'll be gone much longer?" Catherine asked, sipping her coffee. Pickett sat beside her, blowing on his.

"Oh, no. Not much longer. But I bet he's feeling a little overwhelmed, being in the wild so long. Just give him some time," Pickett said.

"Thank you for staying, Mr. Pickett," she said, smiling at him. "That's very kind of you."

"Kind is my middle name. My first is Owen. You can call me that."

Catherine let herself relax. She had seen a pay phone by the coffee machine and left a message with Richard's assistant, but didn't have any more change after the coffees to call Lewis. He would be worried. But she didn't want anything to complicate Tucker's recovery or Jackson's safety. Lewis could wait.

"I left a message for Tucker's dad. Turns out he's on his honeymoon in Thailand. Not a business trip," Catherine paused and shook her head. "I wouldn't expect him to think twice about me, but it's nice to know he'd miss his own son's funeral." She paused and stared into the dark liquid in her cup. "I talk to him now and wonder how I could ever have been..." Catherine spoke as if in a trance.

"Seems to me like your ex-husband should be the last thing on your mind," Pickett interrupted. "You'll have time later for that."

"He is. Just thought he'd like to know his son was in the hospital."

"You'll find people don't always think like they should."

"The weird thing is, when we were up in the mountains, I felt safe. For the first time in ages. Because of Jackson. I'm ashamed to admit it, but, if Tucker doesn't make it, I don't think I can face it without him." Catherine hunched forward, willing Tucker to survive. Pickett patted her back gently.

"I lost a son. In Iraq," he said. Catherine turned to look at him, brought out of her own grief. She searched for words, but none came. She waited.

"I know that doesn't help any. I just figured I'd wait here with Jackson and you, seeing as I know something about losing people, and being alone after."

Catherine sat up and dried her tears with a tissue.

"My wife couldn't stand losing her only son and her health began going downhill. She died nine months after our son. Died of a broken heart."

"Oh, Mr...Owen. I'm so sorry." Catherine took a deep breath. "It does help. Thank you."

"And I get the feeling Jackson cares about Tucker. He wouldn't leave without knowing he's okay."

"Tucker is a different kid since he's been with Jackson. It's hard to describe," she said, but Pickett sensed she was including herself in the comparison too.

"You love Jackson, don't you?"

"I just want him to be happy," she replied quietly. "He deserves to be happy."

"Come what may, you'll get by. I only known you a couple hours, but you're about the strongest woman I've come across. Ya know? You remind me of my son a lot." Pickett squeezed her arm and Catherine smiled, feeling as though it was the greatest compliment she could have ever received. The room was nearly empty yet Pickett's presence there filled the space with hope.

"But Jackson, yes, I don't want to lose him."

"The Lord will guide the way. Trust in Him," Pickett said. They were quiet a long while. Catherine let the stillness settle over her, calm her heart.

"I want Tucker to get well. That's most important."

"Life is full of peaks and valleys," Pickett said. "When I lost my son and wife, the world was dark for me. I found that I could face the world two ways. Either fill in the grief with positivity or crawl into a hole and feel sorry for myself. I chose the positive approach. It's allowed me the chance to help others. You're one of those people who make my life productive. Thank you."

Catherine gave Pickett a warm grin and patted his knee.

Chapter 25

"Sign here, please," a woman handed her a clipboard with a paper attached to it. The lavender woman was nowhere to be seen.

"What is this?" Catherine asked, taking it from the woman and sitting down by the front desk.

"Consent form." Catherine scanned the page and realized that the form indicated that Tucker could lose his leg in the course of surgery and the hospital and all its agents could not be held liable.

"May I speak with the doctor, please?" Catherine asked.

"It'll be awhile," the administrator responded.

"Please. I'd like to speak with the doctor first." The woman nodded and picked up the phone. After she was finished and hung up, she turned to Catherine and said that the doctor would be right out.

"Thank you." Catherine stood up and went over near the door to the ER, looking from the form to the sliding doors to the outside. Within ten minutes, a man came through another set of doors and looked around the room. "Mrs. Esquivel?"

"Hi, I'm Catherine," she said, stepping up to him.

"I'm Dr. Flores. I'll be looking after Tucker. You have a question?"

"Yes," she said. "What is happening with his leg? He just cut it a few days ago. How could he lose it?"

"These staph infections are quite dangerous," the doctor began. "I can't promise to save his leg." Hearing it from the surgeon made it seem even more real. Catherine swallowed a gasp.

"Your son will be in surgery for the next few hours. We'll keep you posted." Dr. Flores held out his hand to take the clipboard from Catherine. She signed the form slowly and with so much effort, feeling as though she was signing her son's leg away, then handed it to him. Without another word, the doctor turned toward the door. When he was opening it, he turned back and asked, "By the way, who gave him the *arnica foliosa*?" Full of despair, it took Catherine a moment to consider the question.

"I did," she said, then, suddenly unsure, "Was that wrong?"

"He wouldn't have made it otherwise," the doctor answered, then disappeared down the hall.

"Why don't you go find him?" Pickett said, noting the indecision on Catherine's face. She dithered for half an hour. She didn't want to crowd Jackson, especially just as he was acclimating to the new surroundings. But she really needed to see him. "I'll be back soon," she said, finally resolved, and she headed out through the sliding doors.

She almost passed him as she walked along the hospital sidewalk.

"Catherine." Jackson's bright smile against his deeply tanned face and trimmed beard caught her by surprise. It took her a full ten seconds to recover as she looked him up and down. He was carrying a full plastic bag from the store, and he'd looked like a regular guy on the street.

"Say it again."

"What?"

"My name."

"Catherine," he said, again, almost in a whisper. She threw her arms around his shoulders. He gripped her tightly to his chest and stroked her hair before he released her.

"You came back." He nodded.

"Your boy." Jackson said it as a question.

"Tucker is going into surgery," she said. Jackson nodded again and took her hand. They began walking back toward the waiting room doors. Catherine stopped short and sat down on a low wall, keeping to the shadows. She didn't want to go in yet. Tucker wouldn't be awake for a while, she thought. We can spare some alone time.

Jackson sat beside her and let her lean against his arm. They sat for an hour or more, not speaking and barely moving. Neither knew the next time they would be able to share a quiet moment. Finally, Catherine rose and held out her hand to Jackson as they walked through the sliders. Pickett waved them over to where he was sitting.

They barely noticed Dr. Flores as he approached a few minutes later.

"Ms. Esquivel?"

"Yes," she said, standing quickly.

"We cleaned and repaired the infected tissue, particularly around a ligament in Tucker's heel. It'll take some time, but he's out of the woods. So to speak."

Catherine bent over with relief. When she stood up again, she asked, "What about his leg?"

"We were able to save his leg."

"So it's all over?" Pickett asked.

"For you, maybe," Dr. Flores said, stepping away. "I got a tumor to skewer. Your son will be awake in an hour or so. Someone will come find you then."

Catherine plopped down in her chair, letting the feeling of relief wash over her. Jackson put his arm tenderly around her and closed his eyes.

Pickett rounded up some food from the vending machines and the three feasted. Catherine laughed as Pickett shared stories of hunting misadventures with his son. It turned out that Mr. Owen Pickett was a marvelous storyteller. They'd already known that he was kind and generous, but he'd seemed to be a man of few words. But when he got talking about his son, he became animated and jolly.

Jackson relaxed enough to close his eyes for a while after they ate. He slumped against the wall and fell into a deep sleep.

"You mentioned something about knowing the forests better than most hunters," Catherine whispered to Pickett. "What did you mean?"

"Well, that's 'cause I worked in the lumber industry for nearly my whole working life. I got to know them fields of trees out there quite well," replied Pickett.

"Really? What did you do?"

"Why, I was a prospector a ways back. Determined which forests were ripe for harvesting," he said.

"You're kidding." When Catherine said nothing else and simply stared at the man, Pickett grew uncomfortable. "Oh boy, I've stepped in it this time," he thought to himself.

"No, I'm not kidding," he finally said.

"But that's what I do. Kind of," Catherine exclaimed.

It was Pickett's turn to be surprised. Before he could say anything, Catherine added, "I survey for harvesting for Roseburg. Ever heard of it?"

"Heard of it?! Roseburg split off from the company I worked for 30 years ago. I remember when those guys got started. How about that!?"

Catherine smiled and regarded Pickett as a colleague, as well as a new friend.

"Course, in my day, we didn't fly around so much. I'd be given a grid map and a walking stick and told to get moving," Pickett grinned. "It was lonely work. Before I got into prospecting, I'd been a tracker. My experience in the wilderness tracking animals made me a good hire for the lumber company." He didn't mention that he'd begun tracking people for the county Sheriff. They'd pulled him out of retirement. It wasn't public knowledge.

Catherine sensed he had more to say, so she waited.

Pickett looked down at his hands. "That regular paycheck from the lumber company settled me down. My wife and I just married and our son was on the way. I didn't realize I'd be off on my own so much, like when I was tracking. But it was good to come home to them. The loneliness during work made it that much sweeter when I was with them. We were a team, the three of us. Fixed up the house together, did yard work together, went to church and ball games together. We were each other's whole world. That boy meant everything to my wife. Me too." Pickett was quiet then.

"I know that feeling," Catherine whispered, almost too softly to be heard. Both were silent for a while.

"I'm going to go clean up a little," Catherine said. "Will you keep watch again?"

"Go on ahead," Pickett responded.

When she returned ten minutes later, Pickett and Jackson were standing by their chairs.

"The nurse was just here," Pickett said. "Tucker has left post-op and has been moved to Room 2023." Catherine led Jackson toward the doors to the patient rooms, then looked back. Pickett stood by the sliders, grinning. He gave her two thumbs up.

"Well, aren't you coming?" she asked playfully. He grinned bigger and followed the pair through the doors and up a flight of stairs. A nurse greeted them at the reception area, shared how often Tucker would be checked on and what the doctor prescribed, and took them to Tucker's room. His leg in a cast, Tucker looked so small among all the blankets and wires. The three stood looking at him, trying to stay quiet, while he slept. Catherine wiped away a tear and Jackson patted her shoulder.

Drowsily, Tucker opened his eyes. He grinned at his mom and Pickett.

"Mom? I dreamt I was falling. Into a black hole..." his words were slurred and his eyes started to slide closed.

"You woke up, baby. That's all that matters." Tucker squinted to focus on her face. "A giant bird flew by and caught me." His eyes slid almost imperceptibly to look at Jackson standing by his mom. It took him a moment to register that Jackson was still with them. He looked so different. He was in his hospital room! He smiled a big smile and Jackson grinned back at him.

"Are you feeling okay? Does anything hurt?" Catherine asked anxiously.

"Mmm mmmm," he said, closing his eyes. "I'm okay, Mom. Don't worry." He fell asleep a moment later, unable to fight the sedative. Catherine leaned over and gave him a kiss on his forehead. He looked okay. Peaceful. Jackson lingered by Tucker's bedside as Pickett and Catherine turned toward the door. He pressed something into Tucker's hand.

"Looks like your boy is being well cared for," Pickett said as they returned to the second-floor reception desk. "It's time you took care of yourself. You are both welcome at my place," Pickett said and nodded at Jackson. "You can clean up and rest up while the boy recuperates." The two looked at each other then out the window. The sun was already beginning to set.

"Hey, it's after dinnertime," Pickett added. "Already gave the nurse my contact info so there's no reason to turn me down. I got a big house with no one in it but me, and you're both hurting for a good night's sleep." The two shrugged and nodded at Pickett.

"I need to call Diane," Jackson said. A shadow of worry crossed Catherine's face. Even after fifteen years, she wondered whether the sheriff would still be watching for him to make contact. Pickett figured Diane must be a relative. He hoped she wasn't Jackson's wife.

"Why don't you take care of that in the morning, son?" Pickett offered. When Jackson nodded, the three headed to the parking lot. As they walked toward Pickett's old Chevy, they passed a police officer leaning against his squad car and sipping coffee. The cop nodded politely and Jackson nodded back.

Moonlight through the thick pines around Pickett's wood frame house gave the home a slightly mysterious look. Most of it was plunged in darkness by the time they arrived, but the front door and one window were illuminated by the moon's brilliance, making the pair feel welcome. Pickett led Catherine and Jackson up to the porch and through the simple wooden door.

"It ain't much," Pickett said as he flipped on the light switch and closed the door behind them. Jackson and Catherine took in the living room and dining area. Newspapers were strewn on a small table by a recliner facing a TV. A gun cleaning kit was spread out on a few other newspapers on the coffee table.

"Two bedrooms," Pickett said, taking off his hat and rubbing the top of his head. "You've had a lot of nights together. No need to change that."

Catherine and Jackson followed the old man down a wood-paneled hallway. He pointed out the kitchen near the front door and the bathroom, inviting them to take whatever they wanted from the refrigerator and the linen closet. He arrived at the closed door of one of the bedrooms near the end of the hall. Pickett paused and took a deep breath before he reached out and turned the handle.

He opened the door to the bedroom and led Catherine in. Jackson stood at the door, hesitant. Pickett took a moment to look around. It was still decorated like a teen boy's bedroom, with ball gloves, trophies, medals, and posters of sports heroes adorning the shelves and walls. It reminded Jackson of his room back home at Diane's. Collecting dust, but still tidy.

A framed picture of Pickett's son in his military uniform rested on the desk. Catherine and Jackson exchanged a brief glance at one another, aware that this was a solemn and significant moment for the older gentleman who endured so much.

"I kept most everything how it was," Pickett said. "For no reason, other'n I don't much like coming in here. You feel free to make yourselves at home any way you can." He smiled meekly, edged past Jackson, and went back down the hallway.

They stood in silence looking into the room. One bed. It looked like it was queen-sized, but still. Catherine decided to break the tension.

"You've lived fifteen years without modern conveniences, so I take it you can go another fifteen minutes?" she asked with a laugh, pulling an old shirt off a hanger in the closet. Jackson looked at her quizzically. This was the smallest room he'd been in yet. He didn't know if he could stand it. Catherine sensed his discomfort.

"I'm not taking any chances that you'll use up all the hot water. Bathroom's mine!"

She grabbed the toothbrush he'd bought for her and sprinted past him.

Chapter 26

Pickett wandered through the house, checking the front door and shutting off lights. He could hear his new guests muffled voices, but couldn't make out what they were saying. Catherine's voice had the same lilt, like a songbird, that his late wife's had. It lifted his spirits to hear the sound of it in the house. A moment later, he heard the shower running.

As he got ready for bed, Pickett thought about how he hadn't been too social after she'd passed. Folks didn't bother him, but he just preferred to keep his own company. The "Casserole Brigade" made its assault right before the funeral and came in waves for several months, until it was clear he wasn't looking for a replacement for his beloved.

The death of his son followed so quickly by his wife's passing had taken it all out of him. In recent years, though, Pickett began dating again and he'd met some interesting people. None of them quite filled the void, though. He touched a photograph of the two of them on their wedding day that stood on the bedside table. Then he switched off the light and said a wee prayer for the lovebirds in the room down the hall.

Catherine showered, loving the feel of the warm water on her face. The water swirling around her feet turned a murky brown. Her palms stung at first, but she gently cleaned them and they felt much better as she washed her hair. She examined her arms, legs, and stomach. They were all badly bruised, but none of the cuts were too deep. The resident did a good job patching her up. She didn't think she would need to bandage them again tonight.

Standing before the well-lit mirror in a towel, she brushed her teeth for the first time in weeks. She took her time and was meticulous, spitting often. She stared at herself, leaning in to get a closer look. The cut on her head from the crash was closed, but the bruise around it turned yellow. She looked like she was beaten up. Catherine touched her jawline and turned her face from side to side. Despite the tan, she was thin and a little gaunt. A stranger.

Jackson examined every surface in the room. "Frozen in time," he thought. "Just like me." He saw a photo collage of a preteen boy displaying various game, sometimes fish, sometimes rabbit or bigger animals, with a younger Pickett grinning proudly beside him. It reminded Jackson of his own father and his granddad. Jackson felt the profound loss that Pickett must feel.

He finished his circuit around the room in front of a full-length mirror. He checked out the Walmart restroom haircut he'd given himself. Still past his chin, but remarkably even. He pulled a few strands back behind his ears, then admired the work he'd done on his beard. It was trimmed neat, but he would scrape his face clean with the razor he bought. He thought of Catherine then. He wondered what she would think when she saw what he looked like under fifteen years of solitude.

The rawhide around Jackson's neck caught his eye. The ring. Was it time to let it go? Or had its meaning changed after all these years? A moment later, she came through the door, the bundle of dirty clothes and boots under her arm, smiling at him. "Wow," he thought. She's beautiful." Her skin glistened as she looked up at him, and she smelled like heaven.

"Your turn," she said, coming close to him. He grinned at her, then took the bag with him and headed down the hall.

The house had grown quiet. Catherine figured Pickett went right to bed after such a long day. She turned on the bedside lamp, its base in the shape of a football, then shut off the overhead light and climbed under the sheets. A five-star hotel would have paled in comparison. She nimbly braided her still-wet hair into two plaits and wicked the water away with a clean washcloth she found in the linen closet. Then she rested her head on the so-soft pillow and closed her eyes.

She didn't know what time it was, but she knew it was just a little later when she awoke, maybe just a few minutes after she closed her eyes. The light of the moon filtered through the sheer covering the only window. She reached out her hand across the bed. No Jackson. Her heart thumped a single beat hard in her chest and she swallowed. She leaned over slowly and saw him on his back on the floor. He looked up at her, his hands behind his head, and smiled. Even in the dimness of the room, she could see that he had no beard. His face was striking. She wondered where the ring had gone as she scanned his bare neck and chest. His eyes stayed on her face as she drank him in.

"Come to bed," Catherine said, and moved back to her side, folding down the covers. Jackson obliged.

Her touch, the warmth of her skin, the lingering scent of shampoo in her hair all converged on Jackson's senses at once. He felt scattered for a moment, trying to adjust to the feeling of his own body so close to another's. To hers.

He felt different now. As he drifted off to sleep, one thought crept through. "What would it be like to live with people again?"

She felt like she had been asleep for days. She was immobile, couldn't move a muscle. She could sense the morning light filtering through the curtains and her eyelids. It took a few minutes for her to blink them open. Her vision filled with the corner of her pillow and, beyond, Jackson's profile as he slept. She couldn't imagine what sleeping in a bed felt like to him. For her, it had been the best night of her life.

Tucker. "I need to get up and go to him," she thought. She laid there a moment, organizing her thoughts. Their life had been as normal as it could be. They were a team, Tucker and her. He was the light of her life and she was settled. Went to PTO meetings and school outings. Helped with his homework, had movie nights, baked together. They had a routine.

And now, here was Jackson. So strong-willed and self-sufficient. "Like us. But on steroids." Catherine felt like she had to reassess her worldview. From the work she did to the way she raised Tucker. To the woman she'd become. She could feel the hard edges getting rubbed away. Her heart swelled to include him, envelope him. She reached out her hand.

Despite the slight chill outside the covers, Jackson felt warm all over. It wasn't the warmth he felt on the coldest nights when Akasha and Blue crawled up onto the bed and pinned him down on both sides, snuggling as close as they could. No, this was a heat that radiated from his core, and from hers. It was smooth and comfortable. Safe.

His mind couldn't help but conjure images from his youth, pushing himself so hard, all his military training, never satisfied, always craving more. He became a warrior, delivering death, surviving destruction. Then he ran to the most remote corner of the world he could find. More animal than man for years. Now here he was, a fugitive on the edge of society, hiding out in a room with four walls. He heard her take a deep breath and it pulled him out of his reverie. Her fingers brushed his hand under the covers. He took it in his and pressed it against his heart.

"She does this. Finds me. Like at the campfire," he thought. Jackson kept his eyes closed a moment longer and remembered the electricity that shot through him when she hugged him that night. The thought aroused him. He opened his eyes and turned to her. They studied each other's faces to recognize in them what they'd felt the night before. It was still there.

Catherine drew her fingers over his face and along his jawline. They both smiled. He raised his arm and she laid her head on it, her arm across his chest. Her bare skin against his tingled, aroused her desire as she looked into his eyes. He brought his face close to hers, breathing her in and feeling her heat. A feeling he hadn't experienced in years infiltrated his every nerve.

Slowly their lips touched, lighting a fire between them. Hungry for one another, their mouths locked together. His lips worked their way down to her chin, her neck.

He kissed her deeply and allowed himself to relax. Her kisses, more insistent now, showed him all he needed to know. His desire galloped, fully in charge, and he squeezed her tightly. Their animal instincts took over and the world faded away, replaced by a passionate desire to connect after years of hibernation. When they were done, Jackson laid back, exhausted.

Weak from the physical exertion they were deprived of for so long, they rested their heads on their pillows and replayed the experience silently for a few minutes.

"Not many around like you. Thank you," Catherine said, trying to catch her breath.

"No thanks needed," Jackson said, "Twenty years is a long time."

Catherine smiled. They laid side by side, reminded of each other's kisses and bodies against their skin. Catherine turned toward him and nestled against his arm.

"Jackson, I've fallen in love with you," she whispered into his ear, so softly he almost didn't hear. He started to speak, but hesitated. After a moment, he pulled back to look at her and tried again.

"Catherine, thank you. I don't feel like I deserve your love. It's humbling. You make me feel something I never expected to feel." Jackson rolled over onto his back and looked up at the ceiling.

"I've been on a roller coaster for so many years. To have another human love me like this sends my head spinning. You're such a strong woman and mother. You have a future. I don't want to spoil anything for you and Tucker." Jackson turned back to look Catherine in the eyes. She continued to study him and listen.

"Would I be able to adapt? I don't know. I wish I could find comfort in a human world and in a human way. Do you see what I'm saying?" Jackson paused, but Catherine knew he had more to say so she waited.

"I'm wild, living a day-to-day existence. To be with you and Tucker would be great, but do I fit into your future? I might be arrested. I'm struggling with how my past would fit into your lives." Jackson paused again. Catherine knew this had been building in Jackson for days. But she just needed him to know how she felt, no matter the consequences. She sensed he was getting to the consequences. It was the most he'd ever said to her.

"Catherine, you give me so much joy just to look at you. I can feel your love. I think about actually having that joy and love forever," Jackson let his fingers trace a path down her shoulder. "But let's be realistic. We don't know what I'm about to face. And we don't know what living as a normal family would be like. We're attached by surviving together. How will we continue that under different circumstances?"

He took a deep breath and came to it, "I love you too, but I don't want to hurt you or Tucker by messing up your chance for a happy life. My whole life has been difficult. Would we make each other completely happy? I just don't know."

He took another deep breath. Catherine waited, wishing it could be easier.

"We better get up so we can check on Tucker," he said and stood, turning to look at Catherine. He knelt down by the side of the bed, took her hand in his, and held it up to his lips. "You are very special to me," he said, and kissed her fingers gently.

Chapter 27

As Jackson walked into the kitchen, he saw Pickett pouring two mugs of coffee.

"I thought I heard you coming down the hall," Pickett said. He sat down at the kitchen table and handed him the mug. Two fresh apples, an orange, a grapefruit, and three plums sat in an earthenware bowl in center of the table. The whole kitchen gleamed. It looked as though Pickett had gone grocery shopping at the crack of dawn.

Jackson's mug read "World's Greatest Dad." He smiled across the table from Pickett as he sat down.

"You don't look like a cream-and-sugar man, but I can get them for you, if you like."

"No, thanks. This is great." Jackson studied the hot liquid filled almost to the brim. He breathed in the scent that he'd only faintly noticed in the waiting room the night before. This was strong. His first cup of coffee in 15 years. It reminded him of home, looking out at the lush forest after he had returned from Walter Reed.

Pickett watched him, a smile spreading across his face as he gauged Jackson's reaction. When Jackson grinned and nodded after his first sip, Pickett gave a hearty laugh. "This fella is all right," he thought.

"Sleep okay?" Jackson grinned again. "Good. Have everything you need?"

"Yeah, I think so." Jackson considered a moment. "You mind if I make a call?"

"Sure. It's right over there," Pickett said. When Jackson looked at the phone and didn't move, Pickett added, "I'll give you some privacy. Gotta go check something in the garage."

Jackson continued to sip his coffee and look toward the phone. Pickett sat back down.

"You remember the number, don't ya?"

"Yeah."

"Is she going to be mad?" The question took Jackson by surprise. There was no telling how Diane would respond.

"I did something, Mr. Pickett..." Jackson started.

"Owen."

"Okay. Owen." Jackson looked out through the window and cleared his throat, but the words wouldn't come.

"Jack, you've had some tough experiences. Only yourself and nature. I know you have adapted, but how did you handle being alone?" This was safe territory, Pickett thought. The conflict on Jackson's face vanished, replaced by deep introspection.

"Well, Mr. P...Owen," Jackson began, "it was an emotional merry-go-round. I missed the military and the brothers I fought with. We tried not to get too attached to each other because one of us could die tomorrow. At any moment, we were sitting ducks for a sniper or an IED. You protect each other and take a bullet for one another. It hurt...it hurt a lot to see a brother zipped up in a body bag. You never get over it," Jackson paused and looked out at the morning mist evaporating on the surface of the pond across the gravel road. He thought of Pickett's son. Wondered what had happened. "I was captured…" Jackson stopped abruptly. Pickett waited, cradling his coffee mug.

"I was captured," Jackson began again. "Tortured. It was brutal. There was never a question of selling out just so I could stop hurting. Or sleep. Or breathe." Jackson paused again. The chatter of squirrels on the front porch broke the silence. Both men looked in their direction. Jackson then looked Pickett straight in the eyes.

"Total darkness. Beatings. It's not anything you ever want to endure again. I lost track of time…days. What little I was given to eat was sporadic. I lost hope. I never expected to be rescued. To survive."

Pickett remained motionless. He wondered whether Jackson had ever shared this with anyone else. Pickett knew his own loss qualified him in some way as a person Jackson could trust.

"When I was rescued, I was a zombie. I changed. It took months of rehab just to function. My senses came back slowly. Diane helped." Jackson registered the confused look that briefly crossed Pickett's face. "My sister."

"Oh. Well, that's good." Both men looked through the kitchen door toward the hallway. Jackson chuckled and Pickett followed with another hearty laugh.

"The thing is, I longed to be alone. To get back to my old self. My dad and granddad raised me in these woods. I planned to go camping and meditate on things for a few days after I came home. Then, the incident with Diane. I lost all reason. I just knew I couldn't be confined again. Nothing else mattered." Jackson looked at Pickett for reassurance. His gaze was met with confusion again.

"When I said I did something, I meant that…Diane was being attacked. I accidentally killed a man when I pulled him off her. We struggled and his gun went off." Jackson hung his head, afraid of the look of recrimination in the old man's eyes. "He was a sheriff's deputy."

The whistling of a mockingbird in a shrub by the driveway was the only sound for several minutes. Pickett sat back in his chair and set his mug on the table.

"I think I remember that incident," he said, weaving his fingers together in his lap. "Happened not too far, two or three towns over from here, right?" Jackson nodded without looking at him.

"Had a friend who was a cop over there before he retired. Arapaho Glades. He told me a story, kinda like yours," Pickett paused and squinted at Jackson. The younger man looked up at him. He had to be ready for anything.

"See, the thing is," Pickett began, "the reason my buddy would tell this story, is he thought it was funny. Probably heard it a dozen times." Jackson didn't expect this reaction. He frowned and furrowed his brow.

"Doesn't seem funny to me."

"Well, son, the punch line was that the killer disappeared into the woods never to be heard nor seen again, but the thing of it was that there was no murder. The victim didn't die. Turns out it was just a flesh wound…he was a bleeder," Pickett barked a laugh, remembering how his friend told the story. Jackson leaned forward and looked intently at the old man.

"What are you saying?"

"Loss of blood was the worst of his injuries. They sewed

him up and he was out of the hospital in a week. But the funny part, at least to my buddy, the cop, was that the poor bastard who pulled the trigger fled the scene, never to be found again. Rumor was that he fled into the woods." Pickett grinned and shook his head. "Turns out it was true. Everyone thought the poor soul died the first night or two out there. Cops have a sick sense of humor, I guess, but I just thought you might want to look into that. Seems to me you're running from nothing...paying for something that didn't happen."

"No charges were filed?"

"No," Pickett started to smile.

"What? What's funny?" Jackson was taken aback by the look on Pickett's face.

"Well, the joke's on him. The deputy. He tried the same thing on the ex-wife of the high school football coach. Bunch of other women came forward. He'd been doing it for years. DA had an open-and-shut case."

Jackson looked at the pond, now glinting in the bright sunshine. The light flashed on every crest of the ripples. It made him think of the peaks and valleys his mind had been somersaulting through, from isolation to independence, need to want. The TV images played in front of him, flickering like the light. The virus, war, mobs, hostility, uncertainty. Should he avoid adjusting to this new world? Or should he accept love? He felt like he was going insane.

"They mean a lot to you, don't they?" When Jackson didn't respond, Pickett added, "You gave up your fear to save them. You're a part of their lives now."

"She deserves better."

"She doesn't *want* better, son. She wants you. And believe

me, that woman sure as heck wouldn't waste her time on a man who wasn't worthy."

Jackson leaned back in his chair.

"Days became weeks, Owen. Weeks became months. Months, years. I don't even know what I was, animal or man." Jackson took a deep breath and held it. The first truly deep breath he'd taken in 15 years. Longer. He let it out slowly, savoring the freedom.

"Helping them changed me. Made me more human. I feared them at first, then I started enjoying the boy...Tucker. She calls him T," he smiled and looked at the old man. "I was confused, but then I thought, 'I can't let this boy become me.'" He glanced back toward the hallway.

"I rejected Catherine. I couldn't figure her out. I was her only hope and yet she challenged me constantly. She's a fighter, but they were babes in the woods. She was suspicious of me... she should have been. She acted like I might hurt them."

Jackson smiled for a moment, then said very quietly, "I wanted them out of my life. Now I don't know what I think. I almost feel human again." Jackson looked at Pickett, who recognized a look of pleading on the younger man's face. "I'm really messed up about them, Owen," Jackson continued. "My life is not like they want theirs, if that makes any sense."

Pickett pressed his weathered hands against his knees and rose to pour another cup. He gripped Jackson's shoulder and looked into the mountain man's clean-shaven face. "Sounds like you've got some soul searching to do," he said, then turned toward the counter. "You may not agree, but it seems like somebody up there thinks you earned a second chance. It'd be a shame to see it go to waste."

Chapter 28

Lewis couldn't believe it. He laid on his dining room rug so he wouldn't fall off his chair.

Catherine's voice came through strong and clear. It was a miracle.

"What...*happened*?" was all he could utter.

"Oh, Lewis. So much. I can't explain everything now, but I hope Roseburg had insurance on that Piper." When Lewis didn't respond, Catherine forged ahead. "We crashed deep in the forest, but we got out. Tucker's in the hospital, though, and I need to go check on him."

"Where are you?" Lewis recovered a bit and sat up.

"Charleston, or near it, I think," she said. "It was dark."

"Are you okay?"

"Oh, I'm fine. A little the worse for wear, given that I just trekked through valleys and over mountains to get here, after getting pretty banged up in the crash. Tucker is the one I'm worried about. But the surgery went well."

"Surgery?!"

"We're okay, Lewis. But I lost my cell phone, so you can't

reach me. I promise I'll call you later."

"You promise? You're kidding, right?"

"No, really," Catherine rummaged through a drawer and found an old pair of sweatpants. She pulled them on and cinched them as tightly as she could. They still hung down on her hips.

"Catherine, I'm going to need to call Missy and Frank and give them the story here. What am I going to say?"

"Don't say anything yet, Lewis, okay? I need to sort things out here, but I will call you. Just sit tight." Catherine hung up the phone, cringing. She knew she had a lot to answer for, but she must keep her priorities straight. She pulled a sweatshirt over her head and walked through the quiet house toward the kitchen, where she heard the low murmur of the men's voices.

"Good morning," Catherine said brightly.

"Well, good morning," Pickett said, starting to rise. Jackson nodded and smiled.

"Good morning," she said, looking at him. Pickett noted that she said it a little softer, like a secret.

Jackson looked at her through his eyelashes and said, "'Morning." Both Catherine and Pickett noticed the dimples as he grinned at her.

"Mmm, coffee," she said and went to the counter. While she poured, she kept her back to the men at the table. She couldn't help her wide smile. "Keep cool, Catherine." She smoothed out her face and tried to act natural.

But as she turned around, her eyes met Jackson's for the briefest moment. Pickett looked between them as she sat down and concentrated on sipping her coffee. The glow was unmistakable. It radiated from them both and he smiled to himself. "The garage. That's right. Gotta get something from the garage." Without a word, he got up and headed out. It was still silent in the kitchen as he closed the front door.

"Yesterday I was going hunting," Pickett thought to himself. "Today is…different. Better." He opened the side door to the garage and leaned against the tool bench, feeling a little amazed. For the first time in a long time, he felt connected. These two new people crash landed into his life. After years of loneliness, he felt a sense of belonging. Like he was starting this journey with them. Like he could contribute somehow.

"Sleep okay?" Jackson asked. He rested his hand near her coffee mug—"16th Annual Bass Fishing Tournament"—and she placed her hand in his.

"When I slept, yes," she laughed. She marveled at his strong jawline and peekaboo dimples. He was already getting a five o' clock shadow. He held her fingers to his lips and kissed them softly, just for a moment. She smiled, enjoying the moment, then she broke their gaze and looked out the window. He got up and poured himself another cup.

"I was dead. For weeks," she said quietly. She looked like she was dreaming. Catherine turned to him. "Everyone thought I was dead. And the world just goes on. It really made me think."

"It is hard to get used to."

"When the plane went down, I thought for sure we were going to die. But it was different when we met you. You're… comfortable," she took his hand again. "You're connected to something so, so natural. When I'm with you, when we were out there, I was a part of it. I don't want that to go away when you leave."

"You have your faith. I have nature."

"That's how I know your finding us wasn't luck. You were brought to that place, at that time, for a reason."

"Fifteen years ago, I shot a man because eventually it'd save you?"

"Maybe coming back is part of it too. Maybe you're meant to stay here."

Jackson looked at her for a long time. She could tell there was something he wanted to share with her. She told herself to be patient for a change.

"My sister. I have to call her," Jackson said, glancing at the clock on the wall. "I'm looking at clocks now." He shuddered. Catherine grew concerned.

"It's going to be okay. She'll understand," she gave him a quick kiss on the cheek and started to walk toward the front door. "I'll still be here. Come find me after."

Pickett was just coming out of the garage as Catherine approached.

"Great coffee! Thank you. Hey, any chance I could impose upon you some more?" Catherine looked at Pickett hopefully.

"Why, sure. What do you need?"

"A ride back to the hospital," she snaked her arm through his and they began walking down the driveway toward the pond across the road.

"Well, that's built into the plan, m'dear," he said and laughed.

"You sure? You really don't mind? I don't want to spoil your plans."

"Plans? What plans?" he chuckled again and patted her hand on his forearm. They stopped and looked across the meadow at the shimmering pond.

"He's calling his sister."

"They have a lot to talk about," Pickett said and turned to her. She turned and smiled at him. Was there something he wanted to tell her too? When he didn't say anything, she said, "I'm in awe of him, you know."

"Yes, I can see that," he replied. "Catherine, what would you like to see him do?"

She looked out across the water and said, "Stay with me." Then she looked back at Pickett. "But I don't think that's going to happen. He's afraid of being part of society again. I know he likes me and he knows I like him. I can't be the one who ties him to a world so broken and wind up making him unhappy. I'll have to let him go, if that's his choice." Catherine dropped her arm from Pickett's and turned away. He sensed her grief.

"Owen, I've never felt so helpless..." she said softly. Her words were clear yet not without emotion. Pickett gave her hand a quick squeeze. They stood without speaking for a long time. When she brightened, they returned to the house. Pickett sat on the porch while Catherine went in and down the hall to the bedroom.

Jackson sat on the bed, the old phone cradled in his hands.

"You okay?" she asked.

"Yeah, she's coming. We'll meet her at the hospital. It's getting toward 9. We had better get going."

Catherine sat down beside Jackson and took his hand.

"Any chance you'd stay with us?"

Jackson opened his mouth, but then closed it again. After a long moment, he replied, "I've never known anyone like you. But I'm not sure that I can. This world..."

Pickett had to wind his way through the news vans just to get to the parking lot.

"Someone tipped them off," Jackson said. At least he wouldn't be part of the story, he reassured himself.

"I'll drop you by the emergency room doors, like yesterday," Pickett said, executing a perfect U-turn. "I've got to run an errand, but I'll meet you on the second floor in a little while."

"Thanks, Owen," Catherine said, and gave the old man's arm a squeeze. She fluffed out her hair around her face so she wouldn't be easily recognized. Jackson held out his hand as she stepped out of the cab. He looked normal in Pickett's old hunting jacket and the Walmart clothes from yesterday. Catherine felt a little self-conscious in the baggy sweats, but she couldn't think about that now. She was clean and alive and that's the best she could expect at this moment.

As Catherine and Jackson rounded the second-floor desk, they spotted Tucker in a wheelchair, talking to two young nurses in front of his room. Jackson stretched out his arm to hang back a moment and together they watched Tucker, smiling and laughing, his cheeks flushed and healthy. Catherine's heart filled with love for the boy who had made it through.

"It was wicked," Tucker was saying as they approached. "I was hanging off a cliff, like, 500 feet in the air!" The girls—they looked like student interns around Tucker's own age—wowed and giggled. Tucker caught sight of his mom and Jackson. "And this guy...this guy, well, he saved..."

"Hi, I'm Tucker's mom," Catherine cut him off. She didn't want Jackson to be exposed. "How are you doing today, honey?" She bent and gave him a kiss while Jackson took the handles of the wheelchair and wheeled him back into his room.

"See ya!" Tucker waved and the girls said they would check on him later. He turned to his mom. "How do you like my new wheels?"

"Pretty fancy, though I was hoping for a couple more years before I started worrying that you'll run me over." They both laughed, then Tucker got serious.

"The therapist guy was just here. Said I can't walk on it for a few weeks."

"I'll go find the doctor," Jackson said. "If Diane comes, I'll be right back."

"It's good that you have to take it easy, T. It's a good hospital and I'm sure you can come home soon." Catherine dropped her voice a little. The door to the room was still open. "But be careful, honey. There are news vans out front and I have a feeling they are here to interview us. Please don't tell anyone anything about Jackson. Okay?"

"Yeah, of course. You're right. I wasn't thinking."

"That's okay, honey. Has anyone talked to you yet?"

"No, Doc Flores just asked me questions about how it happened, but I didn't say anything about Jackson. I told him you'd put on the herbs. But he was curious about the moose-hock shoe. That was a tough one to get out of."

"You're doing great, T, and don't worry," Catherine hugged her son and then sat in the room's only chair. A few minutes later, Dr. Flores walked in, looking a little nervous.

"You have questions?" he asked and Catherine launched into a series of concerns. By the end of their conversation, Catherine knew that Tucker would be in the hospital for nearly a week, then released to her care and the care of an orthopedist, physical therapist, and, possibly, an occupational therapist in Denver. Tucker might expect to walk without cast or crutches in about six weeks.

"Just when school lets out," Tucker said with a grin, thinking of summer and missing school.

"Oh, you'll be ambulatory in just a few weeks, Mr. Esquivel," Dr. Flores said. "You won't miss much. And you'll have a heck of a story to tell your friends."

"Thank you, doctor," Catherine said as Dr. Flores headed for the door. He turned and added, "And, uh, your friend told me to tell you he's found his sister. He'll be along shortly."

He caught sight of her at the nurses' station, leaning against the counter and asking a question. He stopped and waited for her to look up as the receptionist pointed toward Tucker's room. Besides a little gray at her temples, she looked exactly the same as she did by the edge of the forest 15 years ago. Same olive skin, deeply tanned, same long, straight black hair, same sparkling dark eyes. It was immediately clear that they were siblings to the nurses who stood nearby. She broke into a grin as soon as she saw him and ran into his bear-hug embrace like she had at the airport all those years ago.

It took them a full minute to speak. Diane looked Jackson up and down and he studied her face for any sign of anger, disappointment, or sadness. He couldn't find a trace.

"You look...normal," she said, stepping back from him.

"You look fantastic," he said, and Diane blushed a little.

"Oh, c'mon, little brother. No, seriously, you look like you've just come back from a day of hunting. Like no time has passed."

"Like I told you," Jackson said, and pulled Diane into a seating area near the desk and sat down, "this old gent helped us in the woods and drove us here. He gave us a place to stay, and I got to clean up a bit."

"Wow, well, fifteen years in the mountains has been good to you, brother," Diane admired him again, then frowned. "Denny was out in no time. If I'd had any way to be in touch with you…"

"I'm sorry. And I'm okay saying it every day for the rest of my life. I wish I had known, Diane. I could have saved us both a lot of grief." Jackson rested his hand on her upper arm. "Listen, I have to find the doctor. I'll be right over there."

Diane turned to watch him. She didn't want to take her eyes off her little brother again. After he spoke to the receptionist, Dr. Flores approached him at the desk. Diane watched as the doctor seemed a little put-off by Jackson, but then Jackson leaned in close and said a word or two into the doctor's ear. The doctor immediately straightened up and made a beeline for a patient's room. Diane assumed it was the boy's.

"What did you say to him?" Diane asked as Jackson resumed his seat.

"Ah, I just told him they'd been through a lot and, if he didn't show some respect and a little hustle, I'd talk to the reporters he'd called."

"Huh. It was already on the radio this morning. Sounds like Catherine and Tucker Esquivel went through an ordeal."

"They did. You want to meet them?" Jackson started to stand, but Diane pulled him back down. "In a minute. Let them have time with the doctor. Now, you don't have to give me the day-by-day or even the year-by-year, but give me some of the details. How did you make it all those years?"

"I'll tell you if you tell me what happened after that night."

Chapter 29

Diane followed Jackson into Tucker's room nearly an hour later. Catherine rose and smiled, extending her hand to Diane, who returned the smile and handshake warmly. Jackson introduced everyone, then went over to Tucker's bedside.

"I'm so sorry that you crashed, but I have to feel a little lucky that you landed near my brother," Diane said smiling and nudging Jackson. Catherine marveled at the same beautiful dark eyes and dimples that Jackson had. Diane had an easy-going way about her that was a little less intense than her brother's.

"You feel lucky? Imagine how we feel. We would be just another sad news story if it hadn't been for your brother," Catherine said.

"Yeah, there are no roads where we were, where Jackson and the wolves live," added Tucker.

"Wolves?" Diane's eyebrows shot up.

"Another time," Jackson grinned.

"Well, you brought my brother back and I am so grateful to you," Diane said. "Tucker, how are you feeling?"

"I'm a little banged up, but I'll be okay. I already miss the forest. Jackson was teaching me how to track and hunt. I was getting a hang of the survival thing," Tucker said and looked at his mom. Catherine caught the look.

"Jackson excels at the survival thing. He always has. I'm glad you're doing okay," Diane responded.

"Diane, would you like to join me for a cup of coffee downstairs? I'd like to learn more about how you two grew up." Catherine led Diane out the door and down the hall. "I think Tucker wants a little time with Jackson," Catherine said as they approached the stairs.

"He's an amazing kid, Catherine," Diane replied. "He reminds me of Jackson at that age. Fascinated by nature, very observant, witty."

Jackson watched them chatting like old friends as they walked down the hall and into the stairwell. He felt uneasy, conflicted about his future. The world was so screwed up and he had a sweet life in the woods. He felt a moment of sadness thinking about Akasha and Blue, wondering where he was and when he would return. They were his family. He felt a kinship to them that no one could understand.

But here were his sister and this new family, Tucker and Catherine. And, strangely, Owen Pickett, like a father figure. Each person was a little damaged somehow, but, together they made him feel whole. New.

"Hey, do you want this green stuff?" Tucker called to him, breaking into his thoughts.

"I'm sorry, Tucker. What stuff?" Jackson turned and took a seat across from Tucker's wheelchair and lunch tray on a stand.

"This," Tucker said, pointing. "They gave it to me last night too. Yuck. I mean, it's not for me, but you can have it."

"I'm okay, buddy. I grabbed something at Mr. Pickett's house." Jackson watched the boy as he ate, glad that he was feeling better. The bruises and cuts had gone down significantly. He still had a little welt above his left eye. He was a handsome boy. Jackson listened for wheezing or any struggle for air and couldn't sense any.

"I thought you'd be gone." Tucker didn't look at Jackson as he spoke.

"I wouldn't leave without saying goodbye. You're my bud, Tucker." When Tucker didn't respond, Jackson added, "You had a tough time getting through that infection."

"I didn't want you to think I wasn't tough," Tucker paused and put down his spoon. "I didn't want to be more of a burden to you."

"Tucker, you were never a burden to me," Jackson felt such a strong connection to the boy, possibly the strongest he had ever felt with anyone. He fought back that welling-up feeling and put his hand on Tucker's shoulder. "You're one of the toughest young men I've met. And I've met a lot. I was very proud of the way you handled such a rough trip."

Tucker ate quietly for a few minutes. He reached under the covers of his bed and pulled out the bird—a crow maybe?— that Jackson had pressed into his hand while he slept. Tucker turned it over in his hands and then looked at Jackson.

"Our deer hunt, felling that tree, and living off the land… you showing me how…it made me want to grow up to be just like you. You made me feel like I was worthy of being with you. You treated me like a man," Tucker bowed his head and muttered, almost to himself, "No one has ever made me feel so strong, like a normal person."

Jackson tried to keep his face calm and still. But his heart hammered in his chest.

"Will you take me hunting again?" Tucker's words hung in the air. The boy had no idea the firestorm such an innocent question created in Jackson's psyche.

"Sometime?" Tucker repeated.

"Let's see," Jackson said, not meeting the boy's eyes. He wasn't going to make a promise he couldn't keep. Despite being a free man, he was not part of society. He didn't know if he could be or wanted to be.

"I wish my dad was like you. You've taught me so much in a week!"

Pickett stopped in the doorway and caught sight of the two locked in serious conversation. "Am I interrupting something?"

Tucker and Jackson shook their heads as Jackson rose to offer their new friend a seat. Pickett studied Jackson's face as he sat down. Something was definitely wrong.

"We were just talking about the trip and what we went through," Jackson said, taking a deep breath and backing toward the door. "Listen, I'm going to see if they have an extra chair. I'll be back in a moment."

"Take your time," Pickett called and turned to Tucker. "I want to get to know this remarkable young man a little better anyway." He patted Tucker on the hand.

Catherine and Diane sat at a table off a hallway on the first floor. A TV on a wall nearby was turned down low, but they could still hear the newscast.

"And it's a happy ending for the Roseburg forest surveyor whose plane went down more than three weeks ago. Catherine Esquivel and her teenage son were returned safely last night thanks to a local hunter who found them in the woods. Now the search is on for the aircraft…" The image switched from the reporter in front of the hospital to the scene of a vast, unending forest.

Catherine turned back to Diane.

"He risked his freedom for us," she said, turning the cup on the table.

"He hasn't told you?"

"Told me what?"

Diane considered, then smiled. "I think you like my brother."

"Yes, but I don't think he wants to stay."

"I can't imagine what you went through, but you made an impression on him that I don't think he's going to shake. At least not for a while." Diane liked Catherine instantly. She was nothing like many of her contemporaries in Arapaho Glades. She was smart, resourceful, economical in her choice of words, yet warm and self-effacing. And she seemed to have Jackson's number.

"What I went through?!" Catherine laughed. "It was a rough month. You've been dealing with his disappearance for fifteen years!"

Diane shared many of the details she gave Jackson earlier in the morning. How she called her boss as soon as she went home that evening. Reg Stewart counseled her and stayed by her side as she gave her statement to the police. Reg made sure she wasn't implicated. Diane decided it was Jackson's place to tell Catherine the rest, that Denny lived and that Jackson was never charged. It was curious that he hadn't already.

"He died just a few years later. Reg Stewart was my rock. The whole office pulled me through."

Far down the corridor, a man with a microphone and a cameraman in tow was rushing toward them.

"Excuse me, Mrs. Esquivel, may I just have a word?" he called.

The two women grabbed their cups and ducked into the stairwell before they could catch up with them.

When they reached Tucker's room a few minutes later, they found the three men laughing.

"You laugh, but I'm half moose now after wearing that sock," Tucker laughed as he spoke. "The doc didn't buy it, but it was worth a shot."

Pickett wiped tears of laughter from his eyes and smiled at the women as they walked into the room a little out of breath. No one had followed them to the second floor.

"Thanks, wild man, for taking care of me," Tucker said. Jackson smiled and patted Tucker's knee. But Catherine could tell he felt uncomfortable. Maybe claustrophobic.

"Mrs. Esquivel, may I please speak with you?" a hospital administrator, a woman she had never seen before, appeared by her side. Catherine nodded and the woman led her out into the hallway while Diane stayed to chat with the fellows.

"Mrs. Esquivel, I'm sorry to bother you, but the news people simply won't go away until they speak with you. Will you please address them? We've given them all the information we legally can, without giving away anything about Tucker's condition, and we just need to be fully functioning again."

"Of course, I understand," Catherine replied. "I'll need to check in with my boss first, though. Do you have a phone I can use?"

The administrator, Ms. Wheeler, led Catherine down the back stairwell and into her office. After she instructed her on how to make a long-distance call and was shutting the door behind her, Catherine asked, "Do you know how the press found out?"

"We are definitely looking into that now," Ms. Wheeler said. Catherine didn't want to be around when the poor soul was discovered.

The phone rang once and Lewis picked up.

"Oh, thank God. Catherine, you have got to tell me what's going on," Lewis sounded frantic.

"We're at the Charleston hospital and the news vans are here."

"Right, so Frank drafted a press release saying how relieved Roseburg is that you've been rescued."

"Is it okay for me to speak to the press?"

"Yes, it's fine. Just don't comment on the condition of the plane, the weather, or anything. Focus on how there's an element of danger anytime you work with nature, as we do. Just say how grateful you are that Roseburg has been so supportive. And that you're okay," Lewis was calmer and starting to sound like his old self. "Is Tucker okay?"

"Yes, we're both fine. But I have to stay here a few more days. He may not get out of the hospital for almost a week."

Lewis was quiet.

"Lewis? Are you still there?"

When he spoke, his voice sounded more measured, almost somber. "Missy is very impressed by your resilience. She told me to commend you. I told her you need more than a commendation. You need a medal for surviving a month in the wilderness after a plane crash. And maybe some compensation too."

"Oh, Lewis, but…"

"Let me finish. She agreed. We want you to head up the project out there. With your new knowledge of the terrain, you are the best person for the job."

"You want me to be the project lead?" Catherine was incredulous. This was like two steps above her paygrade.

"I've always known you can handle yourself, but now the whole world knows and, more importantly, the muckety-mucks in the C suite know. Take as much time as you need to heal and care for Tucker."

"Thank you, Lewis. You're a true gem," Catherine said, choking up.

"And don't ever forget it," he replied. "And while you're convalescing, you should check out the real estate so you're ahead of the game when you move."

Catherine smiled as she said goodbye and hung up. She wondered if caves got wifi.

Chapter 30

Ms. Wheeler turned out to be a true gem too. A little before four o'clock that afternoon, she found Catherine a comfortable, but stylish pair of jeans, sweater, and boots that fit her. Then she arranged for a very brief press conference in the media room of the hospital. She chose the questions and cut it off after ten minutes. Then she ordered the news vans off her hospital's property.

Jackson met Catherine just outside the door of the media room. He looked like a caged animal.

"What's wrong? You looked so happy a little while ago," she asked.

"It's nothing. I'm fine. Just need a little fresh air."

"Me too. Would you mind some company?"

Jackson smiled and took Catherine's hand. They stood just inside the front sliders until the last van had pulled away. Jackson strode out into the brisk late-afternoon air. He didn't give two police cruisers parked side by side a second look.

"How did it go?"

"Oh, fine. That Ms. Wheeler is a peach. Like my new outfit?" Catherine twirled in front of Jackson and he laughed.

"Yes, but you always look good, even in rain-soaked rags."

She smiled and gave him a peck on the cheek. They walked a block before Catherine got up the nerve to speak again.

"I talked to my boss."

"Oh, yeah? Everything okay?"

"Do you know how many years I've busted my ass to prove I can manage my own site? Apparently all I had to do was take a nosedive in the mountains..."

Jackson stopped on the sidewalk and let go of her hand. He looked disappointed.

"It's good," she said, taking his hand again and trying to reassure him. "I'll be nearby. This way I can make sure no one goes near your little hideaway."

Jackson gripped her hand and began walking again. He couldn't express to Catherine what he was feeling because he could barely comprehend it himself. "The best course is to keep quiet," he told himself.

"Hey, look at me," Catherine said as they neared the corner. "You saved my life, and Tucker's. So, in my eyes, you're the exact opposite of a killer."

He looked into her eyes. He couldn't keep the truth from her any longer, but he couldn't let her knowing influence his decision to stay or go. His isolation was a part of him. He clung to it because it was the only way he knew how to survive.

They did a lap around the block in silence as Jackson collected his thoughts. When they neared the hospital, they found Tucker, Diane, and Pickett in the courtyard off the front entrance, enjoying the late-day sun.

"Wow, look at you!" Catherine said.

"Doc thought it'd be okay," Tucker said. "I got bored and Diane and Mr. Pickett offered to bring me down to wait for you. Once you've slept outside for a long time, it's hard getting used to being inside." Jackson smiled while the others laughed at the irony.

Pickett got up from the stone bench and went over to Jackson while Diane and Catherine chatted with Tucker.

"You're a free man now," he said, gesturing for Jackson to stand with him under a blooming tree out of earshot of the other three. "What are your plans?"

"I don't think I belong here."

"What about Diane and Catherine?"

"They're pretty special. Diane knows the truth, but I can't bring myself to tell Catherine that I don't have a bounty hanging over me. If she knows, she may not give up on me so easily."

Pickett nodded. He understood the predicament Jackson found himself in. He wouldn't want to have to make such a decision.

"I don't know how to be a normal person."

"Give it time. Catherine and Tucker will wait."

Jackson walked over to the trio, with Pickett trailing behind him.

"Listen, I need to take care of a few things. Diane, do you mind driving me so Catherine has a ride home with Mr. Pickett?"

When Diane nodded, surprised, Jackson turned to Tucker, "I'll see you later, buddy, okay?"

Tucker held out his hand and Jackson clapped and grasped it. Tucker had the fleeting sense that Jackson wouldn't be back. He swallowed hard but didn't betray his suspicions.

After dinner, Catherine, Pickett, and Tucker played cards and recounted their adventures. Catherine stepped out briefly to purchase new clothes and acquire a new cell phone, while Pickett let the boy nap while he read the paper. He was happy to see the boy was out of the woods, both literally and figuratively. He only wished he could fix everyone's worries over Jackson. "Be patient," Pickett told himself, "and help them to be patient too. Jackson needs to feel safe before he allows himself to reconnect completely," he thought.

It was starting to get late when Catherine told Pickett she would stay and wait for Jackson and Diane, if he wanted to head home.

"Just call me if you decide you want to come back to my place sooner," Pickett said. He was careful not to concern her over Jackson's return.

"I'll see you tomorrow, Tucker, and this time be ready for a rematch!" he laughed as he headed out the door. Both Catherine and Tucker said goodbye to the old man.

"What do you think of him?" Catherine asked.

"He's funny. And nice. I like him," Tucker said.

"He has surely helped us out," Catherine said, adjusting Tucker's pillows so he could keep his leg elevated while eating dessert in bed.

"Mom…"

Catherine's new phone rang. She held up her finger to pause as she answered it. Diane had written down her number before they had left, in case something came up. But it was Jackson's voice on the other end of the line.

"Catherine."

"Is everything okay?" Catherine's worst fears cascaded through her mind in the half-second since she'd seen Diane's name on her phone. Was this his one phone call? Had he been picked up by the police so fast?

"Yeah, we're fine. Listen, I'm going to stay at Diane's for a few nights. We have a lot to catch up on and I've got to sort some things out."

"Sure. Of course."

"Tell Owen thanks and we'll see Tucker and you soon, okay?"

Catherine agreed, said goodnight, and pressed the off button.

"He's staying at his house? Isn't that really far away?" Tucker asked. He had clearly overheard.

"No, it's not so far and yes, he is."

"Mom, do you think he's ever coming back?"

"He said he would. But if he doesn't, we have to be okay with that. Do you understand?"

Tucker nodded. He'd eaten only half his dessert, but he scrunched down in his covers and closed his eyes. Catherine kissed his forehead, shut off the overhead light, and called Pickett to come pick her up.

Thinking about the past few days, Jackson stood at the large window facing the backyard and forest that he'd grown up in. He allowed himself to sleep in a little later each morning, but, this morning, Diane was still in her room. They talked late into the night after she driven him back four nights earlier. Every night since felt like a therapy session for both of them. But they would both be okay. They had never stopped trusting each other.

Two days ago, she had taken him to restock his cave. He'd marveled at the newest hunting rifles, bows, and camping equipment. When he had mustered out back east, he already had had plenty of money. But even though he had never been declared dead, the government had made sure she had received ample compensation for his service. He felt like he'd bought one of everything, including new clothes and food. He'd splurged on a real haircut and shave at the barbershop too.

Yesterday, he had walked into the police station with Diane and one of her law firm's associates. Barry Petrus had arranged for an assistant district attorney and a sheriff's representative to meet them there as well. Jackson felt like he needed to clear the air and give his statement. Diane supported him. Petrus saw no risk and was happy to do a little pro bono for his favorite paralegal and her brother.

"But you fled the scene, Mr. Eagle," the ADA had said after ten minutes of questioning.

"Yes, I did," Jackson sat a conference table in a large, window-filled room. Petrus had made sure that they didn't confine Jackson to an interrogation room.

"Why?" the assistant from the sheriff's office had asked. "Why didn't you stay close and find out what was happening?"

"Like Diane said, I was planning a camping trip anyway. And…" Jackson had looked into each of the faces around the table. "I couldn't get locked up again."

"With all you've gone through, Mr. Eagle, from serving your country to defending your sister, who is a well-respected member of this community, my office and I want you to know that you have nothing to worry about from us," a police detective had offered. She held out her hand and Jackson rose and took it.

"We closed that case years ago, Mr. Eagle," the ADA had
said, also extending a hand. "The worst that could happen
is that Denny could file a civil suit, if he finds out you're
alive. And I don't think he wants to go up against a war
hero in a court of law. With the amount of cases stacked
against him, I doubt if he ever wants to see the inside of a
courthouse again."

The others had chuckled and shaken hands. Jackson turned
to the sheriff's rep.

"Denny was a stain on our office. It was good to get the
full story. We are very sorry about what happened to your
sister...and to you. If you ever need anything, Sarge, please
don't hesitate to reach out," the rep had clasped Jackson on
the shoulder and led him out to the reception area. After the
others had left, Jackson, Diane, and Barry Petrus had stood
on the front steps of the Arapaho Glades PD.

"Told ya," Petrus had said, grinning.

"Thanks, we really appreciate it," Jackson had shaken the
young attorney's hand. Diane had given Barry a hug.

"So, what's next?" he'd asked.

Jackson had put his hands in his pockets and looked
up into the bright sky, then out at the mountains beyond
the town. He had glanced back at his sister and Petrus and
shrugged.

Now Lucky sat on a low stool beside him, looking out as
if contemplating all the same problems. He was larger than
Lady had been but had similar markings. His big, soulful eyes
looked up at Jackson, then he turned and leaped off the chair
as Diane walked into the kitchen.

"Tell me you haven't been up long," she said.

"No, just long enough to run out for muffins and coffee. Don't worry. I wore a ball cap and sunglasses. No one recognized me."

"Good. I'm not ready to start explaining things," Diane helped herself and sat down at the table. Jackson sat down next to her and smiled.

"Thanks, sis. You're one in a million. And, just so I don't forget, I'll say today's 'I'm sorry' now."

"You don't have to apologize, Jack. We're good." They sat in silence for a while.

"It's time to go find Akasha and Blue," he said.

Diane sat back and brushed the crumbs from her fingers. She studied Jackson for a long moment. He could feel a tongue-lashing coming on. She was still his big sister.

"You're a free man. Why not stay?"

"I told you last night. I don't belong here."

"Catherine is rare. Look how far you've come. She and Tucker can help you. Do you really want to lose them?"

Jackson shook his head. But he could feel his resolve starting to wane.

"I can help you," she said. Jackson looked at Diane. Maybe. Diane latched onto his indecision. "You said Catherine will be moving here, right? And Tucker needs you, not someone like you, but you, in his life. Why not give it a shot?"

"I'll think about it," he said. Jackson pulled on his new jacket and headed out the back door. Diane watched as his back retreated into the still-dark shadows of the huge trees. She knew he would return, but with only ninety percent certainty.

Chapter 31

"Your mom is talking with the doctor. She asked me to come on in. Is that okay?"

"Yeah, I'm just not feeling great," Tucker was laying partially on his side, facing the window. Pickett took a few steps into the room and paused.

"Tough getting comfortable, huh?" he asked.

"I didn't sleep great."

Pickett could see something in Tucker's hand. He was looking at it and turning it over. Tucker readjusted to be able to see the old man better.

"Thanks for bringing Mom every day. How is she doing? Do you think she needs to see a doctor?"

"I tried, but she seems to be doing okay. I have a pretty well-stocked first-aid kit and she's been bandaging her hands and looking after her scrapes. She's a fast healer."

Tucker smiled and tucked the object under his pillow. He reached for the cards.

"Rematch?"

"You bet," Pickett said and pulled a chair close to the tray by Tucker's bed.

The two had played a round, when he asked Pickett about his own son. "What was he like?"

"Oh, well, he was a good boy. He loved his mother and me very much. He studied hard in school and played sports. We went out hunting and fishing every chance we got."

"You miss him?"

"Yes, I do. Every day. But I'm glad to have gotten to know you. I think you and he would've been friends."

"Really?!"

"Yep. You both like nature and have an adventurous spirit."

"I didn't know I liked adventure until spring break." Tucker was quiet for several minutes while Pickett continued to shuffle.

"Do you think it's wrong to like Jackson more than my dad?"

"Give yourself time," Pickett replied. "You'll figure it out."

It was late the following day and many hands of cards later when Jackson tapped gently on the door to Tucker's room. The boy and his mom were sitting by the window, Tucker in his wheelchair, playing Speed and struggling not to laugh out loud. Pickett dozed in a chair near the door.

Jackson crept quietly into the room and Tucker's face brightened. Catherine rose and hugged him, overjoyed to feel his touch again. After looking into his eyes for a brief moment, she still couldn't be sure what their future would hold. "He is playing it close to the vest," she thought.

"Here, take my seat," she whispered, and Jackson sat down across from Tucker. "Do either of you need anything?" When they replied no, she said she needed to stretch her legs and would be back soon. Pickett didn't stir.

"Foot giving you any trouble?" Jackson asked. He was in a fresh flannel shirt and his hair looked even shorter, trimmed on the sides. Not even a shadow of a beard. It took Tucker a moment to process that this was the mountain man who had saved their lives.

"A little, but I'm okay. I was worried you weren't really coming back."

"Listen, Tucker. I need to talk to you about that." Tucker took a deep breath and looked out the window. Then he looked back at Jackson.

"I knew it."

"It's difficult to explain, but I'm not part of any of this anymore. I kind of wonder if I ever really was."

"Is it because of the man you killed? 'Cause Mom said she thinks the judge, or whatever, would give you leniency."

"It turns out I didn't kill that deputy. It was self-defense and no charges were brought."

Tucker sat quietly. Every response he could think of would be hurtful and he didn't want to drive Jackson away. He felt selfish, wanting Jackson to stay. And he thought Jackson was being selfish for wanting to be on his own.

"I can't let the wolves stay out there on their own much longer. They'll stop hunting if they are waiting for me too long."

"I get it. But I don't have to like it," Tucker said and tried to muster a grin.

"Thanks, Tucker. I'm sorry," Jackson had witnessed Tucker's resilience first-hand. He knew he'd be all right. He wondered if he would be all right without Tucker.

"I need to go tell your mom."

"Does she know about the non-murder?"

"No, not yet."

Catherine sat on the low wall by the hospital entrance where they had shared an hour the day they'd brought Tucker in. She could tell from his posture that she wasn't going to like what he had to say.

"I talked to Tucker and told him that I can't stay," Jackson began. He stood several paces away from her, his hands tucked into his jean pockets.

Catherine looked out at the range in the distance. "This is going to break Tucker's heart," she thought. "Mine too."

"I need to go. I can't let the wolves stay out there alone. It's time to go back."

Catherine wiped a tear from her cheek and nodded. Sniffling a bit, she said, "I really hate to see you go." Jackson sat down beside her. He didn't want to reach for her. It was too painful. That was the main reason he had stayed at his old house for so many nights. His resolve would have foundered if he had spent even one more night with her.

"I've fallen in love with you," she added after another moment. She gathered her strength and looked at him for the first time. Her gaze was met with the exact same emotion.

"I know. I feel it too, but it isn't enough."

"Stay." Jackson continued looking into her eyes. He had never felt weak like this before.

"I'll help you fight it. Tucker, Pickett, and me. We'll all serve as witnesses. Roseburg will help me find the best lawyer."

"The deputy lived. Pickett told me and Diane confirmed it."

"You're free?"

"Completely free."

Catherine burst into tears. The stress of the week and the relief for Jackson nearly crushed her. He pulled her close and held her for a long time. When she'd regained control, he loosened his grip a little and whispered, "Are you going to be okay?"

"I'm so glad for you, Jackson, I really am. And I'm happy we're safe and Tucker is healing. But, no. No, it's going to take a long time for me to be okay."

"If it's any consolation, it's going to take me a long time too. You've changed me, Catherine. You and Tucker."

"Not enough."

Jackson shook his head. "No, not enough."

The next day, Pickett pulled up to the front entrance of the hospital. One news van was parked nearby, but Ms. Wheeler was speaking with the reporter and it didn't look like he would get any closer. Nurses, doctors, visitors, and even other patients had stopped by Tucker's room throughout his stay to congratulate him on surviving and keeping his mom safe. His physical therapist, who had gotten him up on crutches the day before, had brought him a T-shirt that read, "I survived a month in the wilds of Idaho and all I got was this crummy T-shirt." Now many were lining up inside the door to wave him off.

Pickett and Catherine had taken the big bouquet from Roseburg—roses, naturally—home the previous evening. But Tucker's arms were filled with single buds, cards, and small bouquets. One of the student interns had even given him a little "get well" bear from the florist shop on the first floor.

Tucker stood up from the wheelchair and used his new crutches to make it the last few feet to the door of Pickett's old Chevy. Jackson stood by, holding the door open and helping the boy in next to his mother.

"Diane and I will follow behind," he said, and clicked the door shut.

Cheers faded as the truck rounded the corner and headed out toward the old mining road where they had last seen Akasha and Blue. Catherine looked back and saw Diane, looking grim, both hands gripping the wheel. No one had asked who she or Jackson were and none of them had offered. Jackson's secret was still safe.

The drive was quiet. Pickett sensed the sadness and knew they all would have to deal with their grief in their own way. It was a loss. Like a death. But Catherine and Diane had both arranged to visit Pickett—and each other—often. And Tucker had already challenged him to a re-match "anytime, anywhere" after Pickett had started sweeping the game late yesterday afternoon.

The ground was dry and fresh when they pulled up to the exact spot where Pickett's truck had gotten stuck in the mud. Catherine shuddered thinking about the state they were all in then. She smiled at Tucker and gave him a quick hug. Jackson pulled open the door and offered Tucker his crutches from the truck bed as he got out.

Catherine took Jackson's hand as she stepped out, but she knew that was the last time they would touch. The thought almost made her hold on a little longer, but she turned to Diane instead.

"I'm so glad I got to know you, Diane."

"Me too, but I look forward to seeing you when you're settled. And I hope you'll take me up on my offer to help with the move. And Tucker," Diane turned to the boy. "You are always welcome to stay with me while your mom is painting or arranging furniture."

"Thanks, Diane, but I have a feeling I'll be doing the furniture arranging, hurt foot or not." The women laughed, but Tucker only smiled.

"Once Tucker is mobile again and we figure out where we'll be, Tucker will finish out the school year there. I talked to his school principal this morning. And his father. He called us a few nights ago when he finally got the messages," Catherine said.

Pickett and Jackson had walked off toward the woods a bit. Jackson scanned the brush for any sign of Akasha and Blue.

"Anything I can say to change your mind?"

"No, but I could use a helo to transport all my gear. It's going to be some hard yards back to my hermitage." When Pickett didn't respond, Jackson looked at him and said somberly, "The forest is my home now."

"Suit yourself. Happy trails, Jackson," Pickett held out his hand. "You're always welcome at my house." The two men shook hands and Pickett patted him on the back.

"Thanks again, Owen. I know where to find you."

Diane had opened the trunk of her car. Jackson walked over and began pulling out his hiking pack and bag. She stopped him and gave him a big hug.

"You don't have to do this," she whispered.

"Don't make it harder, sis."

"One more for the road," she relented and hugged him tight again. After he had gotten all his gear, she waved goodbye to the group and drove away. She had to have faith. It had replenished over the last day. She would give it a little nudge with prayer.

Pickett stood by the passenger door where Catherine and Tucker waited.

"Walk out with me," Jackson said. Tucker hung back a moment, but Catherine waited for him. Jackson walked ahead, pack on his back and another bag in his hand. He stopped about twenty yards from the truck but didn't turn around. Catherine walked up beside him and Tucker hobbled next to her. He hopped a little to get his footing on the uneven ground.

"You don't have to go," Tucker said. He pulled the wooden crow from his pocket and held it out to Jackson. Jackson folded Tucker's fingers around it and pushed his hand back toward him. "Yours now. He'll keep you safe." Tucker nodded and put it back in his pocket.

"Will I ever see you again?" Tucker saw the answer in Jackson's eyes. He wiped both his eyes with his hand.

"Breathe deep," Jackson said. Tucker inhaled the crisp, dry air.

"It's so…clear."

"Your gift. From the forest."

Tucker looked down at the ground, fresh tears welling up in his eyes.

Chapter 32

Jackson reached up and pulled the rawhide cord over his head. He put it over Catherine's head and arranged the gold ring along her neckline. It took her a long time to calm herself and be able to speak.

"Thank you for finding us," Catherine choked.

"Couldn't help it. It was part of the plan."

Tucker reached out and hugged Jackson, then made his way slowly back to the truck.

Catherine grabbed Jackson's face between her hands and kissed him hard on the mouth. She let the kiss soften and linger, then she pulled away.

"And someday I'm sure I'll understand why saying goodbye is part of it too." She stepped back a few paces.

Jackson began to walk toward the path winding through the trees. As she watched, she imagined him changing his mind. Then she turned and walked back toward the truck.

It was slow going. Jackson took his time reaching the tree line. He wanted to be sure the wolves caught his scent when they passed this way again. Behind him, he heard the truck's engine start up. "Must keep going," Jackson thought to himself. He willed the lump in his throat to go down. He began to whistle to distract himself and call the wolves. The sound of a plane's engine drowned him out, but he resumed the call after it had flown south. The birds mimicked his call.

In the cab, Tucker sat in the middle with his leg stretched across his mother's lap. They looked out the window at the lush terrain. It was beautiful and abundant. Catherine knew she couldn't compete. A familiar sense of loneliness started to creep in.

He regarded her a moment.

"You seem different now."

"Oh, yeah? Different how?"

"Better different."

"You too," she smiled at her radiant son.

She fingered the ring resting against her breastbone. Something came over her and she leaned over to Pickett.

"Stop."

Pickett slowed the truck and rolled to a stop, careful not to jostle Tucker. Before he was completely stopped, Catherine jumped out of the cab and ran back toward the tree line. Jackson had disappeared into the trees. She stood and looked for a long time. Pickett turned the truck around and pulled up behind her. He and Tucker exchanged looks and peered out the windscreen.

"I just…had a feeling," she said softly to herself. She began to walk back to the truck when a black shadow emerged from her left. Blue. He loped up to her and she bent and stroked his fur, then threw her arms around him and wept. Tucker opened the door and Blue darted over to him, licking his hands as he eased himself down to the ground.

Striking against the deep colors of the forest, Akasha trotted out of the woods along the old trail, followed by Jackson. Catherine ran to Akasha and stroked her ears, then embraced Jackson.

"You don't have to say anything," she said. He grinned back at her.

"I'm struggling, but I can give this a try." She took the bag from him and they walked back to the truck, hand in hand.

Tucker hugged him tight and Pickett gingerly made his way around the wolves to embrace Jackson too. After they tossed his gear into the back of the truck and got Tucker settled in the cab, Catherine pulled Jackson toward the truck bed. With a short whistle from Jackson, Akasha and Blue sprang onto the tailgate and stood along the sides of the bed while Jackson helped Catherine up. He closed the tailgate and turned around to see both wolves licking Catherine's face as she sat down against the back of the cab. He sat beside her and wrapped an arm around her shoulders, scratching Blue between the ears with his free hand.

"You guys are going to have to get used to living with humans…"

Acknowledgements

I want to thank my editor Camille Cline, who helped me give this book its essence. Thanks to her care and guidance, she made this an easy read.

To Karen Badart, my assistant for 43 years. Thank you for your attention to detail and your dedication to this project.

And to my wife, Rita, who gave me the encouragement and support I needed. I am grateful for her love that gave me the ability to truly understand Catherine and Jackson. This book is with reverence to Rita's passing while it was in the works.

To our strong faith in God and the works of the fine charities who will benefit from the proceeds.

And finally, Thanks to Bob Snodgrass and the talented team at Ascend Books for helping to make this book a reality.

-Gene

About the Author

O. Gene Bicknell is a writer, actor, broadcaster, veteran, professor, entrepreneur, and philanthropist. He is well-known for his success in building NPC International, which became the world's largest Pizza Hut franchisee. Bicknell has also raised considerable funds for dozens of charitable causes, taught master-level business courses and lectured at major universities throughout the United States and abroad. Gene founded the O. Gene Bicknell Center for Entrepreneurship. He has authored four books and produced a number of movies. He also owns an entertainment business in Branson, Missouri, and resides in Englewood, Florida, near Tampa.